---- ★ ----

Dean moved a light, startling me back to the scene. His paper jumpsuit crackled as he crouched low to get a close-up photo of the knife, then half stood to lean over the body. The burlap sack seemed a strange item with which to don a corpse. Not big enough to accommodate the entire body, it served to cover only the victim's head and shoulders. Why was it here? I glanced again at the mound of gifts, the gold and silver church pieces on the altar. Had it been a burglary attempt gone wrong? Had the victim been murdered by an accomplice? Why, then, not finish the looting? Why stuff the man into a sack? I stared at the burlap as Dean took another photo. And had the knife been part of the burglar's tools? Why else here and available for murder? Shaking my head, I exhaled loudly. For all the knife spoke of murder, the sack shouted more clearly of hatred.

---- ★ ----

Previously published Worldwide Mystery title by
JO A. HIESTAND

DEATH OF AN ORDINARY GUY

Sainted Murder
Jo A. Hiestand

W🌐RLDWIDE®

TORONTO • NEW YORK • LONDON
AMSTERDAM • PARIS • SYDNEY • HAMBURG
STOCKHOLM • ATHENS • TOKYO • MILAN
MADRID • WARSAW • BUDAPEST • AUCKLAND

To Rob, my long-suffering friend,
who knows all the intricacies of The Badge.

SAINTED MURDER

A Worldwide Mystery/May 2007

First published by Hilliard & Harris.

ISBN-13: 978-0-373-26601-2
ISBN-10:   0-373-26601-4

Printed in U.S.A.

Acknowledgment

As usual, thanks to the many people who helped me create this world and story: Dr. Ruth Anker, for her medical expertise; DS Robert Church and DI David Doxey, for English police procedure; a fame-shunning St. Louis cop, for general police and tactical information. Thanks to the many people who supported and encouraged me: Carol Hiestand, Chris Eisenmayer, Paula Harris, Cindy Greer, and the legion of supporters who showed up at events. I can't do anything without you!

In spite of the best help, some information may have become garbled in the translation to text. Those mistakes are mine.

—Jo A. Hiestand, St. Louis, 2005

ONE

I HAD NEVER believed in ghosts. They seemed more the stuff of fiction and ancient castles than of churches. But as the massive door closed behind me with all the heaviness of a coffin lid settling into place, I considered there might be some basis for the stories after all.

It was the hinges that first startled me—great, metal things groaning into the stillness like an atmospheric prerequisite of a gothic novel. The disturbance echoed against cold stone and hard wood; it multiplied into a dozen voices that tumbled down the aisles or rolled up the tower steps, dying as they nudged a bell into song. A deep tone, soft as an angel's voice, sighed from the tower and cajoled sympathetic ripples from neighboring bells. In the ringing chamber below, their ropes swayed as if pulled by invisible hands, the sallies dancing ghost-like in the dark.

I could relegate these phantoms to their nether lands by flipping on the lights. But I wanted to experience it as it probably had happened. So I sank against the wooden slab, letting my eyes adjust to the gloom, letting my mind reason through my sensations.

Scents of pine, hot candle wax and wood polish floated over to me, and I breathed deeply of the fragrances that stirred a thousand Christmas memories—the pine tree decorated with gingerbread men and orange pomanders, the bayberry candles gleaming against frosted window panes, the tins of homemade chocolates and spiced tea, Uncle Ernie's after shave lotion that clung to me after his bear-hug greeting. Yet, just as quickly as the images rose before me, they dissolved. A window rattled and the candle flames cringed. An organ pipe droned with no mortal hand upon the keys. And a whisper—as though from a great distance—moaned somewhere beyond the pinprick of light. A sighing of wintry wind buffeting the windows, or a lamenting banshee?

I had no real desire to find out, to leave the relative security of the door, however cold it was, and cross the vast expanse of darkened floor. But a path of water droplets taunted me, coaxing me to follow them into the darkness. Remnants of an innocent visitor, or the reason I was there? I tapped the snow from my boots, and pulled on my paper shoe covers and latex gloves. Flicking on my electric torch, I stretched out my arm and felt my way forward as though blind or sleepwalking.

Even through my half-frozen boots I could feel the texture of the flagstone floor, the rough and smooth stones, the grade of the rocky slabs that had tilted during the centuries, asserting their individuality among a sea of apparent flatness. Patches of near-black near the nave altar spoke of centuries of worshiper's feet trafficking the area. Lighter stones shone dove-grey in the dimness, chiseled with ancient names and dates to commemorate or remember.

A rectangle of brass gleamed among the sober tones, repelling the surrounding stone, sanctifying this body-sized space. I detoured from my path and shone the light on it. The monumental brass depicted an armored knight. The wording, as were parts of the tablet's edging, showed slight wear from the thousands of feet that had walked across it. The knight, however, still stared distinct and unmarked into the future. Between the raised lettering above his head small drops of water had accumulated. I bent down to sniff them but could detect nothing odd.

Snow from a recent visitor? If so, how fast had it melted in the mid-50 degree temperature of the chancel?

Clumps of melting snow led me past great, white bulks of carved chests, gargoyles and alabaster statues that jumped out of the shadows. A sliver of gold flashed out as the torch discovered two gold candlesticks, then left them as I threaded my way between the low houseling benches and the white nave altar cloth, floating phantom-like in the gloom, the silvers, peacock and cornflower blues, reds and golds of the needlework mesmerizing. Wondering what it would look like at evensong, I snapped off the torch. The satin cloth shimmered like moonlit white sands; glass beads and gold sequins sparkled as if on fire. Its beauty was almost enough to lure me back to a church service.

But I wasn't there to worship. Shifting shadows thrown by the candlelight gestured toward the murkiest part of the church. On the far side of the wooden pulpit, a black bulk in the gloomy reaches of the chantry screen called to me. Snapping on the torch again, I walked over to the shape.

It revealed itself slowly as the torch's beam crept up its length, bits at a time, as though being pulled from the night. First the ice-encrusted boots, then the black slacks still damp from snow, the dark jacket and finally a ghost-white hand. All part of the inert body lying face-down on the floor. It was a peaceful scene, as though he were napping. An ordinary body— except for the glint of metal above its back. The knife seemed jammed into the flesh, the victim's jacket nearly swallowing the knife blade. Yet, I knelt beside it, reached for the left hand and felt for a pulse. There was nothing I could do.

Had he, before joining his ancestors, been my whispering phantom, urging me to capture his killer? I gazed again at the knife blade, and waited in dead silence for Graham's arrival.

TWO

'FLASHY' WAS NOT a word to describe Mrs. Lindbergh, nor did she covet notoriety, but she glowed with an inner spark of self importance when relating how she had discovered the corpse.

"I'd just finished with the holly, Miss," Mrs. Lindbergh said, not knowing whether to look at me or her handiwork. Her voice trembled slightly as she related the event. I had been the first police officer on the scene, called from my warm office in Buxton for a preliminary investigation in this snow-wrapped village in England's upland Derbyshire. She had been calm enough when I had met her half an hour ago, but now that it appeared official, complete with written statements, she was seized with nerves. I let her take a deep breath and smiled encouragingly. She charged on. "I always likes a bit of holly on the altar on St. Nicholas Day. Though there are *some* in this village that calls it *heathen* to put Druid greenery there, so close to God. But I say God made it and we've come to embrace other heathen symbols. Can't see the church bein' the worse off for a bit of holly. Not when we here have been doin' it for better than 400 years. And if it's so heathen, why *are* we still here? Why's not the church smote down by now?"

We were inside St. Nicholas Church, a limestone edifice warding off sin and evil with all its stalwart enthusiasm of medieval gargoyles, buttresses and towers. In the half-darkness at the foot of the nave altar, the vicar remained mute, staring at the ancient gold rood as though seeking divine explanation. Or help. The rood was flanked by two statues—though of whom, I couldn't tell—that gazed at the crucified Christ. We waited in the quiet, expecting a flash of lightning or a rumbling Voice, but only a tree branch scraping against a window spoke. The statues, as realistic as they looked, weren't imparting any theological answers.

Silently, I agreed with her assessment. Besides, holly did seem made for Christmas—red berries and green foliage. Mrs. Lindbergh glanced at the vicar, as if expecting his approval. Getting no admonishment from him, she said, "I brought it from home, that holly. Cut just before I come, so it's fresh. Though I was havin' that much trouble with it, with the snow fallin' and the branches weighed down and all. Lost some berries shakin' off the snow. Stuck, for all my pains, too. *And* drawin' blood. But I endure it all, for that's what makes holly—and the church—so lovely, I think."

I nodded, recalling the church as I had seen it on my arrival.

A path had been shoveled from the lych gate to the church porch, yet even now nature was reclaiming this land, for snow continued to settle into the faint depressions scattered along the walkway. A red bow, starched from icy wind, stood crisply on the south door. A sprig of holly, already defeated by Nature's blast, sagged in the bow's knot. Below it, as though shaken by the force of the door's closing, several berries dotted the snow, blood-red drops on white.

"Anyway," Mrs. Lindbergh said, tugging her well-worn cardigan around her hips, "I got a good armful, then took up the basket with the boughs of yew and boxwood, and come on over. That's when I seen it. The body. When I was tyin' up the greenery on the chantry screen." Her bravado wavered under the retelling of the event. "I screamed," she added, as though that told me everything.

The vicar, a mid-30s pillar of strength with a take-charge

voice, must have thought I needed more elucidation, for he said, "I had just finished with the last of the St. Nicolas gifts when I heard her. Well, at first I couldn't tell where it was coming from, the scream. It echoes rather badly in these all-stone edifices, you know. Hard walls, lofty ceilings."

I nodded, thinking it a blessing and a curse. One solo voice echoing in a cappella song sounded as near to angelic music as I could imagine, but sermonic speech was rather difficult to understand at times. Taking my nod as a sign of understanding, he said, "I walked about a bit, calling. I was of a mind to flip on the lights when I found Olive by the nave altar. That's here, just behind us."

We turned as if one body, I imagining the shaken woman over the body, Olive reiterating her scare, and the vicar acting as guide as he pointed to the spot. I asked, "Was the body there? Is that why you crouched there, Mrs. Lindbergh, trying to comfort the dying man, perhaps?"

"I *never* touched him, Miss. Lord love you, I would have done so if he'd been breathin', but he never was. He was that dead, he was. And him with that great whackin'—?" She clamped a work-roughened hand over her mouth, as though speaking the word would inflict more painful memories. A shake of her head induced me to ask, "Did either of you move the body to the screen, then?"

The vicar blanched at my question, uttering an emphatic assertion—nearly an oath—that the body was exactly where and how they had seen it. I tended to agree, for there was no accusing trail of blood that suggested the attack had been other than the place of his death. And the vicar wouldn't lie, for he was a man of God. But he was also a man of the world, so he had pulled the frightened, prostrated Mrs. Lindbergh from the altar, given her a cup of tea, locked the south door, restrained his curiosity, and phoned the police. *Nothing,* he swore, had been touched. Not the melting snow on the floor. Nor the knife in the victim's back. Not even the burlap bag that enveloped his head and shoulders.

"Murder, isn't it?" Mrs. Lindbergh said, finally breaking the silence. When I agreed, she said, "Can't think there was much of a struggle, or Vicar would've heard it. Things would've been disturbed. Don't like the idea of fightin' for life, strugglin' against man and nature." Rather nervously we turned quickly, rather edgy, as a window rattled under a buffeting of wind. Mrs. Lindbergh sighed deeply, then said, "I only hope *your* lot aren't havin' too much of a struggle gettin' here, Miss." Her eyes shifted from me to the south door as though she expected the whole of the Derbyshire Constabulary B Division to suddenly appear. "I wouldn't fancy the drive from Buxton myself, not through these twisty roads. I always say, for all the fancy gadgets the police has these days, a car's a car. And you *still* can't drive on ice. *And* it's blowin' up a storm fit to smother us all inside our homes!"

December was blowing into the village of Bramwell in a swirl of snow and wind laced with North Sea coldness as sharp as village gossip. Snow shrouded rooftop, car top and treetop. It christened the pub sign, a wind-driven splatter flocking the already white swan and masking the pallid letters that read "The Snowy Cygnet." Snow lay like a vast winding sheet over the churchyard, camouflaged tombstones, nestled against the building.

The church itself, an expansive pile of medieval architecture with Victorian 'improvements', stood dark against this snowy whiteness. Doors and bell louvers were closed as much against the elements as against burglary, and the building seemed a carcass silhouetted on the bleak hill. Yet, a glimpse of life called the traveler from the storm, the believer to the play. A whisper slipped from the tower shutters, the faint voice of a bell singing to Aeolus. A lancet window glowed with welcoming candlelight. Like a cat's eye in the darkness. Watching your journey across the frozen ground, assuring you of a sanctuary. The window danced within the solid black shape. Yellow, purple, blue and red diamonds spilled onto the snow, their jeweled shapes stretching and convulsing as the candlelight behind the windows flickered...

Within the church walls, pine roping looped across choir stall and pews, scenting the cold air with hints of the season. Garlands of tiny silver bells twined amongst the greenery while, hanging from the wooden rafters and suspended from the railing of the west gallery, groups of three golden balls threw back the candlelight. The church's acknowledgement to its namesake, St. Nicholas.

"And you are decorating already for Christmas?" I asked, trying to keep the astonishment from my voice. "Isn't December 6 a bit early?"

"It's St. Nicholas Day," the vicar, Trueman deMere, explained. He was a frail-looking man, all elbows and knees, which a wisp of wind might have swept away. But his physique belied an inner strength that took no nonsense from villager, squire or police. "It's for tonight's St. Nicholas festivity. Or, rather, it was for the festivity. I suppose that now, with the, uh, difficulty..."

"St. Nicholas festivity?" I asked, looking up from my notebook.

"A bit of a mix, actually," he said, straightening as though giving formal evidence in court. "We do a bit of reverse role-playing with the stockings. You know, instead of hanging up your stocking tonight, with the list of what you want for Christmas, we give out St. Nicholas gifts."

I replied that the people of Bramwell were starting their Christmas season in the right spirit.

"We try to, Sergeant—Miss Taylor—" he said, stumbling momentarily over the correct usage of rank or name or acknowledgement of gender. I smiled, saying either was fine, and he went on, relieved to have put that confusion behind him. "Oh, but they're nothing extravagant! They can't be." He said it so forcefully that I half expected to see the stone pillars tremble and the ceiling collapse. "The church ledger bleeds every time I open it. So we limit the gifts to just a few things for the children. Trinkets, small toys and books. We have a lot of help with the buying and the wrapping. Most of the boxes are rather plain I'm afraid, just red and green paper and a ribbon run around the box. But those silver-paper ones with the wired bows are done up by Joel Twiss, a parishioner who excels at anything creative. Pity I'm not like that, but God gave us different talents, didn't he? Olive, as you see, is rather good with the holly and carnations, and Colin Hale likes to help with the banners and penning a brass fanfare or two."

I said that it was fortunate he had so many talented helpers.

"Yes, isn't it? But the gifts and decorations are only part of it, of course. We must see to it that our needy parishioners have a bit of bread."

It was certainly more than 'a bit.' I gazed at the foot of the altar with the baskets of freshly baked bread piled mountain-high, and tried not to focus on the aroma.

"Yes," he said, noticing my attention to the small baker's shop. "St. Nicholas was real, certainly. More than our cartoon Santa Claus. Martyred in 305 A.D., we believe. He aided the poor, gave money, bread. We, bearing his name, do the same. Little things in their way, but it means so much to those on the receiving end. Especially during the Christmas season when the rest of the world seems to be wallowing in excess. But, then, that's what the church is really for. Relieving suffering and trying to overcome the blatant commercialism of late."

"As long as the jobs are decent and law abiding," Mrs. Lindbergh said, "you shouldn't judge how others make their bread,

Vicar. People have got to live, too." Her words rose like the bitter wind outside, speaking with an insistence that whispered of her own struggle to make bread. She mirrored that toil—skin coarsened by weather, fingernails cracked and broken, a back bent by too-heavy toil. But her eyes held a sparkle that mirrored her loyalty and love of life, faith and family. She seemed content with the inner gift; why bother, then, about the outer wrapping?

"I'm not saying no one can live," the vicar began. Then, as though realizing his statement, he looked in the direction of the victim, and coughed.

I followed his gaze, straining my eyes against the dimness beyond the altar and tubs of wrapped packages. The body was no gift from Santa Claus, as most of us call the saint. It had been difficult to see at first, dressed in dark colored clothes and slumped in a shadowy section of the church. The vicar had offered to turn on the overhead lights. But I had restrained him, thinking it better to see the scene as it may have been originally. It was dark, nearly pitch black, by the chantry chapel screen, the rectangular, wooden enclosure that sits in the north aisle. A splendid spot to delay the discovery of a body if one needed time to escape the scene. Or establish an alibi.

Scattered pinpricks of candlelight stood out like spotlights in the gloom. Like the pockets of warmth issuing from the space heaters that slowly, valiantly chased away the chill. They had been turned on, I had been informed, that lunchtime, so the church would be comfortable for the evening's St. Nicholas celebration. But for all of the vicar's foresight, the murder team would still have a cold job processing the scene.

I had taken a step toward the body but stopped just outside the shadowy region of the chantry. The vicar stood several yards behind me, his voice low yet echoing in the stillness of the vast interior, hesitant at first to speak, as though unsure if I should be disturbed. When I turned and looked interested, he continued.

"It's not our bread knife, Miss Taylor." I must have looked bewildered that he had read my thoughts, for he added, "We don't keep one on the altar for the St. Nicholas bread. The killer must have brought his own."

THREE

PREMEDITATED MURDER, then. I had not given voice to the supposition whispering in my head for, even though murder itself was usually calculated, this one, inside this church at this seasonal time, seemed especially so. I trembled.

Mistaking my reaction, Mrs. Lindbergh came over to me and rubbed my arms. "You're all of a shiver, dear. Go stand by one of them heaters. There, by the bell tower. I stands there myself when I gets here early for service. Nice and warm you'll be in no time."

I thanked her, declined the suggestion, and pulled my jacket about me. "So, you don't cut the bread."

"No," the vicar said. Then, taking up my meaning, added, "We give out the entire loaf. That's why they're all of the same size and shape. Saves time, handing them out whole."

"And so Mrs. So-and-so can't grouse that her bit was smaller than Mrs. Whozit," Mrs. Lindbergh said, her voice sharp with hints of past experiences.

I replied that it was a good idea, let them sort out to whose statement I was referring, and asked, "Who supplies the bread? Surely your parishioners have enough to do with wrapping gifts and decorating, Vicar."

Trueman deMere smiled, as though remembering some emphatic discussion on the subject. "Owen Parnell. He's a professional baker. Works for Magdalína Dent who owns and runs the village tearoom."

"Nicest person you'd ever want to meet," Mrs. Lindbergh put

in. "Busy from early morn till late at night. Though never too busy to have a kind word with you." I must have raised my eyebrow, for Mrs. Lindbergh said, "Magdalína, that is. Owen, now, he's a fine man, but I never have had much say with him. Always in the kitchen, baking," she said, as though that explained why she didn't speak with him outside business hours.

"And Owen Parnell," I said, jotting furiously in my notebook, "supplies all this bread out of the goodness of his heart—or his pocket?"

"Could do, I suppose," mused the vicar. "But it's actually a united effort by several people. Owen, Magdalína, a bit of the church's Parish Bread fund, Francis Rice—he's a retired physician, worked until June this year, in fact—and one or two other contributors." His brown eyes never wavered as I looked up to see if he was one of the contributors. Not that it mattered, but it told me Trueman deMere could hold a well of secrets.

"Well, after Olive found the body…" Trueman reminded me.

I turned to Mrs. Lindbergh, acknowledging her importance in the event.

"Yes," I returned, rather glad of the change of subject. "And this was…"

"Near enough to half six to call it that. Weren't it, Trueman?" Mrs. Lindbergh searched the vicar's eyes for verification, then, receiving it, added, "I was here from one-ish on. Came right after luncheon, I believe it were."

"That's right, Olive. I'd just finished my meal. The clock struck the hour, and you knocked on the rectory door."

Olive Lindbergh seemed to brighten at remembering these ordinary, homey touches. "That's right. One. The others were just arriving."

"And," I interrupted, "these others were…"

As if we were reading from a radio drama script, a pounding on the south door punctuated my question. Hoping it was some of the lads from the constabulary, I opened the door. Karol Mattox's cold face hovered ghost-like in the feeble lantern light. The rest of her was nearly invisible, dressed as she was in the constabulary's white working jumpsuit. I opened the door wider to let her and Dean Hargreaves enter. Karol stomped her feet, dislodging the snow, then looked up at the lofty ceiling beams and whistled. I knew what she meant.

"Thank God you're here," I said, rather too pitifully. Karol was B Division's police surgeon and Dean was a Scenes of Crime Officer. After the sergeant—in this case, me—they usually processed the scene next, examining the body, photographing the body and area before evidence was destroyed. It was comforting to have them here, to get the work underway. "You're all here, then," I asked, looking at the white world beyond the church door. I must have lingered too long at the opening, for Karol said, "He's coming, don't worry. Held up at the office."

She didn't need to explain further. Superintendent Simcock usually had to flex his muscle by telling his officers how to process a case—even if he hadn't seen it yet. I grimaced and wondered how many beers Graham would down before the case was solved.

"Pity, that," Karol said, her eyes searching the dimness for the body. "If Simcock'd leave Graham alone he'd probably get better work done all around. But no, not our Super. Has to stick his oar in the water and splash about a bit."

"Just as long as he doesn't upset the boat."

"What's his problem, then? Loveless marriage, poor self image, promotion itch?"

I shrugged, hardly caring what drove Simcock's surges of bullying. It only touched me when Graham let it filter through him.

And even then I was more concerned with Graham's well being than with mine. I wanted to spare him the headaches and pain. "Could be pressure from Above."

"I suppose there's no psychiatric report lying about some-place," Karol said, straightening up from putting on her shoe covers.

"I can't see him leaving it on his desk, if there is," I replied, my eyes scanning the road for signs of Graham's car. Several detective constables, including my friend Margo Lynch, swarmed like ants over the street and churchyard, searching for the odd scrap of paper, the lost button, the drop of blood. DC Byrd carefully cordoned the church within a ring of blue-and-white police tape, establishing the twenty-meter limit of the crime scene.

"No. Not the sort of thing you'd advertise. Shut that door, will you? It's damned cold out there."

Apologizing, I let the door shut with a bang, now that Dean had all his photographic equipment inside. He, too, leaned against the wall and pulled on his shoe covers. I watched him, as though for the first time, until Karol said, "How's your safe cracking skill, Brenna? Any good with picklocks?"

"You tired of me already? You want me demoted or kicked off the Force?"

"If you're any good, you won't suffer either. Besides, haven't you got a pal to stand watch? How about Margo?"

I replied that I hardly thought O-Level Burglary a fitting course to teach Margo. She had dreams of promotion, too.

"Fine. If that's all you think about your mates… We'll all have to put up with Simcock until he retires, then."

"Speaking of which… He's not coming?" Frankly, I was surprised. Along with the police surgeon, senior detective—in this case, Graham—and the Scientific Officers, the detective superintendent usually attended the scene. Though it wasn't unheard of for Simcock not to be here, it was unusual.

"Not from what I understand. He'll view the crime scene video later. It's up to Graham and me."

"No pressure there."

"Well," she said, adjusting her facemask. "You say it's murder, then? Why so certain? Do we have a witness?"

"Unless he's a contortionist, I can't see it being suicide. And it's hardly an accident. Knifed. In the back. Don't know a thing beyond the obvious."

"Well, I'm not going to wait. Dean and I had a hard enough time getting here. Who knows how long it'll take Jens?"

"Or *if* he'll even get here," I said, imagining the roads from Sheffield snowbound and iced over. Dr. Jens Nielsen, the Home Office forensic pathologist, would examine the scene and do the post mortem. And while Karol's presence wasn't outside strictest police procedure, I had called her in for this very reason. Wintry roads and a long drive didn't always combine well. It was best to have Karol here in case Nielsen couldn't make it. "Thanks for coming, Karol."

Muttering that at least this murder was indoors, Karol waited for me to put down the milk crates. Like a miniature archipelago, these overturned cartons offered safe, uncontaminated passage to and from the crime scene. I led the way to the chantry screen, my white shoe covers seeming to hover above the floor, and indicated the victim in the shadowy depths.

Dean, a strange collection of tripods, lights and cameras, set up the photographic lights around the screen, destroying the earlier ambiance of candlelight and shadow. The blaze of brightness was out of place in such dim surroundings. As our presence was an intrusion on the church's St. Nicholas festivity. But we were only doing our duty. Murder had decided all this. I tried to watch—disengaged, analytical—ignoring the sacrilege I felt over our presence and the death. But I couldn't. The baskets of bread and gifts whispered of the disappointment of hundreds of people. They say Christmas is for children, but old age pensioners can tell you that it means as much to them. It brightened lives and filled the cupboards.

Dean moved a light, startling me back to the scene. His paper jumpsuit crackled as he crouched low to get a close-up photo of the knife, then half stood to lean over the body. The burlap sack seemed a strange item with which to don a corpse. Not big enough to accommodate the entire body, it served to cover only the victim's head and shoulders. Why was it here? I glanced again at the mound of gifts, the gold and silver church pieces on the altar. Had it been a burglary attempt gone wrong? Had the victim been murdered by an accomplice? Why, then, not finish the looting? Why stuff the man into a sack? I stared at the burlap as Dean took another photo. And had the knife been part of the burglar's tools? Why else here and available for murder? Shaking my head, I exhaled loudly. For all the knife spoke of murder, the sack shouted more clearly of hatred.

THAT HAD BEEN an hour ago. Now I stood outside, having retraced my path back to the lych gate. The temperature had fallen in those two hours, and the wind had picked up, as though claiming the night hours as its habitation. It carried the clouds of my breath over the church roof and into the night. I pulled my woolen hat down over my ears and tried not to look cold and impatient. Though the snowfall had abated somewhat, the sky showed no rift in its vast, sober mantle. I was glad the murder team had arrived when they had, that Dean had photographed the foot-printed path before the wind swept away any damning evidence, if any was there.

Feeling the hour, temperature and situation, I stamped my feet. Of course I was apprehensive. I was still suffering the pangs of "pleasing teacher," if that's how to describe my partnership with Detective Chief Inspector Geoffrey Graham. But what do you expect from a mere detective sergeant of less than six months? Graham has always been patient with me, praising and criticizing as my conduct warrants. Yet I was still in awe of his intelligence. Still concerned with his power to bust me back to constable. Still fearful and wondering if I was falling in love with him. So I was over keen. I didn't want to mess up when my career was blossoming.

Hearing a door slam, I turned to see the vicar and Mrs. Lindbergh step outside and duck under the crime scene tape. They were garbed in the same white paper work suits as the rest of the Force—a necessity to keep the crime scene free of witness cross-contamination. The vicar must have felt self conscious for he turned his back to Mrs. Lindbergh before removing the overalls. Mrs. Lindbergh had stepped over to a tombstone and leaned against its upper edge as she shed the outer garment. Handing the garments to the nearest constable, they began talking of their experience, wondering at the identity of the murdered man. They nodded to me in passing and I watched them destroy the smoothness of the snow as they trudged into the night.

It was barely quarter to nine, but I felt it was nearer midnight.

The blackness of the evening, the anxiety of safe travel on the hilly roads, and the strange, almost irreligious setting of the murder drained me of any energy to continue with taking statements. But I reasoned if I didn't, Graham would have good reason to assign me elsewhere, or demote me. And I didn't want either.

Where was Graham? The main contingent of our police division had arrived half an hour ago. Had the roads become impassable in that short time, or was he delayed further by Simcock? Surely he would still arrive! I fought a panic sharper than any I had known on imagining Graham's dismissal from the case, and wondered how I would survive as a detective, how I would survive as a person. I took a deep lungful of cold air. Simcock had done this before, if I remembered office gossip. And Graham, after nodding and yesing, did just as he pleased. He would be here.

The village was dark except for occasional houses alive with light and curiosity. They shone sharply in the blackness, vivid testaments to the village telegraph system. The vicar had contributed mere basics when canceling the St. Nicholas festivity; the system had contributed the details. I knocked the snow off the wing mirror of my Corsa—now looking more like a blue bobsleigh than a car—and struck out for the first of my interviews.

Fifteen minutes later I sat in Magdalína Dent's dwelling. It was a simple 4-room flat above the tearoom in which she took such obvious pride. Parlor, kitchen, bedroom and an office converted from a dining room seemed large enough to house the proprietor's life. The walls of the parlor, in which we sat, showcased her culinary creativity in the form of awards, autographed celebrity photos and framed memorabilia. They were also the color of butter, a rich, golden yellow that befit the shop's name, The Pineapple Slice.

Magdalína sat on a chair upholstered in brocade fabric of tiny pineapples. The small settee I sat on was a mass of crewelworked pineapples and pomegranates. I ran my fingertip over a French knot and asked about her part in the St. Nicholas festivity.

"I contribute the ingredients for the bread," she said, offering me a cup of tea. I accepted it readily, for even the short walk from the church had chilled me. "Shortbread?" She waited until I had taken one of the delicate biscuits before saying, "Of course, I can't force Owen to bake, but he seems willing enough to help. And we have the ingredients. So it seems a natural donation. Where did you hear about my part in the Bread Dole?" She tilted her head, looking at me with wide, grey eyes. They were serious even when she smiled. I thought she would be a sharp businesswoman.

"From the vicar."

"Of course. You came from St. Nicholas, didn't you? I

would've remembered if my mind wasn't still reeling from that dreadful news. I suppose it is murder..." Her words nearly echoed Mrs. Lindbergh's and I wondered how many more echoes I would hear the next day. "Who is it, may I ask?"

"I can't tell you. I don't know."

"You don't—" She caught herself before she snapped in exasperation. "Well, surely, Sergeant, if Trueman and Olive were there, they could've told you. We're not that large a village that we have strangers in our midst."

"I don't know, Miss Dent, because the body is camouflaged. A sack was thrust over his head. Makes identification rather difficult."

"Over his *head?*" she said, her voice rising, her fingers gripping the arms of her chair. "But you'll know soon, won't you?"

"You think it may be someone you know?"

"What? Oh, no. I know everyone—that is I can't imagine who would have been killed. Or who would do such a thing. Especially in a church. And to spoil the celebration."

I agreed it was a bit of a facer, then asked how many people take part in the festivity.

"Workers or participants?"

"Both. Either."

"Well, as to workers, there's Olive Lindbergh, of course. She and Trueman are the backbone of this whole thing. They do an incredible amount of work. Just staggering. Never seem to tire. Perpetual helpers. And there's Owen, as I said. And one or two others who show up when the spirit calls, if you know what I mean."

"Can't hear too well at times?"

Magdalína smiled. "And there's Joel Twiss, a retired police officer. You look interested, Sergeant, but I'm afraid I don't remember where he was stationed. Bakewell, perhaps? Anyway, he's our dog's-body. Every committee should have one. Such wonderful people. What they accomplish, doing all those odd jobs! Saves us hundreds of little errands, don't they? Joel's usually around to hang the greens when Olive can't manage a ladder. Does all the heavier work. You know. And that's it, I think. No! Nearly forgot Sylvia Hale. She's the village do-gooder with all the money. She's fallen in love with her name on plaques, I'm afraid."

"Directing the putterer and the rest from afar?" I asked, suddenly interested in this group.

"You'd never know her hands were chapped from holding reins, Sergeant, but they are."

FOUR

"DOES SHE CONTROL other aspects of village life?"

Magdalína was gazing out of the window, clutching the neckline of her Aran-knit jumper. The wind and snow had stopped, leaving a soundless world beyond the stone walls. No rush of traffic, no bird song, no laughter from patrons leaving the pubs, no dogs barking. The village sat as though deserted of all life. It was as bizarre a scenario as the body in the church. Magdalína turned back to me, briefly closed her eyes, and said, "Not so as you'd notice. Nothing very blatant. Just little things."

"Such as?"

"Choosing the date for the annual flower festival, presiding at the competition for Wakes Week queen, judging the pet show."

"Sounds as though she is May Queen, I agree. How'd she become so authoritative? Birth right or dying request?"

"Significant money, I'm afraid. She and her husband, Colin. He's a dear. Don't let anyone tell you differently. It's just that he's normally shy around people. A product, I fear, of Sylvia's dictatorial personality. But he's more affirmative on his own, away from her."

"More like mother and child, then?"

"A bit too strong, Sergeant, but that's the idea. He sits mutely in her shadow and watches her direct events and people's lives. Don't know if he's just that sort who prefers to let others do the hard work or if she's beaten him into the role. Colin never serves on any village committees, either. Here, again, it may be that he enjoys his solitary time when she's gone. Or it could be he's not interested. Not everyone gives a hand."

"Is he the sort to pull strings from the background? Does he impress you as the real power behind the throne?"

"I'd be surprised if he was. Of course, he may write the checks, for all I know. When she started donating to local charities, as a way of imparting thanks, several of them asked her to sit on committees, lend a hand or ideas. That help escalated into chairing the concern when either no one volunteered or there was wide spread opinion she should get the honor since she had pumped time and money into the thing. Now it's become a way of life. She's so firmly entrenched that most people don't give it a thought."

"Just you and other democratically-minded people."

"It's not so much the hand on the rein that I find annoying as it is her assumption she should be doing it. Enough money poured into anything lets you buy it, I assume. It's obscene." Magdalína uttered the last statement so quietly I nearly missed it, but there was no mistaking the bitterness in her voice. She sounded like my mum after one of my brother's piano competitions. Although his sonata had been the more technically difficult, he'd lost to a showier piece. That was when mum had forsaken Chopin and taken refuge in wine. "I suppose," Magdalína said, "we committee members are as much to blame as Sylvia Hale is—we let her settle into her complacency without raising a hue and cry about elections."

"It's easy when one works nine-to-five," I said, thinking how little energy I had when I walked into my house at the end of the workday. Letting someone else take charge and do the hard bits was one less stress in life.

"That still doesn't excuse us. That's how countries are overtaken."

A silence fell between us as we were busy with our own thoughts. My dad had fallen into the easiness of collapsing on the sofa at the end of his work shift, turning off his brain, shifting household decisions and duties to mum. My brother had been too ensconced in his music to be disturbed; my sister had been too young, so I had stepped in to help run the house. Dad, absorbed in the telly and his own hypochondria, ignored the new hand at the helm. Anything was fine with him as long as it didn't bother him. Overthrown country, indeed. Finally, Magdalína said, "I'm afraid I've painted a rather harsh picture of Sylvia. She's really not Hitler incarnate, and she really does do splendid work. It's just that one gets…" She drew a breath as though considering her feelings.

"Tired?" I suggested.

"That or jealous. Or suspicious."

"Jealous, I can understand," I said, envisioning someone who frittered away her day while the rest of us slaved it out for little more than life sustaining wages. "But why suspicious?"

"She's got money. She's a good-looking woman. And while the former doesn't ensure the latter, it helps."

I nodded. "Help nature along with well-made clothes and cosmetics, weekly trips to the hair dresser."

"I'm not saying that I wouldn't dress better and indulge in membership at the fitness center if I had her money. I suppose I'm sounding rather resentful and spiteful, and I'm not."

She looked at me steadily, as though wondering how I judged her. I said, "You're sounding rather normal, I should say. It's hard to see others obtain so easily what you slave after. And there's that crumb of suspicion as to how they came to be so placed, and why not you?"

Magdalína set her teacup on the small table, between a framed photograph and a porcelain figurine. I commented on the photo.

"That's our dog's-body I was speaking of a moment ago. Joel Twiss."

"The retired police officer," I remarked, jotting a note that I would have to see where he had been stationed.

"Joel's another committee backbone. Donates more than he really should—finances, emotions and time. Lot of good ideas, too, whether for the village well dressing designs or fete themes. Likes to spend his time in the kitchen, doing his bit for the fund-raising bazaars. And there are more of those than you'd imagine. Seems like a village always has something it needs money for—church roof, church organ, school playground, landscaping, village hall repairs. Nearly as bad as home ownership, isn't it! But Joel doesn't mind giving his time and talent, and we're all quite grateful he can. Don't know what we'd do without him. He's quite famous for a few of his original recipes. He helps Hannah Leftridge with the refreshments for the festival. Nothing elaborate, but you have to have lemonade and biscuits for the children, don't you?"

"Owen Parnell doesn't do that? I would have thought—"

"Owen's got enough to do with the bread and with his job at the tearoom. No," Magdalína said, breaking a shortbread biscuit in half and brushing the crumbs off her slacks, "that's where Hannah and Joel shine. They're given complete leeway in that regard. Everyone else has started their own Christmas cakes, I think, so can't be bothered with baking dozens of biscuits and sausage rolls. At least that's the excuse. And Hannah and Joel enjoy it. Though Joel, being retired, has more time for baking than Hannah has. She owns the local bookstore, so you see, she's not got all the time in the world. She does her share, but she leans on Joel a good bit. Which everyone, including Hannah, is just as glad of. He's an exceptional baker. In fact, he always sells out of a particular raspberry scone each year."

I said that they couldn't be much better than the shortbread we were now eating.

As though afraid she was coveting undeserved praise, Magdalína hurriedly explained, "Owen's baking, those shortbread. Of course, I can match him there, but Owen's the backbone of my shop."

"And the St. Nicholas festival," I said, bringing the discussion around again to the reason for the interview.

"Well, we *do* need the bread, that's certain. So Owen's important in that sense. But we all do our part, like I said. Trueman and I see to the gifts, several people help wrap, and David Willett plays St. Nicholas."

"David—"

"He's a school teacher. History. He hands out the gifts."

"I take it he has a proper costume for this."

"Wonderfully accurate. At least it seems so to me. Not a Father Christmas red coat but a true 4th century bishop-style cape and staff. The children seem awed by him. Well, so do we all."

"I should think so," I said, glad that Father Christmas, as much as I liked him, was relegated to later in the month.

"And there's Olive, of course. Olive Lindbergh does the greater part of the decorating. And you said that was…"

"Yes, when the body was discovered. So you hadn't been up to the church yet, Ms. Dent?"

Magdalína pressed her fingertips against her lips, as though considering what to answer. Shaking her head slowly, she said, "I'd finished with the gift buying Monday. I wrapped them here, thinking Trueman had enough to do getting the church ready for this evening."

"And what did you do with the gifts, then?"

"Kept them here, on the sofa."

I glanced to my right, half expecting to see remaining wrapping paper and ribbon. The space was tidy. "Until…"

"This noon time. I didn't want to take them over too early,

for they'd only be in the way—and perhaps be too strong a temptation."

"Some children are like that," I agreed. "Can't wait a day or two if they see a gift."

"Actually, Sergeant, I was thinking more of theft."

"Had trouble, then?"

"The odd problem. Collection box broken into at various times. Small things gone missing. Nothing like the altar cross or candlesticks, thank God. But Trueman can tell you better about that."

I scribbled a note in my book and asked, "Was there anyone else in the church at noon? I'm thinking more of someone who shouldn't have been there."

"Like our sporadic thief or Colin Hale, for instance?" she said, nearly smiling. "No. No black cloaked figures lurking. I left the bag of gifts in the vestry—Trueman knew I was going to do that. He was going to get another bucket from someplace. That's why I couldn't just put them out, near the nave altar. Olive was due to decorate around 1:00. That's been her set routine for years. Owen was to deliver the bread around tea time, after he'd finished with the baking and the rush of lunch at the shop, here."

"And you?"

"For my alibi, you mean? I didn't kill him."

"You just asked me for his identity."

"I didn't kill *anyone*. I haven't a way of proving it, but I didn't. I was here, in the shop, all afternoon until nearly 6:30, when Trueman rang me up to tell me about the festivity cancellation. Other than that…" Her eyes half closed, as though weary from remembering or shutting out the mental image of the body.

I set my tea cup on the table, closed my notebook and stood up. A small golden-toned clock on the fireplace mantleshelf chimed the half hour.

"Half past nine," Magdalína said quietly, staring at the clock face. "Festival would have been over by now. All our hard work..."

"That's the way with most things, isn't it, Ms. Dent? Weeks of preparation, then it's over in a matter of an hour or two."

"At least Olive found the body before the children came."

I left, agreeing that some things were indeed fortunate.

OWEN PARNELL WAS JUST getting ready to go to bed, but he willingly gave me a few minutes. He was large and muscular—the perfect build, I thought, for heaving cumbersome, heavy pans in and out of the ovens. His florid face spoke of natural coloring that wouldn't be flushed in the heat of baking. We sat in his kitchen, for he was just brewing a cup of tea. I declined the offer, gave him a minute to feed his dog, then asked when he had delivered the festival bread.

"'Round tea time," he said, watching me open my notebook. He paused, as though afraid he had implicated himself in the killing. When I merely smiled at him, he said, "That's when I always do it. Each year, I mean. Four-ish, so the bread's fresh and I have the lunch crowd over with."

"You didn't have the rush of tea time patrons to worry with?"

Owen grunted and slapped the face of the clock as he walked over to the table. The chair banged against the table legs as he pulled it out. He swore. "We close early on St. Nicholas day. People understand. Even if they don't—" He shrugged, as if to say 'damn them.'

"And you didn't see—"

"Not likely to see anything, am I? Heavin' that lot about."

"Lot of bread, then?"

"'Round about ten dozen loaves."

"Should think that would take—"

"It takes how long it takes," Owen said, yanking out a neighboring chair and resting his legs on it. The chair was white, as was most everything else in the room. Flour white. The table at which we sat occupied the wall along the back. Cupboards and appliances spread over the remaining walls, the sole splash of color a few framed awards on the walls and the springs of holly in an apple-red vase. A few berries lay on the counter, fallen and forgotten—like the berries in the snow outside the church door. The stove was the usual domestic variety. Odd for a man who lives by baking, I thought. Or maybe in response to. If I cooked all day, would I want to cook for myself? "Can't get it all done in one day. So I freeze it. I just finish it up today. Still, bread's fresh enough. Never heard any complaints. Especially so, since it's free."

"There are a lot of things that are free that people still find they can complain about. A gift doesn't erase ill humor or discourtesy."

"My hospitality's worn thin at times, I do admit," he said after taking a long swallow of tea.

"And you didn't notice anything unusual in the church when you delivered the bread…"

"The gifts were wrapped, the greens put about. What is there to see that's unusual?"

"Oh, something out of place, a window open, snow where someone had—"

"I'm not interested in somethin' out of place or a window open. I had tubs of bread to get in and I had to get back to the shop. And that's where I spent the rest of the time until I left around 5:00. And I don't know if anyone saw me in the kitchen or walkin' home. But it you wanna check my whereabouts— or lack of—to link me to this murder—"

"I haven't accused you of murder, Mr. Parnell. I'm asking if you saw anything unusual in the church when you were there."

"I had no time to be noticin' snow in front of the west gallery, if that's what you mean. I was that glad to get rid of the bread,

Miss, without standin' about lookin' for open windows. I do the bread and that's all."

"Well, most people are thankful for it, I shouldn't wonder."

"Seems like I just get done with this lot and I have to start again." He got up and refilled his mug from the teapot. In passing the vase of holly, he swept the dropped berries into his hand and let them trickle onto the saucer before sitting back down.

"Oh? I understood that the bread-giving only occurred during the festival. Does the village give—"

"First of all, the *village* don't give nothin'. It's a few hard-working *souls* who do all the givin'. And second, the bread ceremony has finished, yes. I'm talkin' about *bakin'*, *not* bread. Got another large bakin' job comin' up in three days' time— Saturday. A party. Pub party for one of our people."

"Pub party?"

"Publishin' party, if that means more to you, though it didn't to me when I first heard it."

"Publishing, as in 'book'?"

Owen sniffed, finished the last of his tea, and stared at the clock. I asked the question again before he answered in the affirmative. "Lot of nonsense, a party for a book. But it's his first, so I suppose it's a big thing."

"And whose book would this be?"

"Suppose it would be just about anyone's, but it's Dave Willett's. Teacher up at the school. History. Wrote a book on local history, though why we have to have that—"

"You don't *have* to," I said, wondering if the murder or the late hour was putting Owen out of sorts. "But it's nice. It's an awfully exciting thing when your first book is published."

"Well, I suppose it is, but it makes more work for others, don't it? All this bakin' for the party…"

"Is Mr. Willett's publisher footing the bill for the party?"

"Don't think so. At least, not all of it. I heard Dave talkin' to Magdalína about cost and number of people and food and such. So he's obviously got to watch the quids even if the publisher is helpin' out. But it won't be all that hard, I guess," he relinquished, stretching. "I like Dave well enough. And he's a hard workin' chap, so give him his party, I say. There aren't that many times we can celebrate in this life, are there?"

"So you grab on to St. Nicholas and the book party while you can."

"At least his book's out before Christmas. Should help with sales. People'll buy them for gifts if for nothin' else."

"You don't think David Willett's book will be all that popular?"

Owen shrugged again. "At least it'll get read once. Not in the same league as the satin pillow bought on holiday in Crete."

"You said he wrote about local history. That could cover a large area—anything from geographical formation to local politics. What's the book's subject? Do you know?"

"Think it's on local customs. Not just the village. Most all of Derbyshire, I'm thinkin'."

"He should have a large chapter, then, on your St. Nicholas festival. I don't think I've ever encountered that before."

"Vicar feels more or less obligated, what with the church bein' named St. Nicholas. He gave bread to the poor, you know, St. Nick did. Time of famine, it were. Like our Lord's loaves and fishes, only this were just loaves. Miracle, they say, the way the saint procured the bread. But that's Providence, ain't it? Pure, holy Providence. Somebody always providin' for someone else. Anyway, it's kind of nice, at that, havin' a bit of celebration to put us in the Christmas mood. We oughta have more Christmas mood, I'm thinkin', all year 'round. But that's another problem for another day."

"So every 6th of December the village holds its festival,

seeing to the children and to the elderly. Your bread, Mr. Parnell, is very important to these people's lives."

"More so than cherry scones and punch at a book signin' but I ain't complainin' about how Magdalína runs her business. It's kept me fed and clothed." He ran his finger through the holly berries.

It wasn't until I was standing outside his home that I realized Owen hadn't asked about the identity of the body.

FIVE

WHILE NOT EXACTLY Victorian in architectural design, the village bookshop *did* have a Dickensian air. It looked every day of its two hundred years. Stones quarried in George III's reign from the dark limestone veins that run through the Pennine mountain chain had smoothed water-soft through the winters. The shop leaned against the restaurant on its north side with the weariness of enduring Life's battering. Stone-smothering ivy had been clipped enough to accommodate the doors and windows. A bow window, alive with strands of tiny white lights, displayed some of the store's merchandise. Snow-crusted pine roping and red bows framed the window. The sign announcing 'Fact and Fiction Bookshop' creaked from its wrought iron arm above the door.

It could well be Dickens' old curiosity shop. Or Copperfield's boyhood home. Or even Smike's last refuge. But not Scrooge's house, for the joy of Christmas was too evident. I rang the bell and leaned against the wall, gazing at the small gaslit park that ran along the shop's southern side. I could almost distinguish the figure of Christmas Present in the shadows beyond the great barren trees. Hearing the door open, I turned from my thoughts of Dickens.

The case was only hours old and already I was hallucinating. A man crowned in a white and gold bishop's miter stood in the doorway. When I had introduced myself he called over his shoulder, "We're rumbled, Hannah. The constabulary are here." Not knowing how he meant that, I murmured my thanks and waited for him to close the door. As I followed him into the bowels of the building, he said, "I'm David Willett, by the way. And this—" he gestured with his coffee mug, "—is Hannah Leftridge, hospitable book shop owner. You want some tea or coffee?" I declined and took the offered chair. He stood behind Hannah as though guarding her from arrest or inquisition or grief.

Hannah Leftridge sat beside a small table lamp, her dark eyes mere pools of blackness in its shadow. The light fell across her hands, pudgy as the rest of her, veined from work. Fingernails of various lengths bore mute evidence of too many uncooperative boxes and too little shop help. Her hair, limp and in need of a good cut, spoke of too little free time. She patted David's hand, which was resting protectively on the back of her chair.

"David had just left his home for the church," she said, glancing at him as though to affirm her story, "when I waved him down. So he stopped in for coffee."

"You were walking, sir?" I asked, eyeing the bishop's garb on a chair. I had walked from Owen's house to Hannah's shop, alternately looking for Graham's car and losing myself in the splendor of the sky. The grey screen of clouds had parted slightly to show a sprinkling of stars, rather like a vein of silver running through lead. The moon, as yet hidden, hinted at a later appearance, for its silvery light shone from behind the edge of the cloud bank. An owl, on some silent journey, sped across the sky.

"No," David said. "Costume's too heavy. Besides, it was snowing and I didn't want to risk its ruin from the storm. I was driving. Hannah had just rung off from talking to the vicar and stepped outside to wait for me. Trueman tried ringing my place, but I'd evidently just missed his call."

"That's why I went outside to look for him," Hannah said. "I didn't want him going to the church."

"And when did the vicar ring you up?"

"Oh, 6:25, 6:30. Somewhere around then."

At least it fit with Trueman's account of discovering the body.

"And until 6:30 when David arrived, you were…"

"I had a customer around 4:00," Hannah said, her voice noticeably strained. "She stayed for nearly half an hour, browsing for a Christmas gift for her niece. When she left, no one came in until David. So I suppose I have no alibi…"

I murmured something non-committal while Hannah gave me the woman's name and address. Turning to David, I said, "And can you vouch for your time from, say, 4:00 until 6:30, sir?"

David shrugged. "Not anything cast iron, if that's what I need. After I got my costume out and had my tea, I had a kip around 4:30. Woke at 5:00, shoveled the driveway, took off for Hannah's and got, like I said, here around 6:30. Why? You suspect old St. Nick of murder?"

"And you've been here ever since?" I said.

"Nothing much else to do," David said after taking a sip from his mug. He seemed the sort who had to be doing something constantly, for he was tall and thin, as though he constantly burned energy. Apparently just realizing he still wore his hat, he took it off, smoothed down his reddish hair, and set the miter on top of his robe. "I thought of going home and marking papers, but when you're in the St. Nick mood everything else seems a let-down."

"You've a marvelous costume," I said, looking at the clusters of tiny gold balls stitched onto the deep-yellow embroidery. Designs of fish, interlocked double rings, crosses and sailing ships—portrayed in metallic thread, beads and imitation gems, mother-of-pearl and silk braiding—covered the white wool robe and cape. I remarked on the handiwork.

"Artist's license," David said. "I've no way of knowing what St. Nicholas' robes looked like, of course, so I designed what I wanted. But it's authentic as to style."

"The three gold balls I understand," I said. "The three bags of gold he threw down the chimney of the three sisters who were about to enter into prostitution for lack of a marriage dowry."

"Yes, the symbol of pawnbrokers—financial help in time of great need—and his most famous deed by which we have turned him into Santa Claus."

"The fish," I said, "I assume are symbolic of Christianity."

"You could read them as such, but I added them in recognition of fishermen. The small sailboats represent sailors. He's the patron saint of both groups."

"And the two linked circles?"

"Represent wedding rings," David said. "He's the patron saint of brides. That's the only thing I could think of. He's also patron saint of spinsters, prisoners, bakers—oh, many more occupations—but I couldn't come up with symbols for those that would be readily identifiable. Besides, I had to stop somewhere."

"It's beautiful," I said, wanting to run my fingers over the embroidery. "Really a work of art. How did you become St. Nicholas?"

"I stepped into my predecessor's shoes when he moved to London. He dressed up, but not authentically."

Hannah said, "I asked David when he took over if he could wear something more in keeping with our image of the saint."

"So," David said, "we both researched it, I sewed the basic costume, Hannah embroidered it, and Trueman created the miter. I've played St. Nick for nine years. This was to have been my tenth..." he said, his words dying away. The shop became quiet. Pulling himself from his thoughts, he rushed on. "But the festival's gone on longer than folks can remember. I'm just one of many, you know."

"The villagers are lucky to have you," I said.

"Don't know about that, but I love doing it. The looks on the little kids' faces when I step out of the shadows near the altar..."

"David devotes a lot of time to it all," Hannah said.

"Time I should be off," he said, putting his cup on a small table. "Or do you need me, Sergeant?"

I said I could talk to him later and watched him gather up his costume.

After thanking Hannah for the coffee, David bid us both good evening and left the shop in a flurry of cold wind and snowflakes. The shop felt empty without him.

"He certainly seems made for the part," I said. "Friendly, dedicated to the saint's research, likes children...must make an excellent St. Nick."

Hannah pushed a strand of hair behind her ear and expressed concern for the gift recipients.

"They look forward to it from year to year," she said, her voice as quiet as the evening.

"It does seem like fun—need aside," I agreed, glancing about the room. We sat in the used book section of her shop, a room divided from the new books area by upholstered chairs, small tables and foot stools clustered on opposite sides of the walls, allowing an opening into each region. It was a comfortable way to divide the books, and one that begged the browser to read and then buy. Smaller tables throughout both areas displayed the current offerings or small flyers of events such as author signings or book reviews, but offered no seating. Bookshelves clambered up the walls. In each book section a skylight counteracting the claustrophobic, cave-like atmosphere, would spill sunlight into the store. Now it hinted of starlight. I breathed deeply of the scents of old books and pinecones.

"I suppose there's no alternative date set," Hannah said, leaning forward in the chair so that I could see her eyes. They held the color of night, black and infinitely deep. When I shook my head, she said, "No, early days yet. Of course. It's just that with everyone looking forward to it so, and Owen's already baked the bread..."

"He told me you're about to hold a book party."

Hannah smiled slightly and gestured to a nearby table with a display of books. The cover showed a photograph of a group of costumed figures, most notably Father Christmas, standing in a semi-circle and staring at a body on the ground. The book's title, *The Ancient Art of Derbyshire Customs,* stood out in embossed red and silver lettering above their heads. "David's latest. Well, his *only* one to date. Just got a shipment in today, in fact."

I said that it was quite a striking cover.

"Oh, yes. Quite first-class. A lot better than some of that 'artistic' muck that's dished out, leaving you to wonder if it's supposed to be a book or a piece of art suitable for framing. But I'm of the old school, thinking a cover should give you an idea of the book's contents."

"Mummers are a great favorite of mine. Especially the Christmas ones. Somehow the ones at Easter just don't seem as traditional or as mysterious."

"And that's a big part of mumming plays, isn't it? The doctor with his nonsensical, mystical power to resurrect the body." She stopped abruptly and shifted her eyes from mine. I knew what she was thinking. There would be no resurrecting doctor for the body in the church. After a rather strained silence, she said, "Will your investigation postpone the publishing party?"

"I shouldn't think so, Ms. Leftridge. We don't like disrupting people's lives more than we have to."

"And unless David turns out to be the killer...yes," she said, her voice ringing with forced cheerfulness. "We cook our eggs, wash our clothes, watch our sitcoms and buy David's book. Everyday life. All guaranteed to bring on the sunshine and eradicate the tragedy."

"I don't think a celebration of a new book is exactly eradicating the tragedy, Ms. Leftridge. And I don't see any harm in going on with life. Just so people show a proper respect for the victim."

"Of course. I apologize. I didn't mean to sound flippant. It's just so sudden. So unbelievable. And you don't know who…" She nodded as I said we weren't able to identify the victim yet. Leaning back in her chair, she said, "Well, I don't envy Owen's lot in all this. First he works his fingers to the bone for tonight's festival, then he has to supplement what Joel Twiss and I make for the book party."

"And the party is…"

"Saturday evening."

"And this is Wednesday. Only gives you—"

"Tomorrow and Friday evenings. Yes, not much time. Luckily, I've done some advance baking. And Joel's retired, so he'll do the bulk of his baking Friday evening and Saturday morning."

"Sounds like a lot of work," I said, getting up to leaf through David's book. I passed a small display of Advent and Christmas books, the most prominent one featuring Father Christmas through the ages. All very timely. I promised myself I'd buy a copy before I left the village.

"It *is* work, I admit. But I'm leaving on holiday next week, so I can rest up then. Greece."

"Must be nice," I said, thinking of the present snow. "Never been myself. Your first time?"

"Yes. I wouldn't know where to go, ordinarily speaking, but I've got a good tour guide."

Taking up David's book, I said, "I'm surprised the publisher isn't having the event catered. Or am I hopelessly out of date?"

"It's up to the author and the store where he's signing. Most stores supply the refreshments. We count it as a business expense, a slight out-of-pocket to sell more books. God, it sounds awful! I never spoke of it in those terms before! But that's the gist of it. Takes money to make money. Anyway, Sergeant, I don't begrudge David a party, even if the publisher doesn't throw in a bit. David's well liked in this town, and Joel, Owen and I won't miss the few hours of cooking to ensure a successful party for his new book."

"I hope it *is* a success," I said, putting the book back. "Must be difficult for a new author to get his name out to the public."

"Very difficult. That's why you need help from your family and friends. You count on them to spread the word, recommend the book."

"If you don't mind me saying so, Ms. Leftridge, I'm impressed *you're* so successful. It's nice to see a small, independent store."

"Amazed I'm still head-above-water myself. Actually, I tried competing with the dot-coms and big chains but it wasn't long until I was frantically treading water, so I switched to the present format. Not only does the used book section help with my grocery bill, but also I know my clients well enough to specialize in what sells around here. Local stuff does well— history, local biography, Derbyshire rambling guides and nature, true crime—" She reddened at another verbal blunder.

"Finding one's niche isn't easy," I said by way of glossing over her embarrassment. "But once you've discovered it, entrench yourself and don't budge. How much is Mr. Willett's book selling for?"

Hannah told me and said I should stop by the party for an autographed copy.

"Well, I'm glad I caught you up, Ms. Leftridge," I said, walking toward the door. She followed me, glancing at the clock above the checkout desk. It was later than I had thought, but Graham—if he had arrived—and the rest of the police contingent wouldn't see bed for several hours.

"Wednesdays and Fridays are my late evenings, Sergeant. I'm glad you could find me. I hope you solve your case quickly." She rested with her hand on the edge of the open door, as though eager to close it on my retreating figure. "Sorry I wasn't at the church to see anything, but if there's anything I can do…"

I thanked her, wished her success with the party, and stepped outside. The moment the door closed the shop's light went out.

WHEN I HAD TRUDGED BACK to the church, I learned Graham had arrived. He was, Margo informed me, at the village hall, seeing to setting up the incident room. I exhaled loudly.

"Great. I just spent quarter of an hour fighting knee deep snow drifts to get here and he's at the hall."

"You exaggerate," Margo said. She was a detective constable, in her mid 20s, single and beautiful. She was also slim, which gave her the right, she thought, to advise me on my extra weight. She had her eye on sergeant stripes of her own, so I tutored her as best as I could. Even if she wouldn't have had designs in that direction, we still would've hung out together. She understood me. "It's only calf deep. Anyway, exercise is good for you. You're always saying you'd like slimmer hips, Bren, and now when you've got the opportunity to combat those thighs—"

"Exercise has its time, Margo, and a murder investigation isn't it."

"Fine, but don't grouse around me, then." She handed me a sketch of the village. Like everything else Margo did, the sketch was precise, well-drawn, and researched. She was learning quickly and would soon win her promotion to sergeant. I smoothed the paper and glanced at her handiwork.

Bramwell was laid out along four intersecting streets, like a giant noughts-and-crosses game. On the southwest corner, claiming the highest hill, the church and vicarage sat, predominant and awesome. Traveling north along this street you came upon the tearoom and bookshop. A collection of other establishments—post office, hotel, chemist's, pub and a restaurant—

dotted the same road. The village hall and adjoining playground lay beyond these on the northwest corner. Owen's
house, I didn't need reminding, was on the opposite side of the
village. I angled the paper beneath Margo's electric torch and
asked how far away the hall was. She had neglected to include
a mileage scale.

"Walking or driving?"

"Driving," I said, knocking the wet snow from my wellies.

"Really, Bren, you've got a ready-made exercise right here
if—"

"The tax payers will be thrilled to hear I'm exercising instead
of solving crimes." I turned toward my car. It was boxed in
between a stone-wall and Jens' car. So, our Home Office pathologist had made it over from Sheffield. Karol was probably thrilled
she could go home. But the only mobility I would see right now
was with my feet; even my little Corsa couldn't maneuver out
of this cramped space. I sighed. "All right. Walking."

"Shouldn't think more than ten minutes in this stuff." Margo
bent to pick up a handful of snow. "Fifteen minutes, then. Kind
of heavy going, I guess."

"Great observation for a detective. Well, unless I wait for
Jens to leave…" I eyed the church's south door. "Any idea of
what's going on in there, how soon he'll finish?"

"Haven't an idea. Not been inside. You want a space suit?"

I waved away her offer of the paper jumpsuit. Getting into that
would be almost as much struggle as walking the two blocks to
the hall. "No, thanks. I've done my snowman bit for the evening."

"You could always get a ride down with Dean or someone."

We looked around but couldn't see his car. "Guess he's
already left. Sorry, Bren."

"Well, a walk's better than standing here." I stamped my feet.
They were beginning to feel numb. "Uh, how's Graham? Did
he seem…I mean, after getting an earful from the Super…"

"He mustn't have done. He was all smiles and politeness. His usual self."

I shoved my gloved hand into my slacks pocket. My fingertips hit my car keys. Giving a last look at my car, I turned toward the road.

Margo's voice followed me as I strode off. "Village hall is two blocks down this street. You can't miss it."

GRAHAM'S CAR WAS the last in a long line of police vehicles and rather less snowy, which spoke of recently plowed roads. As I approached the hall I blinked several times, for the brilliant white light spilling onto the fresh snow was a sharp contrast to the dark village. I ran my fingers lightly along the side of his red Honda in passing and walked into the building.

It was a large, rectangular affair, smelling of floor wax and fried bangers, with a main room and several doors leading to what I presumed were the kitchen, storage closets and facilities. The wooden floor creaked under my footsteps as I walked up to Graham, who was standing by a muscular metal table. He had just plugged in his computer but smiled when I came up.

"Hello, TC," he said, pulling out a chair for me. I sat down, thanking him. The use of my nickname boded well. Simcock had not done too much damage. He eyed my snow-flocked boots and slacks. "Been in a fight?"

"The elements, yes."

"By the way, I commend you on calling out Karol. Jens Nielsen finally got here."

I murmured my thanks, suddenly shy at his praise. The local police surgeon was called out only in cases of suspicious death when foul play is suspected at the outset. And this body, if anything, was suspicious. In fact, it screamed bloody murder.

"Jens said something like 'Well, I can rule out accidental

death,'" Graham continued, grinning. "Of course, that was the second comment he made on arrival."

"I don't need to hear his first. I can imagine it."

A short blonde of Danish lineage, Jens Nielsen usually uttered a one or two-word oath on arriving at a crime scene. His word choice was ranked and used depending on the situation or condition of the body. We always knew how bad it was from Jens' profanity.

"Anyway, Karol was just as happy to leave it to Jens. And I'm pleased you enlarged the crime scene barrier beyond our usual five-meter limit. Who knows what we may find beneath all this snow? You showed real foresight, TC."

I said something like my Girl Guide training coming to the fore even when least expected, and pulled out my notebook. He smiled as I handed it to him. "You may want to have a look at this, sir, before I type it up."

Flipping back the notebook cover, Graham said, "You'll make Superintendent before I do, TC, if you continue in this vein. All this already?"

I tried to keep from smiling, tried to keep the pleasure from my voice, but I don't know how successful I was. I was placed in his tutelage, as a newly appointed detective sergeant, to learn, but beyond the lessons I also wanted his praise. Not just so I could move quickly through the ranks but because I feared I was beginning to love him. And through that love I wanted to show him I was worth loving in return. I cleared my voice and said, "Yes, sir. I talked to the vicar and Mrs. Lindbergh—she discovered the body. Then I spoke with Magdalína Dent, Owen Parnell and Hannah Leftridge. While the day's events were still fresh in their minds."

On hearing his own philosophy returned, Graham looked at me, his eyebrow raised. I sat quietly, watching the constables convert the room to an investigation site complete with computers, telephones and fax machines. I wondered if the murder was disturbing some other village function. Billiards and darts, probably. Embroidery classes and local WVI, perhaps. But as much as I felt for the comforts of daily life, I wasn't too disheartened. They would lose a week at most of their life; the murdered victim had lost all.

Complimenting me on the swiftness of my action, Graham handed the notes back to me. His eyes, dark green in the glare of the overhead lights, held my look. I stammered that I had tried to be thorough and that they had seemed like the logical people to question right now.

"And what, in your logical mind, TC, seems like the next step in this bizarre case?" He asked it as a teacher would ask a class prior to a test, making certain the lesson had been learned.

"Establish identity of the victim, sir."

"You may progress to the front row of the class. With Karol's preliminary work finished, I had the vicar take a look at our hooded man."

"Thinking he would know most everyone in the parish," I said, feeling easier now that we were talking shop.

Graham nodded and sat down next to me. "The person who usually comes across all church goers in the course of a year. Even if Mr. Parnell, for instance, never visits the restaurant across the street and therefore may not know the owners, our vicar would know both—assuming they are both God-fearing men of Anglican persuasion."

He paused, as though remembering something in his ministerial days. As a Methodist minister, Graham may have been in a similar position. Minister or vicar, each man would know many people in the village. And know some of the history that perhaps drove someone to murder.

I watched his hands toying with the computer keyboard. They were elegant hands, long fingered and thin, matching the rest of his tall, thin frame. His fingertips ran across the keys as though they might have been the keys of the instrument he played. They came to rest as he said, "We know who the victim is, but we've no idea as to why he's been thrust into a sack." He looked up as I asked who the victim was. "Oh. Hadn't I said? It's a retired police officer. Joel Twiss."

SIX

GRAHAM AND I had talked far into the night, discussing the next steps of the case. I woke Thursday morning to a grey and white world. Along the street, dozens of soot-stained chimneys coughed up grey curls of smoke that drifted lazily into the clearing, leaden sky. Coal and wood scented the air, stirring up my memories of long-ago Christmas Eves and fires against frigid winter nights. Dad with the Yule log he'd spent a week preparing, mum with her baking that perfumed the house, my brother practicing carols on the piano, my sister begging me to sledge with her and engaging me in a snowball fight instead.

I inhaled deeply of the cold, scented air and zipped up my jacket. In the distance, beyond Piebald Tor, a snow plow struggled up the hill, its motor grinding under the effort. Here in the village, car tracks, snaked and twined like great, jumbled vines, had rutted the smoothness of the street. Light from the pallid sun slid down the western sides of the ruts, throwing the eastern walls into dark grey. Footprints dotted the sidewalk and disappeared into the snowy mounds at the corner. Snow flecked windows and doors, and lay like frosting along roof slates and tree branches. I lingered beneath a hawthorn tree, watching a group of waxwings devour the tree's berries. Their pinkish-tan chests stood out boldly among the green leaves, yet their red crests were nearly camouflaged among the red fruit. As one large bird hopped along a branch overhead, he dislodged the snow, and it christened me in cold and wet. Hearing a laugh behind me, I turned. Mark Salt, a fellow detective in B Division, was leaning against the hotel's open doorway, his grey eyes bright with humor. I knocked the snow from my hair.

"Always start the day with a laugh, Mark," I said, feeling the blush invade my cheeks. "Keeps your blood pressure down."

"That's one problem I don't have, Brenna. But I wouldn't mind risking it some night, if you'd like to trot up to my room." He shifted slightly, his shoulders pulled back so they nearly filled the doorway, his eyes still smiling, the humor gone from his lips.

"Purely for scientific research, then?" I said, my voice taking on an edge.

"Well, there might be other benefits…"

I suppressed a retort as I counted to ten. While other women—Margo, for one—may have longed for the invitation, I did not. It would have been easy to accept it, for he was good looking, with grey hair and an upper body that benefited from weekly workouts. But Mark Salt conveyed the air of one-night-stands. I did not want to be another notch on his bedpost. When I made love I wanted it to be special, with the man I would love the rest of my life.

Mark evidently took my silence for deliberation instead of anger, for he added, "Your bed or mine?"

"I've got to get to work, Mark," I said, keeping my voice as steady as I could. "Why don't you plunge your head into a snow bank? It might cool you off."

He stared at me, a smile slowly forming on his lips. "And run the risk of suffocation? Hardly sporting of you, Brenna. But I understand you, all right. Can't say yes right away, can you? It's a woman's place to want to be wooed. Well, darling, I'm willing to pursue as long as you wish."

"God, Mark! I have no wish to be pursued. I work with you because I have to, but I won't sleep with you. Plain enough?"

He stepped backward, making a sweeping bow. "Shall I take that as a 'maybe,' then?"

A cacophony of squealing car brakes and yells killed my answer. I turned toward the sound. A white toy poodle trailing a leather lead had darted into the middle of the street. Several horrified people yelled at the dog or the driver of the car that was skidding in the dog's direction. The half dozen commanding voices only served to confuse the dog, for he stood frozen. I jumped over the snowy curb, ran into the street and scooped up the dog, missing the car's front wing by inches. Mark enveloped my arm with his hand and guided me to the bench outside the hotel. The driver's profuse apologies were lost in Mark's scolding.

"What the *hell* do you think you were doing? Playing at Wonder Woman?"

"I was only—that is, the dog—" I glanced at the car resting diagonally across the street, its bonnet nosed over the curb, and found I couldn't control my legs. The world suddenly began to tilt. Mark pushed me onto the bench. His face floated a very long distance from me.

The dog's owner, ashen-faced and bewildered, stumbled up to me. "Oh, Miss, thank you! My God, what a brave—how can I ever thank you?" He alternately hugged his dog and looked at me, tears threatening to spill from his eyes.

Mark nodded. "You *should* thank Sergeant Taylor, sir. She risked her life just now." He dismissed the man as he bent down to ask if I wanted anything.

A voice that must have been mine said a cup of tea would be nice.

The owner handed his dog to a curious bystander and dashed inside the hotel. Mark sat down next to me and put his hands on my shoulders. His fingertips dug into my flesh. "I've never seen anything so damned bloody stupid! You could've been killed! No." His hand grabbed my chin and turned my face toward his. "You're going to hear this. If I have to repeat this every hour on the hour, you're going to hear this. What the HELL were you thinking? Or weren't you thinking? Obviously not. A skidding car—" He broke off, his face crimson.

I muttered something about saving the dog, and Mark swore. He was still swearing when the dog owner returned with my tea. I thanked him, smiled weakly and offered to pay him.

"Oh, no!" the man said. "I'd die of mortification! Please. It's the least I can do after you saved Laramie's life. The *least*. I only wish I could do something else—"

"Sergeant Taylor appreciates the tea, sir," Mark was saying, giving him a polite but firm nudge to move on. "But right now, she's a bit shaken so if you don't mind…"

"But I can't leave indebted to you." He tucked the dog under his left arm and started fumbling for his wallet. "Please. I know it's not proper, giving presents to the police, but won't you take this as a gift from a thankful citizen—to another citizen?" He pulled out a £50 note and tried to cram it into my hand. I shook my head. "Please!" His voice was nearly a whine, a plea to ease his conscience.

Mark laid his hand on the man's arm, forcibly turning him away from us. Giving a hurried nod, the man thanked me again, then walked down the street, embracing his dog.

I bent over, holding my stomach, afraid I was about to be sick. No one seemed to care. A few men were pushing the car back into the street, but the main knot of interested viewers broke up, the drama now over. A few snippets of conversation heavy with the names 'Laramie' and 'Colin Hale' drifted to me. I shut my eyes.

Mark sat beside me as I choked down my tea. I took longer over it than normal, for my teeth chattered and I clamped them onto the cup's rim to keep them quiet. When I had finished, Mark took the cup and set it on the bench.

I looked down the street, toward the vicarage, where I should have been fifteen minutes ago. Mark's voice seemed as distant as the building. "Perhaps you should spend the night with me if that's the only way I can make certain of your safety." He patted my hand before I could stand up.

"Thanks Mark. I appreciate your concern, if not your method. I'm fine. Honest. It just happened so quickly, that's all. The skid and the dog…"

"Leave the heroics to the comic book characters, Brenna. You can't single handedly save the world."

I thanked him again and started toward St. Nicholas, grateful Mark hadn't made a mocking phrase this time out of my helping an animal.

"IS THIS A BET, or are you out on some endurance test?"

I turned toward the speaker as the car drew alongside me. I would've had difficulty seeing it against the background of snow if it hadn't been for the florescent orange stripe cutting the car horizontally in half. A 'jam sandwich', they were called, these white police vehicles. The man who had spoken to me pointed to my snow-splattered slacks and grinned. "A little more white and you'll have the costume, but you need more of a lurch if you want to be successful as The Mummy."

"You chase me down just to be flippant?"

"*Me?*" He looked so shocked that I laughed. "So you don't believe me. I never was a good liar."

"Is that why you strayed to this side of the law rather than to the other?"

He considered the question for a moment. "It's my body language, Brenna. It always gives me away."

Which was so far from the truth that I coughed. Scott could read the slightest voice inflection or merest eye movement. Noting my reaction, Scott said, "All right. The truth is that I just

don't look my best under those bright lights. Accents my
wrinkle. Get in."

He said it so authoritatively that I opened the door and slid
into the car without thinking. It was barely warmer than it was
outdoors. The car's heater sat mute. I angled the vents of one
of the side window blowers toward my face. "Aren't you cold?
Why don't you put on your blouson?" I said, nodding toward
the dark jacket thrown onto the back seat. It sat beside his cap.

"Too restricting. Anyway, I don't personify that part of the
Motto, Brenna."

"Well, I do," I said, and added that I knew very few police
officers who liked to be wet, hungry or cold. I eyed the dashboard.

"And leave it *alone!*" Scott's hand clamped over the temperature regulator.

I looked at his serious face and smiled. Raven-haired and
green-eyed, Scott Coral was one of three dozen uniformed constables stationed at Buxton. Although I had had only superficial
contact with Scott—talks over lunches in the canteen, a 'hello'
nodded at the local pub—I knew him to be ethical to the point
of stoicism, responsible to the degree of self-imposition. One of
a few officers, in fact, who would answer his pager on his day
off. Loyalty marked his friendships, just as optimism pervaded
his daily routine—unusual in a profession saturated by pessimis-
tic officers. However, for all his saintly qualities there was no
halo above his head. Scott could be very human. Besides being
bonkers about sports, he was fond of a pint and of poker.

"Where you off to, then?" he asked, glancing at my snowy
attire.

"The vicarage. Turn right here, if you don't mind. It's just
up the street a ways. Ta." Though the walk from the hotel hadn't
been long, it had been cold, with a wind that had frosted my
eyelashes and lips and seemed to cut right through my jacket.
A sparrow had chirped its good morning to me as I had walked,

and flew in short hops ahead of me until it rested in a finger of sunlight, basking in its meager warmth. I had left it opposite the tearoom and had trudged on alone through the snow drifts, marveling at the quiet a snowfall always brings. I hadn't heard Scott's car approaching until he had called out. "This is it," I said a minute later.

Scott stopped the car, keeping it running as we finished our talk. "So you're off to interrogate Suspect #1, is it?" He was worse than Graham when it came to humor. At least I was beginning to understand when Graham was joking. Scott was a different problem. "Did you pass that part of the course? I don't want to read about your offence against the discipline code—is that section 60 of the 1984 Act, do you recall? I'm always muddled."

Scott was about as muddled on policy as a duck was muddled about swimming. I wondered if he read the Code of Practice as women might read romance novels. Smiling, I said, "Thanks for the lift, Scott. Murder, as they say, calls. I don't want to keep you from nabbing your jaywalkers."

"There's more to being a response driver than you'd expect, Brenna."

Of course there was. I would be the first person to admit these officers worked extremely hard in a dangerous job. Burglaries, robberies, stolen vehicle pursuits, speeder apprehension, drunken brawls—situations that could themselves be threatening or lead to riskier circumstances.

Scott shoved the gear lever into neutral and set the hand break before angling his tall frame toward me. His left arm lay along the top of his seat. "I, too, have spurts of excitement."

"And that is…"

"Thought I'd found a body this morning."

I hadn't been prepared for that. I coughed and asked where.

"Off the A6. Stone bridge over the River Hol near Piebald Tor. Kind of place where you'd expect to find a body."

An understatement. Besides its association with 16th witches, Piebald Tor reeked Gloom. Winter winds planed heather and grass; grey clouds boiled and threatened rain. Fog, usually so dense in the lowlands, claimed the hill in a somber veil.

"But it wasn't," I said. "You disappointed?"

He shrugged, as if to say it was in his day's routine and was all the same to him if it had or hadn't been a body. "I saw a bit of fabric, like—sticking out of the snow, half in the stream. It'd been difficult to discern at first, being nearly the same color."

"How'd you spot it, then?"

"Bit of paper showed up against the snow. The tissue wrapping had been discarded along with the dress."

"Someone's going to be disappointed to learn she's lost a new dress," I said, wondering how anyone would lose a piece of clothing.

"When I got out of the car to investigate, I found that the dress was torn. Not just torn as you would on a rusty nail, but torn as in an act of rage. Ripped apart. Damned shame. It looked a posh dress."

"How odd. Well, Scott, you have your own mystery to investigate, then. As for me…" I patted his hand and opened the car door. "Let's pray the appeals tribunal won't hear of that Section 76 infringement." Of course I had joked, but many officers discovered to their detriment that witness statements made under oppression or coercion were excluded in court. The case, as they say, could go down the tubes by the unintentional application of thumbscrews.

"My lips are sealed." He waved as I slammed the car door. The voice of the police radio squealed over his words.

"No rest for the wicked, Scott. And just when you were so cozy and warm."

"You'd think by now that people would know not to leave expensive articles lying on the seats of their bleeding vehicle. Gits."

"You'd think the crooks wouldn't be out in this weather."

"Who ever accused crooks of intelligence?"

"Off you go, Scott. Flying squad to the rescue."

He put on his Dutiful Face, straightened his tie, and pulled himself up to his full 6-foot height. "Maybe I've got a candidate for the Neighborhood Watch program."

"Just don't tout the vehicular anti-theft devices. He might think you sell those on the side and have you up on discipline. By the way, Scott, do you prefer reduction in rank or reduction in pay?"

I dodged a spray of snow as the car shot down the road.

SEVEN

"WHAT KIND OF person was Joel Twiss? Did you like him?" I was in Trueman deMere's home study, a cubbyhole added onto the back of the house. It was as though the vicarage had begrudgingly relinquished space for the world; a computer and printer possessed the top of a battered desk, while over-filled bookcases and stacks of worn hymnals, magazines, and papers consumed the sparse floor space. I navigated around a cardboard box marked 'Lost Property' to the visitor's chair—an unyielding wooden monstrosity that must have been bequeathed by St. Nicholas himself—and took out my notebook. Trueman knocked over a knee-high tower of bibles as he squeezed past me. He smelled of after shave and pipe tobacco.

"Sorry," he said, stooping to gather up the books. He piled them into a replica of the leaning tower of Pisa and sat down at his desk. Gesturing around him, he asked when he would be allowed back into the church.

"Soon as we're finished with the scene, sir," I said, knowing that wasn't a precise answer.

"And you can't give me an idea?"

"A day or so. I know you're inconvenienced."

"At least we'll be able to hold worship services Sunday," he said, exhaling loudly. "You all right where you are? Good. Now, you asked about Joel."

I nodded, trying to surreptitiously nudge the corner of a hymnal away from my arm.

"I liked him, yes, although at times he was a bit overbearing. I suppose I shouldn't say that, as one should speak well of the dead, but he was. I can't lie. That would be worse. But he had a way of assuming you would drop everything to do what he wanted. He was full of himself, I believe you'd call it. But whether that stemmed from his profession or from his own personality…" He leaned back in his chair, scratching his chin. "I believe he would have made a great actor if he hadn't given himself to the police force."

"Aside from his pomposity, then…"

Trueman shrugged. "He lowered himself to help with anything that needed doing in the church or village. That sounds dreadful, I know," he said, coloring slightly. "But that's the impression I had. Oh, he was eager enough to lend anyone a hand—take the baking for David Willet's publishing party, for instance. He volunteered to help with that, and not because he liked to bake. There are many people in the village who like to bake and who haven't volunteered. But the impression I had every time Joel helped, Sergeant, was that he had something more important to do, and it was a great privilege he bestowed when he gave you his time. He never grumbled, mind you. Quick to smile and tell you he had nothing else to do. Smooth talker. But I had that feeling…"

I wondered if Joel suffered from low self-esteem and tried to build himself up in others' eyes. Making a note to ask Graham later, I said, "Was he particularly close to anyone in the village? I believe he wasn't married, so I wonder—"

"Lady friends? I wouldn't particularly know about them. He wasn't courting, if that's what you mean. But he did go out with some of the single women. Oh, nothing serious, I don't believe. A movie, concert, dinner. That sort of thing. And as for any particular mate…" Trueman stared up at the ceiling, as though a name was written there. "I believe he and Colin Hale were a bit thick at one time, particularly so when Joel first moved here—"

"When was that?"

"You're asking me to remember ancient history, Sergeant."

"An approximate idea would help, sir."

Trueman shut his eyes, as if that focused his memory. Moments later, he looked at me and said, "Nearly nine years ago. One year after the Hales moved here. Have you spoken with Colin and Sylvia yet? Talk about people who help…Sylvia seems to live for nothing else, and Colin—"

"But he wasn't mates with Colin now?"

Shaking his head, Trueman said, "And I don't know what happened. Oh, there was nothing obvious, such as a quarrel. I would've heard about that. They just drifted apart. Well, you do sometimes, don't you? I mean, we all have former friends in our lives."

"And was there anyone now who was especially close?"

"I've seen him and Owen walking about a fair bit. And Francis Rice. *He* more than Owen, I guess. Why not ask them?"

"But aside from Joel's ego, you found him…" I waited for Trueman to supply the adjective, not wanting him to merely agree with something I said.

"Friendly. A steady church-goer. Good sense of humor. Courageous."

I looked up from my notebook. Trueman nodded. "Yes, courageous. I know first-hand because we have experienced a series of the odd theft in the church."

"Did you report these?"

"Nothing much to them. Thank God they didn't take anything really valuable. But still, a theft is an inconvenience, isn't it? And we have to get the money somewhere to replace the stolen items." He signed heavily, as though reliving the ordeal.

"What type of things were taken? How did Joel's bravery figure into this?"

"Offertory box was tampered with and the money taken. A

new riddel curtain—" Trueman smiled. "I would've liked to have seen their faces when they undid the package. I bet they weren't half surprised at finding curtains instead of silver cups." He chuckled. "Also, a brass vase for flowers. As you can see, Miss, nothing that would break us."

"Still, it *is* a crime, sir. And Joel?"

"After two of these annoyances, Joel was as fed up with the burglaries as any of us. He ran after the thieves one night, nearly caught one of them, too."

"How did he know there was to be a break-in? Did he set up surveillance inside the church?"

"Sheer luck, Sergeant. Joel was working in the church late one evening, doing a bit of plastering in the west gallery, I think. Anyway, the thieves broke in through the vestry door and evidently didn't see his work light. Wouldn't have, would they, as there's no gallery window on the west side of the church."

"So Joel heard the break in and dashed after them," I supplied, thinking it rather a foolhardy thing to do, ex-policeman or not.

"He would've caught one, as I said, if he hadn't tripped over a tombstone. Stump of one, actually. Broke off a hundred years ago, I understand. We try to keep the grass mown around it, but..."

"He *is* courageous. I wonder how many people would run after a burglar."

"As much as I would love to boast I would, I don't believe I have that quality. Though perhaps a confrontation in the church proper..."

His brown eyes clouded and he bowed his head, perhaps dissatisfied with what he knew to be his true self. The no-nonsense voice had softened, as though giving himself absolution for his weakness.

I thanked him and quietly left him to his thoughts.

Eden deMere, empty bucket in hand, was just crossing the

front garden as I emerged from the house. Her footprints inter-
mingled with those left by birds and foxes, a strange pattern on
the otherwise pristine snow. Calling out her good morning, she
knocked the edge of the bucket against the metal pole support-
ing a bird house. The bang of metal against metal rang into the
still air. She tossed the remaining birdseed onto the ground.

She was younger than I had thought, possibly in her early
twenties, teenager slim with baby-smooth complexion. She
wore teenager clothes, too, tight jeans, a baggy yellow sweatshirt with 'Yellow Submarine' stamped across the front, and
gold ear cuffs. A contrast to Trueman, sartorially and physically.
Though short, she moved with the grace of a ballerina. I walked
over to her, aware she was already forming her opinion about
me and the investigation. Smiling, I introduced myself and
extended my hand.

"Eden deMere. Trueman's wife," she said as an afterthought,
then nodded toward the house. "I hope he wasn't too impossible. He gets that way whenever his schedule or environment
is abruptly changed."

"I'm afraid it may be another day or two, yet. It's a bother,
I know, but we haven't finished in the church."

Eden nodded and took off her stocking cap to reveal short-
cropped blonde hair nearly as light as the snow. She set down
the bucket and flexed her fingers. "Feeding the birds. I used to
mind it at first, but now I've come to enjoy it. Can even identify
something other than a robin." She laughed, as though making
fun of herself. Gesturing to the half dozen feeders hanging
from tree branches or sitting on poles, she said, "Today I did it
from respect more than anything. Out of memory for Joel. He
got me interested in watching wildlife. I thought it rather silly
at first, buying seed for birds. I mean, they've been surviving
since Creation, so why give them something they can find on
their own?"

"Normally, they could, Mrs. deMere. But with the loss of their natural habitation, food supplies diminishing either through poisoning of rodents or chemicals put down for weed control, they aren't surviving. And if we want to keep seeing robins, or if we want owls, for example, to control the rodent population, we need birds. We need to help them survive. Providing habitat and food is one step."

"You sound like Joel," she said, fingering the bird feeder. "He was concerned about birds. About all wildlife, actually. I suppose I was, in a vague way. I mean, being the vicar's wife I'm supposed to love all creatures great and small. And I do love the birds and mammals almost without exception. But insects…" She grimaced. "I can't claim sainthood, can I? But I bet there were some times that even ticked off Peter. Anyway, today I fill the feeders in Joel's memory and give a silent prayer that his murderer is found. Oh, yes, Sergeant, I already know it's murder. The village telegraph works extremely well in times of crisis. Or gossip. And no, I didn't kill him, though I have no alibi. I was home baking. Want to see the bread?"

"Aside from his interest in wildlife, what sort of person was Joel?"

Eden leaned against a tree trunk, her eyes staring in the direction of the tearoom. I knew she wasn't thinking of hot scones. Joel's house was in the next street over. She spoke slowly, apparently oblivious to the cold, her eyes never wavering. "I thought Joel Twiss the handsomest man I'd ever seen." She paused, as though picturing him, her eyes unnaturally bright. I had not seen the body but I had seen his photo at Magdalína's. He had looked somewhat like Graham, only older and more aware of his charisma. Eden's voice, when she continued, had a sharpness—regret? resentment?—that the casual listener might have missed. Joel's image vanished under the heat of her words. "And he knew how to use his looks—and charm—to get most everything out of life he wanted."

"Such as?" I said, hoping I wasn't going to hear another tale of police corruption. Instead, her answer surprised me.

"Such as popularity, retirement security, immortality."

I asked how he had obtained these, but Eden only shrugged. "How do good looking men acquire anything? By cultivating vulnerable people into what they perceive as a great friendship, then obtaining favors. When you're in love," she said, sighing slightly, "you'll do anything for your man. And to save you from asking, yes, I suppose I was in love with Joel. I'm not proud of it, Sergeant. But nothing ever came of it. I committed no adultery, I never told Trueman—or Joel—of my feelings."

Not in words, I thought, but there were other ways to declare feelings. "Did Joel ever make any advances to you? Do you think he was aware of how you felt?"

"If he was, he never said anything. We were just friends— brother and sister camaraderie. Nothing the village snoops could shake their heads or tongues at. A vicar's wife—"

I nodded. "Spotless reputation. It must be hard to live up to."

She looked at me, a hint of enmity behind her words. "Don't go to the rock concert—people might hear about it. Don't buy a Harley or get a tattoo—people will get the wrong impression. Don't wear *that*—people will think the worst. So I stay at home, drive my Mini, and wear dull colors, my desires sacrificed for Trueman's career."

"You didn't know what to expect before you married him, then?"

"I had a hint, but you never really know until you're in it, do you?"

"And Joel afforded the escape you needed."

"You're making it sound illicit and indecent!" She took a step toward me, her mouth tightening. "I loved Joel for his own sake. I love Trueman for his. I still couldn't hear U2 or whatever group I wanted, or wear a bikini to sunbathe in even when I went over to Joel's. So that 'escape' didn't exist, miss. I liked being with him, doing things with him, even if he was old enough to be my father. And if there's something wrong with that, with my loving him—"

"Nothing, as far as I'm concerned, Mrs. deMere. But it must've been dreadful for you. What did you do about it?"

She shrugged, the toe of her boot nudging the bucket. "Not a thing. I stayed in my wifely bed, went to church and prayed, and reminded myself I'd destroy Trueman if I strayed. And, as much as I loved Joel, I didn't want to hurt Trueman."

"So, forsaking Joel and Bono, you continue with the church socials."

"Till death us do part, Miss."

I wondered if anyone else in the village had thought the same way but had put the phrase into action.

DR. FRANCIS RICE'S HOUSE sat next door to the tearoom and en route to the incident room, so I stopped to ask the same questions of him. Francis' home implied old money and a liberal hand in the arts. Culture and refinement murmured from the oil painting over the fireplace to the crystal wine decanter and Oriental rug near the hearth. Taking a seat on the brocade-upholstered sofa, I accepted the cup of tea Francis offered. The entire service matched—translucent, eggshell-white china rimmed with gold. The dark-eyed woman of the oil painting frowned down at me, daring me to drop her china. The cup rattled in its saucer as I set it down.

"Last evening I was with Colin Hale in Buxton, dear. We debated about going, but left at 4:00 before the snow had become too bad. Got there early, without any difficulty, and had a drink at the Sun Inn. Then to the Collectors' Club, where we attended a dinner lecture on 16th and 17th century silver." I made a note of the guest speaker's name and the time they returned home before asking about Joel Twiss.

"Strange question," Francis said.

"Why?"

"Because I was thinking of him only this morning—before I heard the news."

"And why were you thinking of him?"

"Oh, merely wondering if he'd like to drive over to Manchester one day, take in the Constable exhibition."

"You did a lot with Joel, then? You liked him?"

"I don't know if I liked Joel Twiss or not, dear. One had to work hard at it, I think."

"Why was that?"

"Of course, I can only talk from my experience…"

I nodded and watched him as he picked up his cup again. Surgery-steady his hand was, free of age spots or protruding veins. Though short and starting a bulge of a tummy, Francis Rice—66 come next week—could've passed for ten years younger. He still carried himself ramrod straight, still had an energy in his voice that suggested orders barked during medical emergencies. I glanced at a portrait done in pastels of a woman with dark hair and smooth, pink cheeks, and wondered if it was his wife. I commented on the beauty of the drawing.

"That's what drew us together at first," he said after thanking me. "Not my wife—she's been gone now for five years. The love of fine things. Joel had come over, suffering from an infected cut on his hand, and started commenting on my silver collection." He waved to the shelves housing several dozen tankards, covered dishes and salvers. I suddenly coveted the chocolate pot on the middle shelf and asked about it.

"Nice, isn't it? 1697, crafted by Isaac Dighton. Anyway, we got to talking about the pieces, as one does, discovered we had a mutual passion, and things took off from there. We'd run down to London occasionally, do a bit of fossiking along the Portobello Road or when something good was being sold at auction. Or we'd talk over tea about tapestries and paintings. Joel was quite knowledgeable about it, even knew market prices. Of course, I never sell any of my pieces—I collect to keep. But still, it was smashing to have a mate who was conversant in the things I liked. Not since my wife died had I been able to talk like this. It gave me a new energy."

My dad hadn't understood about collections. Money supplied life's necessities; sometimes treated you to a film or short holiday. Frittering it away on items that you couldn't use, that you kept in glass cages—well, that was why we had museums. Dad never understood and he would've been appalled at the apparent amount of money Francis poured into his glass-front cupboards. I asked, "And why did you have to work at liking Joel Twiss? I would think that finding someone to share your interest—"

"Joel's main interest was himself, dear, no matter how he carried on about a Samuel Edwards coffeepot. He had cultured taste, obviously, and a discernment in clothes and home furnishings, but the pride of his cultivation was himself."

"Bit overbearing, was he?" I said, recalling Trueman's opinion.

Francis snorted. "You could call him egotistical and not be pinched for slander, yes. But I'm painting a black picture of him. Joel was also a light-hearted chap, jovial and ready with a joke if you were a bit down. No matter the weather, no matter the day *he* had had, he always seemed to be without cares. Always having a lark wherever he was. Even before his retirement," Francis added, as though people could be happy only when freed from the daily grind.

I remarked that it was too bad there weren't more like Joel, and left, not sure if I heard Francis agree with me.

EIGHT

EVEN THOUGH The Pineapple Slice tearoom was situated next to Francis Rice's house, I didn't want to disturb Owen during work hours. Walking back to the incident room, I made a note that I would question him later about his friendship with Joel Twiss.

I was wrestling with an uncooperative computer in the village hall when Margo came up to me. She seemed uncommonly reserved. At first, I thought she was going to add her scolding for the dog incident, but when I saw a man standing several yards behind her I knew she was immersed in her Police Mode, as she called it.

"Man to see you, Bren."

"Knows something about the murder, does he?" I said, glancing at him. "Who is he?"

"Andrew Bayley. Oh, you won't find him there," she returned as I flipped through my notebook of villagers' names. "Isn't a local. Lives in Buxton."

"*Buxton?* Then what's—"

"Let him tell you." She stepped to the side and asked Mr. Bayley to the table.

He was dressed in a three piece suit and a woolen full-length coat. Hat, scarf and gloves matched. His hair, though thin, was neatly trimmed as was his moustache. I rose as he approached. For once I held my own with height, for Andrew Bayley and I were of similar short stature, though he was older than I. He waited, hat in hand, until I was seated before seating himself. He also waited for me to speak first.

"What brings you out so early on so cold a morning, Mr. Bayley?"

"Yes, it is that," he said, as though hesitant to come to the reason for his appearance. He stared at the far table, evidently intrigued by the number of phones and computers.

I tried nudging him. "Constable Lynch tells me you're from Buxton."

"What? Oh, yes." He turned his gaze toward me, ready to talk. "But I'm here in Bramwell on business. Well, what I hope will be future business, though right now it's preliminary business." He grimaced and sat back in the folding metal chair. "Oh, dear. Not making a very good start, am I?"

"I understand. You're here on business in regards to what you hope will lead to future business, right?"

Bayley nodded. "I own a tour company. You may have seen my buses in Buxton—Idyllic Outings." On seeing my nod, he gathered strength. "I arrived last week to scout the village. I do that—check places I think may have something unusual to offer, be of interest to my clients."

"And Bramwell has something in the way of sightseeing you wish to include on a tour?"

"Most certainly. The Dark Man, for one, and the St. Nicholas festivity, for another. While other parishes in Derbyshire may have Guy Fawkes celebrations and All Saints Day and well dressings, I do believe the Dark Man is unique to Bramwell."

"The Dark Man…" I said, trying to recall the event.

"Halloween night." As he lost himself to the custom, his voice slowed, becoming a faint, curious blend of nasal tone and sing-song cadence. His eyes held a dreamy quality, as though, in a past life, he conjured up a remembrance. He reminded me of Merlin. "Well, correctly stated, it's 1st of November, beginning one minute after midnight. The Beating of the Devil. You've not heard of it?" he said, astonished at my expression.

"Afraid not. It's a local custom, then?"

"Started in the middle ages, I believe, and has only survived in Bramwell, unless there's some obscure place I have yet to detect." He stroked his moustache. "Villagers assemble a Dark Man, as they call it, from any dark fabric or old clothes. I've seen Dark Men made from gunny sacks, potato sacks, university gowns, discarded clothing…usually filled with straw or crumpled newspaper to give it body. Then, accompanied by torchlight and singing of hymns, they parade it about the town on a long pole."

"And it ends up…"

"They bring it to the church yard, set it on the south porch or prop it against the church door and beat it with sticks. They try their best to destroy the thing, leaving no lump in the dummy that could be construed as part of the devil's body. They may not use their hands or feet, for they must not come in bodily contact with the devil, so they use sticks to disgorge the straw or newspapers from the clothing. When they are finished, the devil should be destroyed and the porch floor merely a litter of straw and the dark clothing. Then they sing a hymn, as though sealing the devil's fate and praising God. It's really very interesting."

I said it sounded like it, and could mentally see it. Superstition, rowdiness and Christian faith conveniently mixed for a good time.

"So I came to see that," Bayley continued, "then returned to the St. Nicholas festivity. That's rather singular, too, you know."

"And it is the researching of these events," I said, "which brings you here?"

"Unfortunately, yes." His voice lowered, as though he was frightened. "I'm not pointing the finger at anyone, Officer, and I didn't see the murder—oh, yes," he said suddenly, his eyes narrowing. He pronounced each word emphatically, separately, giving weight not only to his part in this but also to the village telegraph. "I know there was a murder last evening. The hotel's ablaze with the talk."

It would be. Why else would a contingent of police take up residence there, confiscate the use of the village hall, and light up the village with work lamps till the wee small hours? I asked him to continue.

"Well, I was just thinking, Officer, that I may have seen the murderer."

"Really? When and where was this?"

"Tea time, I should think. Yes." He scratched his chin. "Big, stout man comes up to the church carrying something large in a sack. Oh, I know about that, too. Murdered man found in a sack. I—I'm sure he didn't see me, though."

"Why is that?"

"Well, I was just coming up from the tearoom, so his back was toward me. And he didn't look back at me. I would've seen that, too."

"And you saw this man…"

"I know what you're thinking, Officer. Tea time, already dark outside. But I saw what I saw. And besides, the man stood out against the snow."

I could believe it. It had been snowing at 4:00, but not as it had been later that afternoon. Bayley could have seen Owen Parnell—for I assumed that's who he meant. But to make certain…I thanked Bayley and asked if he would remain in Bramwell for a while longer in case I needed to question him. The man stood up, said most solemnly that he would ask my permission to leave the village, and left.

I gathered up my notebook and purse, and thought, purposes aside, both amusements used sacks.

I HAD CAUGHT OWEN during lunch break at the tearoom. It had been a short session due to his boisterous denial of having murdered Joel Twiss. I hadn't asked him if he had murdered Joel Twiss, but it was a logical assumption for my visit. Last night we had discussed his bread delivery, so what else would have brought me to the tearoom's kitchen during the late morning? I told as much to Graham when I had poured myself a cup of tea back at the incident room.

Handing me the sugar, Graham said, "I could probably recite his entire monologue to you, Taylor. The innocent protestations never seem to vary much. Why is it we've lost all creativity?"

I noticed he used my last name that morning—a sign he was all business. It was just as well. After the adventure with the dog, I was ready for some brain work. "I've no doubt you're able to recite his monologue, sir," I said, "but you may not do so well with his recital of feelings for Joel Twiss."

"Not Castor and Pollux, then, from your prologue."

"Not even Gilbert and Sullivan. Owen told me Joel was someone to run around with. He liked his daring—physical and financial. That's what he first saw in Joel."

"Financial?"

"Joel took chances that Owen, living on the cheap, could only marvel at. Rash flings with shares of media and tech companies, race track bettings on long shots—that sort of thing."

"To hell with the pension and live while you can, I take it."

"Whether it was his pension or an inheritance Joel was gambling with, in the truest sense of the word, he seemed unconcerned and out for a good time."

"I didn't know a police retirement pension offered that sort of fun. Obviously we're in the wrong job, Taylor."

"Joel also took a lot of pride in his creativity. Although he could be showy, bordering on pomposity, he usually went about his artistic endeavors as though everyone could do it, not thinking overmuch of his work."

"Humble?"

I shook my head. "Owen says he definitely was not modest about his achievements. Merely shrugged them off as a natural thing anyone could do."

"So in all this, what was Owen's feelings toward the man?"

"Attracted and envious of his cavalier attitude toward money, grateful of the small gifts Joel would hand out after a big win."

"Handouts? What did he do, pass out cigars when his horse ran in the money?"

"Peeled off part of the winnings and handed it to Owen. Dropped off small gifts, such as bottles of wine and tins of caviar. Stuffed 'change,' as he called notes under £100, into Owen's jacket pocket, which Owen wouldn't find until days later."

"Where'd Joel learn slight of hand?" Graham mused, suddenly looking serious.

"But Owen's ardency for Joel's gifts soon stopped when Owen began feeling indebted and embarrassed. He got up enough nerve to demand the outpouring stop, which put a brief strain on the friendship. But they'd still go out for a pint or to the races. Owen could always count on Joel's wit to bring him up from the doldrums."

"He should've been a physical therapist," Graham said. "Certainly seems to have the knack for playing the Lord of Misrule."

"Speaking of knacks..." I handed him a white bag and leaned back in the chair. Even the cold metal frame felt good after half an hour outside.

"What's this?" He opened the bag cautiously, as though expecting something grisly from the crime scene.

"Biscuits from the tearoom. They're called Flying Saucers. The shop's quite famous for them, selling them hand over fist, and even packaging and posting overseas. Owen developed the recipe. Thought you'd like some for your elevenses."

Graham needed no urging, plunging his hand into the bag. When he stopped midway in chewing, he raised a skeptical eyebrow and angled the open bag toward me. I thanked him as I took two biscuits.

"Marvelous," he finally said, having devoured the cinnamon shortbread. "Why the name?" He reached for another biscuit.

"There's your answer."

He swallowed quickly. "I applaud your guilty conscience."

"*What* guilt? I merely thought—"

"You thought to ease Mr. Owen Parnell's ruffled feathers and soothe over any future ruffling by spending a bit of hard-earned copper. Not a bad idea," he said before licking his fingers. "See any more similar situations arising?"

"I try to do something reeking of kindness—"

"By the way, Taylor, I heard about that incident this morning."

My face flushed instantly and I sought refuge in my tea.

Graham placed a biscuit on my saucer and said, rather slowly, "Kindness and love of animals is one thing, TC, but risking your life is quite another. What if it hadn't ended as in the fairy tales? What would I do without you?"

I knew he referred to me as his right-arm-sergeant, but I wished he meant it more personally. I wished he meant it as a concerned friend, even more as Mark had meant it this morning. He could always get another sergeant, but could he always get another friend? I looked at him from over the rim of my teacup and found I couldn't return his stare. I took the biscuit and said faintly that Margo was showing a lot of promise.

"Margo's a fine constable, but she doesn't have your skill of observation. Nor your sensitivity."

He was not smiling when I finally looked up. His green eyes, the hue of his turtle neck pullover, held a solemnity I had never seen. I asked him what success he had had that morning.

"The sack covering Joel's head is a flour sack. And while that doesn't confirm Owen as the murderer, it suggests star role."

I agreed, trying to picture Owen lurking around the church,

waiting for Joel's arrival, then knifing him. I said, "Flour sack and bread knife—tools of his art, but are they too obvious?"

"We'll know as we get further along, Taylor. Unfortunately, the few hairs found on the sack don't pinpoint our murderer, either. Blonde and reddish-brown."

"How many people in this village, with a tie to Joel Twiss, have blonde and reddish-brown hair? You want me to work on that?"

"Perhaps later, Taylor. The blood beneath Joel's body had pooled, proving he died where he fell. The front of his shirt and jacket were also soaked with his blood, and there was a bit around the entrance wound."

"All consistent with an unmoved body," I said.

"I also talked with David Willett, local history teacher thrust swiftly into local fame. He's written a book, TC. And it's about to be lauded at a book signing affair. You're aware of all that, I know. But you may not know that he was first out of the starting gate with it."

"Pardon, sir?"

"Owen Parnell's brother, Nelson, fancies himself a writer and applied pen to paper on the same subject."

"Oh, dear. I know what's coming."

"I should think so. DC Byrd is, hopefully, ensconced in Nelson's cozy front room as we speak, learning just what this means to him. But I don't think Nelson had a publisher, so it's not like two books simultaneously vying for the same custom."

"Nelson's book may take a different approach to the subject. After all, there is more than one book on birds, for example."

"And all to varying degrees of success."

"Does seem odd that two men in the same village would write on the same subject. Is it something in the water, then?"

"I don't know about their water supply, but I do think it's the village itself. Bramwell has several unique customs, just begging to be exploited or canonized—"

"—Or preserved."

"And with the death last year of the local historian, and the inevitable aging of the older generation—"

"It's time to preserve what they have," I repeated. "Not so far fetched, then, these two books. Is there any animosity between them?"

"Neither man is the murder victim, Taylor."

"I understand that, sir. I'm just curious about our key players. Lot of villagers know about the customs hereabout."

"The stage certainly did look set for murder, I grant you. Gloomy setting, stormy weather, pagan-like ritual..." His attention turned to the window as a tree shook in the wind, shedding its snow with an energy that hit the village hall roof.

He sat for several minutes, an intensity in his gaze I had seen once before. He seemed to escape from the world somehow, to project himself out of his surroundings and conjure up another place. Margo had whispered one night over beer and pizza that Graham still yearned for his fiancée. "Might even die of a broken heart," she had prophesized. It looked now as if he might, for his eyes had widened, as though frantically searching for someone. Perhaps it was the weather or the talk about loss. Either might have triggered his melancholia.

A blast of wind blew into the room as someone opened the door. Stormy weather, gloomy setting or pagan-like ritual may have contributed to the murder, I silently agreed. But how many people other than our two authors, the tearoom owner and her baker, the vicar and his trusty assistant, the bookshop owner and our visiting tour operator put this St. Nicholas sack information to murderous use?

NINE

"YOU HAVE ANY more of those biscuits?" Graham asked, pulling his gaze from the snowy world outside. For the briefest of moments, he looked like a small boy.

Rather bewildered or frightened, as though he were trying to make sense of adult situations, reaching for the biscuit tin as one would a mother or—a bit later in life, perhaps—food, as a source of comfort and reassurance that all would be well. I had a strong desire to cradle his head against my breast, stroke his hair, whisper into his ear. But the wildness in his eyes had subsided by this time, and I was left sitting with the very adult, very brilliant Graham who could, if he bothered to look, see through any attempt of mine to mother him. So I let a chance to hold him drop away, as I had before and would no doubt do again. Sleeping my way to promotion was not my style. Nor would it be with Graham, I thought, glancing at him as he rubbed his forehead. If the occasion ever arrived, it would be from love, not from sympathy or resurrections of childhood. I drew a deep breath and prayed my blazing cheeks would not betray my thoughts. Or emotions.

Handing him the bag, I asked about the knife.

"That's Evelyn's baby," he said, referring to Scientific Officer Evelyn Chapman, who was responsible for the victim and anything relating to him. Each SO is accountable for one specific person or scene of a crime; this eliminates cross-contamination of people and scenes, and more easily identifies evidence ownership.

"I know. I wondered if she'd identified it."

"May be harder to do because it's common."

"No one will have one missing from their kitchen, either."

"Bought just for the deed, then? Wouldn't surprise me at all, TC. God, I've a headache." He leaned back in his chair, massaging his forehead.

"It's the late hour you got to sleep last night, sir."

"Damned if it is. I've worked later and longer stretches than this. It's only the beginning. Must be the weather."

"You could get something, I suppose, from Dr. Rice."

"Dr. Francis Rice, lately retired physician of this village, is wallowing in his freedom—which, I don't mind admitting, makes me jealous. And avoiding any patient contact with an exuberance that would shame a politician at election time. Don't look at me like that. I'm not a mind reader—at least not now, with this damned headache. I talked to him this morning outside the bookshop."

"Hannah Leftridge keeps rather early hours."

"Hannah Leftridge needed a strong dose of magic from Dr. Rice's black bag."

"She's ill? I was just with her last—"

"Nothing communicable, Taylor. Lay to rest your fears of measles or bronchitis. She learned of the victim's identity this morning and went to pieces."

I could well believe so. To lose a friend is devastating, but when that friend was as close as a co-worker in an event, and that event only two days away…panic at unfinished work could be as harmful. "The village has been dealt a few shocks in the past twenty-four hours. Hannah was helping Joel with the food preparations for David Willett's book signing party. Wonder how this will affect it."

"Shouldn't think it's the best scenario. A book party seems a bit frivolous in the circumstances at any rate."

"Maybe that's what they all need. Something ordinary to bring them back to their own lives."

"Well, if Hannah can pull herself together…"

"There's always Owen, I suppose."

"There's always a caterer out of Buxton or Bakewell or Chesterfield. Hell, Taylor, I'm all for saving money or helping your friend or whatever it is they're trying to do with this baking marathon, but there comes a time when events force other decisions."

"To hear Hannah talk about Joel Twiss last night," I said, "she must be desolate."

"I think Dr. Rice can give her something to get her through these next days, at least. He didn't seem bothered at being called out, even if he isn't keeping office hours anymore." Graham picked up the last half of his biscuit, looked at it, threw it onto his saucer and leaned back, his arms behind his head. "Just imagine, Taylor, whole days in which to do nothing. Whole days in which to respond to the urges of your spirit and creativity. No alarm clocks, no phones, no Simcocks." He closed his eyes, as though shutting out the daily demands.

His face looked serene, lost in images of retirement, I guessed. And though I had heard of some inspectors chucking the grind of work, I had not envisioned Graham as one of these. True, he was a flyer, as we called a person who moved up quickly through the ranks. But I never viewed him as such, for he was not motivated by promotion, as flyers were. He was just brilliant and wanted to rise in order to direct investigations—another way to help humanity, as he had when he had been a minister. But retirement at his age? He was only 41. I suddenly felt my chest tightening and, using Graham's own question, wondered what I would do without him. There were other detective inspectors under whom I would receive tutelage, but I was certain they did not work a case with Graham's sense of determination to detail and untiring search. Besides, I liked him too much to give him up.

"The vicar's trapped by the phone, too," he said, responding to his own earlier statement.

I abandoned the contemplation of my fingernails to find Graham smiling at me.

"He's explained to the usual group who comes each year that the festivity will be held next week. And your mate, Margo, has tacked a sign on the church doors."

"Village grapevine no doubt caught most of them last evening before they made the trip."

"I should hope. Nasty weather to be out when you didn't have to be."

"Where *are* Margo and party?" I said, looking around the usually busy room. Except for someone in the kitchen, Graham and I were the only ones there.

"Unwrapping Christmas gifts."

"Unwrap—"

"From the St. Nicholas jollies last night. Actually, I exaggerated. They're printing them. The paper, Taylor," he said, reading my expression. "Might have been touched by our murderer, knocked over and picked up. If so, that lovely red and green paper may gift us with incriminating fingerprints."

GRAHAM HAD SUGGESTED we lunch some place civil, like the hotel dining room, instead of eating a sandwich while standing at the computer. We walked up to the hotel where I excused myself, wanting to exchange my wellies for a pair of shoes.

I saw them when I opened my hotel room—a vase of a dozen long-stemmed roses. They were on the dresser. The card simply said 'Because.' No signature. I quickly changed into my shoes and pulled one rose from the bouquet. I was snapping off part of the stem so I could thread the flower into my shirt buttonhole when Margo knocked on my door.

"What bride did you steal those from?" she asked, taking the discarded stem and pulling off the leaves.

"Hardly a bride. More like the father of the bride. Man in his 50s," I explained, grabbing the bare stem from her and dropping it into the waste bin.

"So you're cultivating a romance at last! Awfully fast work, Bren. Or has this been going on for a while and you've only just met?"

"Honestly, Margo. Your ideas of what goes on in my life—"

"E-mail introduction? Or did some friend set you up?"

"There's nothing going on!"

"Not hardly. What's the card say?"

I showed it to her. She looked perplexed so I explained about the dog incident. "These must have set him back a few quid," she said, handing the card back to me.

"He tried to give me £50," I admitted.

"I suppose if he couldn't give it to you one way…"

"Awfully decent thing to do, but honestly, Margo, I'm embarrassed."

"There *is* that no gifts ruling to consider, yes. You going to thank him?"

"I should."

"Just don't let Graham catch you." She left unsaid what would happen if he discovered one of his officers in such a position.

"Must've been a valuable dog."

"Not necessarily. After all, a pet—"

"Right. Now, if anything like that were to happen to Wolf, I'd be wiped out."

I smiled, not at Margo's emotion but at her dog's name. Wolf was a cocker spaniel. "Damn. I wish this hadn't happened. It's liable to muck up something. Nothing is ever easy, you notice that, Margo? The little act of saving this dog has turned into a threat of embarrassment and potential dressing down for me. A card would've been fine."

"It'll make a better person of you, Bren, when you thank him. Now, face to the west and quick march." She shoved me toward the door.

"I'll quick march this afternoon if I can grab a few minutes, I promise. I'm lunching with Graham now." I glanced at my watch and wondered what he must be thinking about my tardiness.

"One woman's cross is another woman's treasure…"

I dragged her out of my room and hurried downstairs.

I DIDN'T HAVE to wait too long to express my thanks to Colin Hale, for I met him in the hotel lobby. Wanting to get this over with, I hurried over.

He was a large, bushy-haired man, bordering on fat, yet able to keep most of the excess at bay. The servility he had expressed over the rescue of his dog was not apparent now; instead, he seemed confident. That quickly turned to puzzlement as I thanked him for the roses.

"I'd *like* to say I sent them, Officer," Colin said, his voice lowering as a villager crossed the floor. "It's been a very long time since I gave flowers to *anyone*. I remember it was such a pleasant thing to do. But, to be truthful about the thing, I didn't."

It was my turn to register confusion. "I…I'm sorry, Mr. Hale. I didn't mean to…" I broke off, feeling my face growing warm. I was 13 again, thanking the most popular boy in my class. He, too, had been as bewildered as Colin was, handing out valentines to the cute girls. I heard the sniggers as I turned away, the rude remarks of the girls clutching their trophies. I should've known he hadn't sent me flowers; should've figured it was a joke to belittle me and emphasize I was not one of them. The walk across the village hall floor had been the longest I had ever taken, the laughter echoing in my ears for weeks afterwards. I flung the flowers onto the snow once I had escaped outside, desperate to be rid of their mockery. Colin's face reappeared before me. I said, "It's just that I received roses this afternoon, and I thought that—"

"A logical assumption, Officer. As I said, as much as I'd like to lay claim to the honor and placate my guilty conscience, I must defer the glory. No apology needed, though I stand chastised at not having thought of thanking you properly. How shall I make amends?"

I assured him that amends were not necessary, and that I had only approached him because I could think of no one else who was likely to thank me for anything.

"Well," Colin said, glancing at his wristwatch, "if you'll excuse me, I must be going. I hope you solve your mystery. And again, apology for my amazingly dull brain. You *do* deserve roses. I'm just sorry I can't claim the tribute."

He left me as nonplused as I had been on first seeing the flowers.

A SHARP WIND had risen, blowing across the park opposite the hotel and moaning as it raced between the alley separating the chemist's and green grocer's. The wind reveled in its freedom, whipping snow against my legs and cheeks until I felt half frozen. I pulled my woolen cap farther down over my ears and held my hands there, needing the extra warmth of another woolen layer. Snow blew into my eyes, and I stumbled into a post-box trying to blink away the irritation. A bus lumbered up the High Street, throwing slush onto the pavement and anyone unfortunate enough not to dodge.

The tearoom's warmth called to me and I made for the building as a bee heads for nectar. Converted from a former dress shop, the tearoom succeeded in forging a pocket of cheer from its stony exterior. Its slate roof was still packed with snow, and icicles hung like fringe from the gutters. Dark and curtained, two small windows peeked from beneath the eaves, while beneath them a large, diamond-paned window, translucent from frost, hinted at shelter and culinary delights within.

I yanked at the door, nearly crusted over with ice. It banged against the wall as it jerked open. Immediately on entering, I began to thaw.

Candles and greenery decorated The Pineapple Slice, in anticipation of the St. Nicholas party. From a long-standing invitation, the old-age pensioners and children gathered there after the church festivity, no one quite ready to relinquish the party feeling or holiday atmosphere. Both were evident here, with pine roping festooning the walls and framing the door. Clusters of golden balls and white paper snowflakes hung from the window tops and ceiling. Red votive candles in frosted glass jars winked from the wreaths of evergreen smothering the tables. It all looked rather ridiculous and misplaced in light of the abandoned amusement. A rack near the cash register held tea towels imprinted with part of a recipe for Flying Saucers. A large sign declared their selling price. Nothing like a spot of commercialism to remind us of life's true goals during this sacred season.

I ordered a pot of tea, and occupied myself with reading the recipe. Reading, however, was soon abandoned as I focused on an animated discussion in the front of the room.

"You'll need the help, Maggie," David Willett said. "With Joel gone—"

"You really are a saint, David," Magdalína said, patting his arm. "But I've contracted with a caterer in Buxton. Thanks all the same."

"But a caterer will cost—" began David, only to be cut off by Magdalína, who said she couldn't infringe on his precious free time. "Besides, you've got enough to do."

"Like what? My Oscar-winning sainted role has been cut, here and at church. What else needs to be seen to?" He waved his hands while speaking, narrowly missing a lit candle by the cash register. I wondered if he displayed as much passion and animation in the classroom. If so, he might be a good teacher.

"I don't know your list, David, but you can't be just sitting about waiting for the party. If you don't have school papers to mark, surely you've got housework. Now, don't argue about the food! Will you shut up and listen to me for once? Even if you and I and Hannah and Owen baked all night, we couldn't get it all finished in time. So I saved us all a sleepless existence and our dispositions, and phoned in the order. It's worth the few quid extra to keep us all friends. Now, toddle on home and get those books over here. You can put them in the back room. They'll not get dirty in there."

"They're in *boxes,* for Christ's sake," David muttered, taking off his spectacles and rubbing the bridge of his nose. "Can I get in the back door?"

A flurry of fur, cashmere and leather blew into the shop, ruffling more than the evergreen boughs and red ribbons. David replaced his glasses, removed them quickly, and continued their cleaning. Magdalína, visibly agitated, forced a smile and gave her attention to the woman.

"You're a hardy soul, Sylvia, to hoof it here. Tea?"

On hearing her name, I peered at the newcomer. Sylvia Hale seemed as dynamic as I had imagined. A woman of 60 who could pass for mid-age, she seemed an embodiment of streamlined efficiency from her sleek, pony-tailed hairstyle to her slim body. I eyed the exuberant fur trim of her coat and hoped it was synthetic.

Sylvia nodded, removing her leather gloves. "And cinnamon toast. I only live the next block up, Maggie. It's not like I walked from Chesterfield. Hello, David. How's our famous author? You faking illness to get off early, or have you chucked it all to live off your royalties?"

David snorted and turned toward the back of the shop.

"Already too famous to remember your old friends, then? Well, I harbor no ill will, no matter how you snub me. I shall buy a book for auld lang syne, if for nothing else. What's it about again?"

"You'll be here for the party, then?" Magdalína said, glancing at David, who had turned back to the group as if to answer Sylvia.

"Darling, I wish I could be, but I've a previous engagement. You must tell me all about it when I get back. You will, won't you, David? Perhaps use it in your next book. But change it, of course. You know how writers do—a kernel of truth enveloped in lies. But you call it fiction, I believe. Take your party, for example." She threw her gloves onto a nearby table and leaned against the counter. "Now, it's easy, David, but pay attention if you can. You start with a kernel. So, let's see…when you're at your typewriter, you picture your party of 5 was really 50 or 100. Then you imagine that everyone had a wonderful time and wasn't compelled to buy your book. Understand?" She smiled, waiting for David to reply, which he did with an improper gesture.

"God, David," she said, breaking into laughter as David walked into the back room, "you do have an imagination after all. Well, break a leg or pencil, darling, or whatever. I suppose," she continued, "he is all nerves and irritated stomach. Could that account for his bad manners? Writers are so emotional."

"I think he has a right to be nervous," Magdalína replied, her fingers tapping the counter top. "Saturday's a big evening. His first book debut. He's put a lot of work into it."

"If you say so, Maggie. Now, I need to cancel my cake order."

"*Cancel?* I'm afraid—"

"My dear, it's *nothing* that reflects unfavorably on you *or* Owen. My plans have just changed. You know how life treats one at times."

Magdalína grimaced, looked over her shoulder as though wishing for support or an interruption, then said rather haltingly, "I'm afraid, Syl, that Owen's just finished with it."

"You mean it's baked all ready?"

The tearoom owner nodded. "Iced an hour ago. It's boxed and waiting. You said you wanted it for tomorrow."

"I know, dear, but I never dreamed it would be—"

"Yours was only one of many special orders, Syl. And with both the children's St. Nicholas party and David's affair…well, Owen had to go ahead with the Friday orders."

"And I suppose you can't just sell it in the case." Sylvia peered into the glass counter top, pointing to the display of macaroons and gingerbread. Exhaling loudly, she fumbled for her wallet. "Too much trouble and expense to ice over the personalization, too. Of course. Well, never let money stand in the way of friendship." She handed Magdalína her credit card. "We'll just have to eat it. Or leave it on the church's doorstep. Thanks, dear." She returned the card to her purse.

I finished my tea and stood up as Magdalína said, "I'm really sorry, Sylvia, but with Owen's schedule—"

"Maggie, *please* don't give it another thought. It's not that important. Believe me. Now, about my tea and cinnamon toast…I'm *perishing* with cold and hunger."

Magdalína apologized for the delay and disappeared into the kitchen. I took my cue and followed an idea, but instead of finding David Willett outside the store, I found only discarded boxes, flour sacks, and other remnants of the baking trade.

TEN

"THERE'S TIME FOR MURDER," Graham said that evening as we sat over dinner. The pub was quiet. Perhaps a combination of the snow and the murder kept folks home.

An Elizabethan building, The Four Marys sheltered azaleas, rhododendrons and magnolias within its cobblestone courtyard. Terra cotta saucers that would hold huge pots of summer flowers now only lined the stone walls, queerly vacant and lonely. Along the courtyard's northern wall, an exuberant evergreen leaned against the edge of the roof, its spent needles like confetti on the snow. Inside the pub, a fire crackled in the fireplace and threw its yellow light across the stone floor. The bottle-glass windows trapped the flames' dance, gifting patrons seated in the back of the room with their own fire. Opposite the bar, a small elevated stage shone under several spotlights. The publican placed a wooden chair behind a microphone stand, and a musician sat down to tune his guitar. I leaned forward, ready to drown in music.

Graham tapped a collection of papers with his pen. "Your time table shows that opportunity, Taylor. Nice job this, by the way."

I thanked him in a barely audible voice, my attention focused on the man behind Graham. "Trueman was very helpful." The singer was blowing into the mike.

"Most likely stemming from his duties to his fellow creatures and his wish to get on with the St. Nick thing," Graham said, grinning so I knew he was joking. At least partially.

"Especially if our killer is local and knows the workers' schedules," I added as the singer ran through a few chords. Graham seemed to wait for me to do something, so I read aloud the timetable for Wednesday.

1-4 pm: church decorated
4 pm: workers home for tea
4-6:30 pm: Vicar and Olive in the rectory, finishing the packages, have tea. Conjectured time of murder
6:30 pm: Olive in church to see to last of holly and car-nations, discovers body
(7:00 pm St. Nicholas festivity scheduled to begin)

The singer, an above average Martin Carthy wanna-be, was launching into his first song with some complicated finger picking. I craned my head, trying to see. When Graham coughed, I looked at him. "Uh, yes, sir. Kind of tight. The murderer would have to know all this, which points to a local. Joel Twiss wasn't killed elsewhere and carted there. The blood tells us that."

Graham said something but I was concentrating on the singer, a forty-ish redhead dressed in black. His face and hands leapt out of the dark surroundings, as if they were the impor-tant objects on which to focus. He played a Martin twelve string, the satin-finished DM model. Good choice for a spot-lighted performance, for it eliminated the glare produced by the polished models. Graham tapped on his beer mug. I blanched. "Pardon, sir?"

"I said we're looking for someone who knew Joel, who could lure him into the church and kill him there."

"Takes in about the whole village, sir. What a surprise."

"I'll tell you something that *may* be a surprise, Taylor." He was watching me, probably to see my expression when he dropped the bombshell. "During our search of Joel's home, we discovered two new wedding rings—a man's and a woman's. Matched set. Do anything for you?"

I frowned, shaking my head. Nobody had seemed overly morose when told of Joel's passing, but then again, I hadn't encountered the entire village. Besides, as Graham would point out if I spoke my thoughts, the proposed spouse didn't have to reside in Bramwell. There was the rest of the world. It remained an intriguing curiosity.

As if knowing of our conversation, the singer began "Rose Connelly," an American folk song of murdered love. I jumped when one of the high E guitar strings snapped. It dangled from the tuning peg, the light running along its silvery thinness. Evidently a common occurrence for the singer, for he didn't miss a word or a note.

Graham touched my arm and I turned toward him. "Jens Nielsen slid the ring on Joel's finger to see if it was indeed his—"

"—as opposed to him playing best man for someone?"

"—and while many people have the same size ring finger, at least Nielsen tells me that the ring fits Joel perfectly. Again I ask, do anything for you?"

"You've no idea as to his bride-to-be? I suppose we can't hope for an autographed photo propped on his bedside table, or an engraved wedding announcement." I must have looked hopeful, for Graham laughed.

"Another mystery, Taylor. Nary a likeness nor name to be found."

"And the birth certificate?" I said, picking up the encased item. The name read Ellery Austin Hale, with a birth date of 60 years ago.

Graham said, "We're checking. Age seems to fit Joel, but..." He shrugged as if to say he couldn't explain the odd name. Grabbing the rings, he said, "Anyway, these are a bit easier to understand. I'll have Lawford hawk the glass slipper around the village."

"Lawford will be smashing as Prince Charming."

The singer was crooning.

I stabbed her with a dagger, which was a bloody knife,
I threw her into the river, it was a dreadful sight.
My father often told me that money would set me free,
If I would murder that dear little girl
whose name was Rose Connelly.

I trembled.

Graham stopped, listening to the words. As the singer launched into an instrumental break, Graham said, "Why don't they write songs about contemporary issues? We've got all this old stuff, which I assume happened, but nothing more recent than 1750 or whenever."

"But we do, sir. We have 'Springhill Mine Disaster,' 'Billy the Kid,' 'The Edmund Fitzgerald'—"

"You go to the clubs, then?"

"When I can."

"You sing? Oh, I know about your stint with Gilbert and Sullivan, TC. You told me. But I mean this kind of thing."

"Not to hear my family tell it." I tried not to think of my dad's ridiculing voice when I had told them I wanted to turn pro.

The folk circuit, he had informed me, was not a respectable career for a Taylor. If I had an operatic-quality voice like my sister, or if I had applied myself to piano lessons as my brother had, I might think of joining them in their careers. But strumming a guitar in a smoke-filled club…I shook off dad's sarcasm.

"You play?" Graham picked up my left hand, turned it palm

up and looked at my fingertips. Running his thumb over the calluses, he said, "Why haven't I noticed?"

"I guess you've never investigated a song I murdered." I withdrew my hand and picked up my glass. Dad grinned up at me through the amber-colored liquid. I quickly asked, "So what do we do with the woman's ring?"

"Keep it neatly wrapped in its plastic bag for now. You want pudding?"

I glanced at my dinner plate, the roast beef and mashed swedes a memory. Dessert was a temptation, but I was working on losing weight. And Christmas and New Year's festivities made it tough enough without indulging in extraneous desserts. "I'll pass, sir. Thanks."

"Surprised the pub doesn't sell Owen Parnell's specialty. What's the name again?"

"Flying Saucers."

"Sounds rather evocative of soaring away to foreign shores. Nice idea right now."

"What brought that on? I thought you liked the winter months."

"I do, Taylor. I was just thinking of the travel folders found today in Joel's house. Spain, Greece, Italy. Wonder if I can wrangle a holiday from Simcock after this case is finished."

"And miss Christmas with m—" I broke off quickly, afraid he had read my mind. I quickly said, "I thought you liked spending Christmas with your sister. The family gathered round the blazing Yule log and all that."

"My sister is a lovely person, Taylor. But sometimes her family is a bit too energetic for me. I wouldn't mind just sitting around in my bathrobe this holiday, sipping a cup of wassail and singing to my CDs."

I shuddered at the bleak picture he painted, so unlike the image his cashmere sweater, wool slacks and suede jacket produced. "Won't you miss them if you did that?"

"I suppose so," he said, his voice registering defeat. "I just find Christmas preparation a chore at times."

I could believe it of a younger Graham, the Graham immersed in his ministerial robes and church. Advent and its preparations were a tiring whirl of planning worship services, church caroling outings, youth sledging parties, staff gift-giving, hanging of the greens party, and donations to the parish poor. It often left the minister exhausted and in anything but the Christmas spirit. Too many demands, too little time, too little help. I wasn't surprised Graham had been burnt out and left the chapel, though office lips whispered that Things Inappropriate for a Clergyman had pushed him into a new career. If taken for his features alone, Graham's lead actor good looks suggested just such improper conduct. He could probably have his pick of women just by asking. But Graham wallowed in a ministerial—if not monastic—mind-set; lack of wife decreed lack of bedroom activity.

The guitar music changed to a slow love song. Graham's voice broke into the singer's pledge of constancy. "Sleepy?"

"Sorry?"

"You sighed. Quite loudly. Didn't sleep well last night?"

"Oh, just tired. It's rather hard going through the snow."

"Strengthens your leg muscles, TC."

"If it doesn't pull them."

We left during the singer's break. The busted string and a broken flat pick littered the stage. I wasn't able to glance at the Martin in passing, for the singer was replacing the string. We walked slowly upstairs, the burgundy colored carpet thick beneath our feet, the wooden banister sleek from centuries of polishing and handling. Halfway up the stairs I paused at the landing. It held a small loveseat drowning in red and green pillows. Hothouse red geraniums in brass pots crowded the windowsill. A handful of paperbacks peeked from beneath the loveseat, which smelled faintly of lavender.

We said good night outside my room. Once inside, I leaned against the closed door, listening to his key jangle in his door lock, the door open and shut, and the sudden silence of his ringing telephone as he evidently answered it. I was feeling uncommonly sorry for myself, but it was hard to shake off. I also knew I had to put the brakes on any thought of falling in love with Graham, for an affair with a superior officer was out of the question. Still, how can you control your heart?

THE SCREAM OF SIRENS woke me hours later from a dream-filled sleep. I reached for the alarm clock at first, thinking it was time to get up. It did look as though the dawn was well advanced, for crimson light filled my room. Yet, it was not early morning light that spilled through my window. The color ebbed and danced, casting immense black shadows on the far wall. I pulled the curtain aside to see the street quickly filling with shouting people silhouetted against a glare of gold and red. The bookshop was on fire.

The first thing I saw on rushing outside was Margo, her arm around Hannah Leftridge's shoulders, her words a stream of quiet, strong comfort—in great contrast to the fiery confusion reaching into the ebony sky. Smoke gushed from the broken windows and gaping roof, rolling into the darkness above our heads. Shadows blacker than midnight stretched behind us, toward the west, melting into the smudges of far-off buildings. Water ran down the street in red veins, like Hannah's lifeblood seeping from the wounded building.

The street was a turmoil of people and fire engines, hoses and water. I fell against Graham as he ran past me, his arms filled with books from the store, his shirtsleeves blackened and singed. Mark was following a fireman to the back of the store. I stood in the midst of this confusion, trying to figure out where I could best help.

Some of the constables and Scientific Officers were creating a safety zone around the building, giving the fire fighters space to work. Doctor Rice had established a first aid center outside the chemist shop, which was just south of the bookshop. Already he was treating burned hands and arms. He glanced up at someone—perhaps the store proprietor—and shoved a small box at the person, then resumed his work. The cotton gauze shone oddly white in the darkness. Water threw back the reflection of crimson flame and inky shadow, puddling the street. It would be ice by morning.

Margo had guided Hannah to the bench outside the hotel, the same bench on which I had sat after the dog incident. Mark was nowhere to be seen—presumably outside the back of the shop. Graham, I noted in horror, was returning to the shop, his arms empty. I tried to follow him but DC Byrd stopped me, his huge hand clamped on my shoulder. As I turned, questions in my face, he pulled me sideways as a blazing bough of a nearby tree crashed to the earth. I quietly thanked him and returned to the bench area where, rather like a strange fire brigade line, I took books from Graham and passed them on to a constable.

How long we worked, I don't know, for I didn't look at the clock when it was finally over. But there was no blush on the eastern horizon as I tumbled into bed, every muscle of my body protesting their cruel treatment.

Morning came too early and with an annoying clatter of the alarm clock. I sat on the edge of the bed, not caring if I never moved again, wanting to dull the clang within my head. The air held the acrid stench of spent fire. I groaned and tried stretching. That only showed me where more miserable muscles were.

After showering and dressing I opened the curtain and looked out. Water that had shone mirror-like on the street and ground last night now was crusted over in dull frost and ice.

The bookshop, though still standing, was a blackened hulk in the grey morning. The major damage, as much as I could ascertain from this distance, seemed to be to the roof and the south side. Still, much of Hannah's stock would have been ruined, despite Graham's heroic effort. I wondered how he was, if he had suffered burns. I let the curtain fall closed, suddenly sick with the destruction and suffering.

I paused in the hotel restaurant only long enough for a cup of tea, my appetite gone. Graham was either still in bed or already at the incident room. I doubted if anything like the late hour and exertion of battling the fire would keep him from his usual schedule.

But he wasn't in the incident room when I arrived fifteen minutes later. Many of the constables were here, nursing their headaches with cups of tea or coffee. I decided not to wait for Graham's instructions, and walked to Hannah's house.

It was a modest cottage of no particular style. A cube of grey with one grey chimney in the center of the roof. Yellow shutters and door broke up the monotony. Perhaps golden mums had enlivened the dullness this autumn. The last blooms of a lemony rose clung to life and the front wall. Not so unusual in early December, this burst of color, if the rose was sheltered. And this one seemed to thrive beneath the porch roof. The front walk was equally utilitarian, leading straight from the sidewalk to the door. As the door opened, I heard a parakeet singing. Obviously he hadn't spent a late night.

"He's uncommonly cheerful," Hannah said, seating me in an over-stuffed chair by the front window. I sank into its softness, afraid I'd never get up. "If his singing bothers you—"

"No. Please don't move him. I'm glad someone's immune to last night's effects." I waited until she took a seat in the rocker across from me. "How are you this morning?"

Lifting her bandaged arm, she said, "Aside from this, you

mean? As well as can be expected. Though I'd be a ray of sunshine if the weather would clear. This cold doesn't help my neuralgia, either." She rubbed her upper arm and peered outside.

A bank of sober clouds edged across the grey sheet of sky, bringing a sharp wind that swept snow before it. A dried flower stalk bowed under the frigid buffeting, upsetting a wren that was trying to land there. I listened to the wind whispering in the chimney, glad for my heavy pullover.

"I hope that burn's not serious," I replied.

"Francis didn't think so. My, how that man worked last night! Bandaging all our heroic wounds. I offered to reimburse him for all the medical supplies, but he refused to listen. Got downright insulted, I think. I was only trying to thank him for his help."

"I think the chemist contributed," I said, recalling Dr. Rice handing a small box to some man. "I shouldn't worry about it, Ms. Leftridge. People were only too glad to help you."

"The entire village must have been there. Several people carried out books and other inventory from the store. I don't know how I'll ever—" She stopped, taking a deep breath as though to swallow her tears.

"People wouldn't have turned out to help if they hadn't wanted to. Remember that. You needn't feel guilty about anything."

"Easier said than done, as they say. Still, with so many people suffering burns…"

I wondered how Graham was, if he had suffered during his rescue work last night. I could still see his singed shirtsleeves, his soot-streaked face. "Even if people were burnt, Ms. Leftridge, there were no major injuries. They had sense enough not to barge into the area that was burning."

"Still, they risked their lives just dragging out books. But I'll be grateful for that the rest of my life. It'll help me more than they can know. Any bit I can salvage…"

I said she seemed to be getting hit rather hard at the moment—shop fire and loss of her friend.

Hannah reached for a tissue as her face screwed up. I let her cry; thinking her sobs an odd contrast to the bird's cheerful singing. Minutes later, she raised her head, dabbed at her eyes and apologized. I assured her that it was unnecessary. "If there's anything I can do for you—personally, even—please let me know."

She forced a smile, said she would, and tossed the damp tissue onto a side table. I let her sit for a moment, composing herself, before I asked if she had suspicions how the fire had started.

"I haven't the least idea, Sergeant."

I asked the standard questions about enemies, jealousies and personnel problems, to which Hannah said, "Other than upsetting a customer yesterday, I haven't a clue."

"A customer?"

"Yes. Bayley, I believe his name is. Here to look over the town. Owns a tour company out of Buxton."

ELEVEN

"IF YOU'RE GOING to take any stock in that daft woman's words," Andrew Bayley said half an hour later, "you're in the wrong profession, Sergeant. Might as well believe in voodoo and spells."

We sat in the hotel's dining room, an oversized replica of blue and white Wedgwood filled with the scents of roses and fried bread. Our cups of tea were forgotten as Bayley talked and I listened. I had found him just as he was finishing breakfast. Remnants of grilled tomato, toast and soft-boiled egg dried on his plate, a white china oval embossed with the hotel name. He pushed it away, wrapped his hands around the teacup, now growing cold, and looked at me. His eyebrows were lowered over glaring eyes.

"Ms. Leftridge says you were upset."

"Too mild, Miss. I was damned angry! Still am. What a bloody stupid way to treat a customer."

"And why are you angry, Mr. Bayley?"

"You suspect me of arson, then?"

"We don't suspect anything at the moment, sir. We're just asking questions—"

"Arson. Gotta be, if you're doing all this questioning."

"We're merely asking people—"

"Those who you suspect might've torched the place, right?"

He took a sip of tea, watching me while I said, "Nothing of the kind, sir. We'd like to know if anyone knows anything about when the fire started, if they saw anything. That sort of thing.

We're not ready to charge anyone—or even if we will. Arson isn't always involved in fires, you know."

"I should think not. However, if I'm to shake you, I suppose I'll have to tell you, then. Yes, I was angry yesterday. I went into her bookshop to see about discounts for my people—when I get the tour set up, that is. I like this village. It has a uniqueness about it, apart from the St. Nick and Dark Man customs. There's a fountain outside the Four Marys—the pub just down from the village hall—that was built before 1100. The youth hostel has a *magnificent* priest hole that's entered by a pivoting wall beam, and the hotel, here, has a splendid original wing, furnished authentically and reputed to be haunted—all dating from—"

"All of which," I said, interrupting Bayley's enthusiasm, "add up to a unique visit for the tourist."

"Maybe not unique, miss, but interesting. Besides the beauty of the Derbyshire dales, a tumulus, and a mine we can tour… makes for a pretty tour, Miss. A *very* nice tour." He settled back in his chair, glancing around the hotel dining room as though imagining it filled with his people, as he termed them, and hearing the cash register ching.

I wondered just how many people would want to tour a coalmine, or even if Andrew Bayley could maneuver it, which I doubted. Bordering Nottinghamshire and South Yorkshire, the Derbyshire coalmines had been big business until 1984, spewing forth the raw material to fuel electric power stations and homes. Now there was not a single mine open, the closed pits having dumped their 6,000 men onto a struggling economy. I had seen the grim reality on their faces, and I could still see the residue two decades later in Mark Salt's face. His eye sockets held the whispers of the coal, the black of a mundane job and physical risks. Mark had told me in a rare moment of seriousness how coal dust was ground into a man's skin, ingrained as firmly as a tattoo.

I had felt the warmth of his grey eyes examining me as I peered at the bridge of his nose. The brand was there, faint black smudges where he had rubbed his eyes. The smudges would have darkened and spread had he stayed longer. But two years had shown him enough, and he realized there was more to life than this repetitive labor. He left the coal face for police work and has never been sorry.

But that was Mark's story. Now I was trying to focus on Andrew Bayley, who had finished his tea and was picking up his bill. I asked about the brush with Hannah.

"The discounts I want," Bayley replied, "should actually result in a profit to her. I wanted to set up a discount plan whereby people with my tour could purchase books on local subjects. I thought the lower prices would induce other sales in the shop. It would be good business for her. I like to see the little fellow make it in this mega-merger world."

"And what do you see for yourself, then? Surely there would be some benefit for you. As much as you may like to lend the helping hand, you wouldn't go to all this trouble without a thought to your own wallet."

Andrew Bayley threw some coins onto the table and stood up, shoving his chair against the table behind him. Looking down at me, he said, "I would have received a flat fee for each tour I brought into the village. But your Ms. Leftridge wanted nothing to do with it or me. In fact, she spoke to me quite abrasively, stopping short of calling me names. I am still amazed at her reaction and unwillingness to do business. She has nothing to lose by this—*nothing!* People on holiday want souvenirs, and post cards, maps, brochures, and books are stunning remembrances. Especially if she coordinates author book signings while we are in the village. The personal touch never fails, miss. How many people wouldn't buy a book if personally autographed by the author? But she wouldn't hear of it!" He dragged his chair back to the table. The silverware jangled from the force of the push. "She wanted no part of additional sales and revenue. Well, I told her where she could go."

He left me open-mouthed and thinking that perhaps, instead of Hannah, he had helped the shop to that destination.

SYLVIA HALE, the invisible hand on the reins, as Magdalína had referred to her Wednesday evening, raised an eyebrow when I asked if I could talk to her, but invited me in anyway.

The house, a centuries-old limestone shell wrapped around modern appointments and enough antiques to convey wealth and heritage, perched on a slight hill on the southeastern edge of the village. Dense woods framed it artistically when approached from the north, but a professional front lawn and garden statuary countered the rustic look. A lordly manor in the 17th century, it still seemed so, with its twisted brick chimneys, slate roof and diamond-latticed windows. Toward the west, a youth hostel backed up to the Hales' woods, while St. Nicholas church spire could just be seen among the winter-bare tree branches.

The drawing room was an extension of Sylvia's taste, an extensive collection of silks, china and artwork. A nod to the approaching Christmas season was by way of an advent calendar and books, branches of red-ribboned evergreen stuck in a large Chinese vase, and a small pyramid of wrapped gifts on an enameled platter. A peaceful rendition of "The Coventry Carol" filtered in from a CD playing in the adjacent room.

"What do you wish to know, Officer?" Sylvia asked, skipping the small talk that normally eased investigation jitters. Anyway, I didn't think she had any. I said I'd heard Colin might have been at the church Wednesday and therefore might be able to furnish information about the murder.

"I don't know where you get your information," she said, her words clipped and quick, "but Colin was in Buxton for most of the evening."

"And you were home, then?"

"I suppose you're subtly asking if I have an alibi. Not so you'd notice. I was decorating the house. A friend came over to help with the festoons above the door. She left close to 4:30. Then around 5:00, I had a trunk call from a friend in London. Haven't spoken to her in ages, so I'm afraid we gabbed a bit. Nearly an hour. At six I had my tea, by myself. So, as you can see, there are holes in my afternoon. And no, I didn't particularly notice when Colin came in. Might have been near 10:00, but you'll need to ask him. I speak to him as little as possible." Her fingers rifled the corner pages of a woman's magazine.

I made a note to confirm her call with Trunk Enquiries. "You don't know—"

"Look, Miss, you may as well hear it from me as from some long-nosed busy-body in this village. Colin and I aren't exactly co-warming our marriage bed. He's in the process of moving out. Taking up residence in the hotel. That's the usual thing, isn't it, after the papers are served?"

I murmured I was sorry to hear of her difficulty and hoped things would turn out amicably.

"Shouldn't think so," she said, gripping the arms of her chair.

"I had all the money coming into this marriage and I'll take all the money leaving it. Colin's been—well, how would you describe him—supportive through our years together. He's turned up at the village fetes, watched from the audience, said 'Good show, old girl' when needed. *Supportive*. Affectionate, in his way, but Casanova's record will still stand. Oh, I know what you're thinking, Sergeant—why did we marry? I'm not sure I know the answer to that anymore." Her right hand moved to the side of her head, and massaged her temple. "Of course it was a physical thing at the offset. God, he was good looking! Poor as a church mouse, but good looking. I suppose our hormones spoke more loudly than our brains. Or I've come to value different qualities after thirty years. But I still abhor lies and deceit, whoever offers it. I may overlook a short affair or overeating. Even cowardice or discourtesy, but I won't tolerate lies." Her fingers dug deeper into her muscle, blanching the skin.

I glanced at the pile of books, not knowing how to respond. Were these personal problems she'd encountered during their wedded years or was she merely citing suppositions? Wishing to leave the Hales' personal problems, I asked if she was involved with the St. Nicholas festivity at the church.

Her hand abandoned her massaging and lay quietly in her lap. "I coordinate it all, yes. It's a very large job, what with deciding on the gifts and designating who will do the shopping and wrapping and so forth...but Owen does the bread baking each year, so that's one less worry. Still, we have the refreshments to see to and all. But yes, I do enjoy it all."

"I've never heard of another parish doing this. It must give you a great deal of satisfaction, especially during Advent."

She stifled a yawn as she made a great show of consulting her watch. "I suppose it does, yes, but I do it more for the tax benefit than for anything."

I pressed my lips together, afraid I would retort ungraciously. It figured. Standing up, I apologized for taking her time.

"Not at all, Miss. I can't think where Colin's got to. He's not one for jogging, and I don't know of anything he has scheduled..." She walked to the small antique desk, glanced at her husband's daily diary and said, "No. Nothing here. It's a mystery, isn't it? But not quite the same magnitude of your case." She stopped me as I opened the front door. "I assume it's murder, being knifed like that. But who is it? Do you know yet?"

"You've not heard?"

"I haven't been out much the last two days, and no one's phoned me with the important news. So, no, I haven't heard."

"Joel Twiss," I said simply, wanting to see the effect on her.

She held onto the corner of the wall for support. Her eyes, when they sought mine, looked suddenly different, as though reflecting the sickness of the murder. In a quiet, almost fearful voice, she said, "Poor Hannah." Then she added, "Poor Colin."

"I know Hannah worked closely with Joel Twiss for the festivity, but why will your husband be particularly saddened by Joel's death?"

"There was this brotherly thing between them. He was that sort of man. Evoked great feelings of some sort in everyone."

If Hannah's emotions were any indication, Joel Twiss would indeed evoke the brotherly twitch in many breasts.

"And what were *your* great feelings, Mrs. Hale?"

Sylvia twined her finger around her ponytail, as though she needed time to consider her answer. Her blonde hair shone even in the dim afternoon light. "I suppose I admired him, mainly. He was only a uniformed sergeant when he retired, you know, but he had this great intellect that could carry him to any height he chose. He applied that to his pastimes, and learned as much about silver as any antiques dealer. But it didn't stop with hobbies. He checked out books from the library, studied all the time." She hesitated, as though remembering an incident. "I admired him for that. When most people vegetate in front of the telly all evening, he was furthering his knowledge."

"Sounds like an ambitious man," I said, wondering why this energy hadn't propelled him higher in his career.

"He was, Officer. But there was also a ruthlessness about his pursuit, whatever he was concentrating on. I found that slightly frightening."

"Had you ever suffered from his inclemency?"

Again she hesitated. The clock in the dining room chimed.

As though it reminded her of the present, Sylvia suddenly said, "No, Miss. Other than a verbal dressing down and a look that would wither the rose on the stem, he treated me well. I suppose he was so focused in his acquisition of knowledge that he rode over us who were too dimwitted or uncaring. I can't believe it was intentional. After all, he was a police officer. You care about people, don't you?"

A door slamming somewhere in the back of the house broke Sylvia's discourse. A male voice shouted, "You got a twenty I can borrow, mum?"

"Borrow?"

"OK. *Have*." The voice, somewhat exasperated, came closer. "What the hell's the difference? You got the twenty or not?"

"It's in my purse, dear. I've got it in here." Sylvia excused herself and walked over to her purse, which was lying on top of the desk. Pulling out her wallet, she said, "I don't know what you do with your money, Ward. You're always asking me for money. I thought you were paid for your hours of employment at that place."

"I am, mum, only it's not enough and not—Oh!" He stopped as he came into the room and saw me.

He was in his mid twenties, I judged, dark, tall and slim, with muscular shoulders. A haze of stubble covered his chin and matched the general unkempt air of his clothes. Though the holes in his jeans might have been part of the current fashion, the smudges on his jacket just spoke of unconcern or poverty. He shook off a stubborn clod of snow and watched it fall onto Sylvia's oriental carpet.

I came back into the room, closed the door, and introduced myself.

"Really!" he said, as though he had never seen a detective before. Or at least a female one. Stepping forward, he extended his hand. "I'm Ward Hale."

"My insolvent, reappearing son," Sylvia said, handing him the note. "I want this back your next pay day, Ward."

"Sure, mum." Shoving the money into his pocket, he leaned against the edge of the desk, unable to take his eyes from me. Either my job or my clean clothing fascinated him, I figured.

"Ward is employed at Hannah Leftridge's shop," Sylvia said. "Has been for…how many years, now, dear?"

"You here about the murder, then?" Ward asked, ignoring his mother.

I said I was.

"You know who did it?"

"It's still under investigation."

"Which means you haven't the foggiest. Well, Scotland Yard can always have a go at it, if your lot needs to give in."

"Really, Ward," Sylvia said, replacing her wallet. "There's no call to be rude."

"Rude?" Ward said, his eyes traveling the length of my body. "Sorry, luv. No intention. But that's one of my few personality defects, isn't it mum? Rushin' ahead without thinkin'. Over-eager. That's me. Not meanin' to insult anyone anytime. Just chargin' ahead. Otherwise, I'm your docile lad. Only meant to give your lot a chance to save face if you can't fathom it all."

"Thank you, dear, for explaining," Sylvia said. Then, stroking her son's shoulder-length hair, said, "You're going to shave before you go to work, aren't you, dear? And have a wash?"

"Half day, mum. Late start today—Friday."

"Oh, yes. I forgot, what with the murder investigation."

Nothing could rattle you, I thought, watching Sylvia caress Ward's cheek. *Cool as the center seed of a cucumber. What's really going on?*

"I just don't want you losing your job because of the way you dress. God, I don't look that bad when I go to my self defense class, even if I do work up a sweat."

"Yeh, well, it's my morning off, as I said, and I'm in a hurry."

"You going somewhere tonight, dear? Is that why you need to borrow money again?"

Ward nudged the snow with the toe of his boot, then pressed it into the rug. "Goin' to a film, then grab something from a take-away."

"I hope you're not going out with—"

"I'm goin' to a *film*, ok?" Ward's voice hardened and he turned toward Sylvia. "Me and a few of the *lads*. Then we're goin' to the Chinky—I'll have cashew chicken, if you need to know. Then to a pub. That's why I need a few quid. You got that straight?"

"I only wanted to know what you were doing, dear. I worry about you when you're out. Especially on these snowy roads."

"Yeh, well, don't. I'm a big boy, mum. If you haven't noticed, there's others as has. Paul's known it for some time. Which reminds me. Better make it twenty-five. You got another five quid?"

Sylvia got the money from her wallet and handed it to Ward. "I really think you should be showing a bit of responsibility about repaying this. Your father thinks—"

"I *know* what His Highness thinks. I know what he says. That's all I ever hear, isn't it? Not 'How are you?' or 'Anything troublin' you?' or 'How's the job?' All the time it's the bleedin' money. When am I gonna pay him back? Do I know how much I've borrowed? Well, I know it down to the last centavo. I know 'cause it sings in my head all night. I know 'cause he's sent me a god-damned letter! So maybe it would be best all around if I crashed and burned on some road. Then His Highness could save his pence *and* the cost of the postage!"

He left the room, brushing past me without a word, and slammed the front door.

"Sorry you had to hear that," Sylvia said, her fingers combing through her pony tail. She followed me to the door.

"Ward's so emotional lately. I don't know if it's his work or something in his life. He's so close-mouthed. Won't talk to me or his father. And they used to be so close. Especially in his younger teens."

"He have any brothers or sisters?"

"No. Perhaps that's his problem, needing someone to talk to. But it didn't seem to bother him before. His father, as I said, and he were great mates. Did everything together. Now, the littlest thing seems to be a storm in a teacup to him."

"Think nothing of it, Mrs. Hale. The weather puts many people out of sorts."

"I hope it doesn't hamper your work. Must be difficult in these conditions."

"We'll get it all sorted."

Sylvia peered at the snow as I stepped outside. "God, what a mess."

I agreed and left her, feeling I had learned more of the Hales than I had wanted to.

GRAHAM LOOKED UP at me when I walked up to our table in the incident room. He had been concentrating on the computer in front of him but smiled when he saw me. I sat down heavily and told him of my morning.

"Kind of a finger-pointer, I agree, Taylor," Graham said, "but how often do angry people think of consequences before acting?"

Not very often, I agreed, thinking of the man who, after an argument in a pub, returned with a scythe and publicly assaulted the other man. Despite dozens of witnesses, his anger had urged him into immediate action. "And jail," I said before realizing I was speaking aloud. Graham had the tact to ignore my sentence, and told me of his busy morning at Joel's house.

"I've got Mark and a few other lads working on the fire, though they can't really do much until it's declared arson. *If* it's declared arson. But I improved my mind and learned more of Mr. Joel Twiss this morning. Care to guess what we found on opening his home safe?"

"How'd you—"

"Never underestimate our abilities, TC." Graham smiled as he tossed a plastic bag at me. It was fastened with Mark's seal. It also held an opened envelope with a nine year old April date penciled on it.

"It's a bit hard to tell, sir, but I quickly rule out water. Could we have papers, here?"

"Your schooling was worth every penny, TC. The envelope, duly opened and photographed, contains a recipe, also photographed. Want to exercise your deductive powers again?" When I shook my head, Graham said, "A recipe for Flying Saucers."

"That's the biscuit—"

"Yes, the biscuit around which The Pineapple Slice rests its fame and fortune."

"Then, if the recipe is in Joel's safe...what are Magdalína and Owen doing with it?"

"Another bit of a puzzle for you to ponder. If that gets boring, employ your talent on this. We found it in Joel's bookshelf." He got up, retrieved a large, leather-bound photo album from a chair seat, and handed it to me. The album was in an oversized plastic bag, also tagged by Mark. Graham remained standing near me as I stared at the cover.

The leather was embossed, gold letters announcing its ten years of memories.

"A mundane collection of photographs," Graham said, "though some of the mementos such as newspaper articles, greeting cards and letters are interesting for their sake alone, never mind the glimpse into Joel's life."

"Why is this marked? What's so special about family photos?"

"Turn to the tabbed page, Taylor. You can do it without breaking Mark's seal. That's why I had him put it in the over-size bag."

I nodded and, with some clumsiness, flipped to the indicated page. The plastic crackled and refused to cooperate at first, and my fingers slid on the slick surface, but at the third attempt I worked my fingernail behind the paper tab and opened the album. The page held family photos, for the inked heading on the left-hand page announced "Christmas, 1953." A decorated tree showed in some of the photographs, the strands of glowing lights barely discernable in the flash of the camera. Gifts in various stages of unwrapping littered floor and table, while in one photo the remnants of Christmas dinner was the main subject. Paper-hatted revelers grinned at me from another image. They all seemed happy, as the 1950s tended to be. And they all seemed to be family, for people hugged or kissed or sat together. Below each color print the names of the photographed were hand printed. All seemed normal and hardly worth this forensic precaution, until I saw what Graham was waiting for me to see: a number of photos with scratches on them. They were group shots—two small children and two adults, presumably parents. One photo showed the same children sitting with three older people—grandparents? But in each photo the face of the smaller—younger?—child was eradicated, scratched off as from a sharp-pointed instrument. My fingertip stroked the plastic covering damaged area, as though trying to heal the wound or feel facial features. I stared at the sacrilege for quite a while, trying to understand, then asked in a small voice, "What does it mean?"

TWELVE

"SOMEONE DISSATISFIED with his family," Graham said, sitting down.

"Yet having emotions strong enough to want to retain his childhood, even if he was rubbing out brother. I assume it is his brother…"

"It says 'Ellery.' But it could be a cousin or some relative."

"Everyone is noted beneath each photograph," I said, "but when it comes to Joel's name, it simply says 'me.' I assume it is Joel who is the 'me.'"

"A logical assumption. I do, too."

"But if these are forty year old photos, is Joel the right age? What was he—fifty, sixty when he was murdered? Is Joel a ten-year-old boy in this snap?"

"About that, I'd say. Maybe 12. Can't tell about the Invisible Man."

"But does Joel have a brother? I haven't heard anyone in the village talk of one, and I've been talking to half a dozen people. People who knew him well. Did you find anything in his desk diary or address file?"

"We're getting to that, TC. Give us time to sort through the house!" He laughed at my eagerness.

I, however, felt far from laughing. The scratched out face chilled me. It was an overwhelming act of rage. Could Joel have followed through with physical violence? And if so, when? Immediately, or had Joel waited years for some type of revenge, planning so it was perfect?

I laid the album on the table, glad to be rid of its hatred and mocking gaiety.

Graham shoved the album off his papers and in so doing I saw the bandage. "Your hand, Mr. Graham," I said, wanting to know about his health as much as I wanted to change the subject. "Last night, did you—"

"Bit of discomfort, but Dr. Rice patched me up. Nothing more serious than second degrees."

"I'm glad," I said, thankful he hadn't landed in hospital. There was a silence between us as I wondered what would become of my career if Graham weren't here. When I looked up, Graham said, "I'm glad, too. Go to lunch."

I DIDN'T GO STRAIGHT to lunch, but talked to several villagers about Joel's family. Every answer was the same. Joel had been a bachelor, no family ever visited him, he never went home—wherever that was—at Christmas. He was little more than a hermit, but he hadn't recluse personality. It was too bad he had never married or had nieces and nephews to whom he could pass on his knowledge and possessions. Tiring of Joel's non-existent brother, I asked the chemist about the fire. His flat, like Magdalína's, was over his shop. No, he hadn't seen anything suspicious that could give us a lead on the fire, but then, how could he, being asleep? Yes, he would've wakened if had heard something next door, but he hadn't. No, he hadn't seen the fire start or smelled anything like paraffin; the first he had known trouble was when the sirens of the fire brigade tender woke him. And he was glad to donate his medical supplies for Hannah. Not enlightened, I left the shop, frustrated and aggravated. I wasn't supposed to be working this case, but I wanted to help Hannah. She might have been a personal friend if I had met her under circumstances other than a murder investigation. That tended to color people's outlook on potential friendships with cops.

Eden deMere was just coming out of the post office as I crossed the street. Upon hearing her name she looked up from the parcel she carried, looking rather confused until I reintroduced myself. She nodded, blushing slightly, and apologized for her atrocious memory. "Normally I have a veritable trap of a mind, Sergeant, and I would've remembered you, but Joel's death and the fire… Shocking, isn't it?" She tucked the package under her arm and waited for me to say something.

I agreed, then replied that it was still too early to know how the fire had started.

"Of course. Just wondering. With all the trouble we've had—" The roar of a motorcycle interrupted her. We watched two black-leathered riders roar down the High Street, skid to a semblance of a stop at the crossroads, then thunder away in a snow-churning rush. Eden shook her head. "Speak of trouble, you've just seen it personified."

"Who are they?"

"Ward Hale and his girlfriend of the moment, Paula Lindbergh."

"Lindbergh? Relation to Olive?"

"Granddaughter. Eighteen going on eight. Regular tearaways, those two, though if they'd been properly reared…"

I murmured something about it being too bad that some kids didn't have the proper upbringing or influences early in life.

Eden said, "For a year or so Trueman worked with them, tried to get them involved in youth activities at the church and at the hall. He spent God knows how many hours talking to them—not as a vicar. That turns off kids faster than anything. But as a friend. Well, he's nearly Ward's age, isn't he? Found out their interests, invited them to concerts—that sort of thing. I thought it was doing some good, but then Ward stopped coming. Lost all interest very quickly."

"And Paula?"

"She stuck it out a bit longer than Ward did. She'd be with Trueman so often that I was becoming a trifle jealous." She laughed, but her eyes held the solemnity of the topic. "Here I bared my soul to you about my love for Joel and I'm now confessing that I was jealous of an 18-year-old. God, am I insecure or daft?"

"Neither, I expect. Jealousy's normal, especially if the intruder seems to offer more youth or beauty or intelligence—"

"Well, I know I shouldn't have worried about Trueman. I mean, he's as solid as the Rock of Gibraltar. But Paula can twist men around her finger. It's not so much her looks, though she doesn't exactly repulse anyone. It's a hint in her eyes and voice."

She looked toward the church, at the road junction where the bike's tire tracks marred the snow. "She gets into your life and leaves traces that you can't easily shake off. Like some hex or illegitimate child."

"So your husband—"

"Trueman turned her over to Joel when he admitted that he wasn't getting anywhere with her."

"Thinking Joel, as a former policeman, could scare her straight?"

"That was the idea." We listened to the clamor as the motorcycle accelerated somewhere beyond the church. "He spent a lot of time with her. Not only on outings, but also at his house. He attacked it differently than Trueman had. He struggled to get her grades up, get her interested in working toward a career, whereas Trueman had focused on people and the village."

"And what was Paula interested in?"

"Besides men? She talked about a lot of things at first. You know—from impossible to mundane as she found the impossible took too much effort or talent."

"Actress and rock star?" I suggested.

"Is it the lure of fame or fortune? I was content with thoughts of singing on the cabaret circuit."

"Doesn't pay as much," I agreed, "but the career lasts longer."

"Anyway, Joel broke it off after a row. Told her where she could go."

"Any idea what happened?"

Shaking her head, she said, "He never said. Happened late one evening, that's all I know. He practically pushed her out of the house and told her that he knew how to incriminate her for *any* crime happening in the area. He wouldn't have, though. It was just the anger talking." She searched my face, as though wondering if I believed her. My concern, however, was if Joel had indeed tried and Paula had responded with murder.

I HAD A HURRIED LUNCH, making up for the hour I'd spent asking about the fire, Joel's phantom brother and Paula's redemption. But I did take a few minutes to dash up to my room in order to make a phone call. The binoculars I had wanted for nearly a year were on sale, the lead item in a local store's Christmas sale. It had taken a lot of saving from my pay, a lot of sacrifice, but I had the money and was now more than eager to part with it. I was imagining where I'd hike to first, what bird I'd like to find, when someone rapped on the door. As I walked over, I found several brochures had been shoved into the room. No one was in sight when I stepped into the hall. Quickly finishing the sales order, I returned to the room, closed the door and threw the phone onto the bed. The brochures advertised holidays in Greece. The hotel with double occupancy room was circled.

I got on the walkie-talkie and asked Margo to come up.

"So, what's the rush?" Margo asked when I closed the door behind her. I shoved the brochures at her, my teeth clenched.

Flipping through the stack, she said, "So? You want me to go on holiday with you? Why not take your mum or sister or—"

"I do *not* want to go on holiday," I nearly yelled. "These were shoved under my door just now. And no, I don't know who by, but I've got a guess."

"You want them checked for fingerprints? Only way you'll be sure, Bren, unless you get him to confess."

"How Mr. Detective Mark Salt could even think of asking me to go with him when we're in the middle of an investigation—"

"You know," Margo said, looking at the front of a cruise brochure, "these are rather like the ones I found at Joel's. Can't say for sure, but how many travel brochures of Greece are there bound to be in this village?"

I know I blanched. In the silence, I looked at Margo, who relinquished her inspection of the brochures to meet my gaze. Dawn, as they say, broke.

"Oh, no, Bren. He wouldn't have! Why, the idea itself is too preposterous. It's too fantastic! You're out on a limb with this one, girl. It'd be worth his badge."

"It'd be worth it to get me to snuggle up with him, if I can read Mr. God's-Gift-to-Women Salt's mind. God, Margo! Of all the berkes I've ever met—" I threw the brochures across the room.

"You know if those are the ones from Joel's house, throwing them about won't do them any good." She picked them up and slid them gingerly into her jacket pocket. "Why don't you go with Mark?"

"*What?*"

"Now, before you tell me to push off, just listen for half a tick. First, you'd get a nice holiday out of it—"

"—Providing I don't end up in Holloway for murder."

"Second, not to appear crass, it wouldn't cost you a single penny, since he invited you."

"It'd cost me my sanity, my good humor, my digestion, my patience, my life—" I ticked the items off on my fingers.

Margo was not deterred. "It'd be very romantic, Bren. Just think of it. Posh hotel, drop-dead scenery, exquisite food, moonlit nights, strolls along the beach…" She sighed and closed her eyes. I didn't know if she was picturing herself or me in the role of Mark's date. I shook her shoulders until she slowly looked at me. "Don't count it out too quickly, Bren. Sounds heavenly. And you might even get to like him a bit more."

"It'd *have* to be a bit more. I don't like him all that much now."

"'Course, you'd like to get some posh clothes. You have a nice dress or two? That hotel didn't look the sort to accommodate jeans and trainers."

"Now you're criticizing my clothes?"

"You know I'm not. I'm just saying that jeans and trainers seem to be leaning toward the standard of dress for any occasion. Last week, I saw a theater-goer in just that." She shuddered, making a face. "'Course, you could always buy some things there. That'd be rather fun, don't you think? Coming home with things to remind you of your, uh, holiday. Even if you buy them off the peg, it's still rather nice. Wonder what the exchange rate of Euros to pounds is…"

"Well, it could be a million to one, for all I care. I'm sticking to my current wardrobe." Before Margo could say anything about her disappointment in my theater-going standards, I added, "I'm not going anywhere with Mark Salt. Not even to the incident room. Can you return those brochures without getting anyone into trouble?"

"That remains to be seen," she said, turning toward the door. "But since I've got them, I'm the one to get nabbed if I mess up. What's lower than a constable?"

"Prisoner."

"Send me a post card from Athens. A moussaka with a nail file in it would help immensely. I suppose Holloway allows us to get mail…"

"Margo." I called as she was about to leave. She stood expectantly. "How did Mark get these brochures? I mean, did he pinch them from Joel's house, or take them out of the evidence bag?"

She shrugged. "I suppose he lifted them from the bag. All he had to do was just break his own seal. He was working that scene, I think. The lounge. The room in which these were found. Nothing could've been easier."

Nodding, I said, "They're his responsibility. Probably was going to pick them up this evening and return them to the bag before Graham knew they'd gone missing."

"Slight chance someone would want to look at them, yes," Margo said, "but I guess he could always stall them."

"Graham doesn't stall."

Margo screwed up her face. "I wouldn't want to try it, but you know Mark."

"Unfortunately, I do. Oh, Margo." She paused, about to close the door behind her. "If you see him—Mark—would you ask if I'm about to become an accessory in all this?"

"What?"

Wriggling my fingers in front of her, I said, "*Prints*. I touched those damned brochures. I'll sleep like a baby tonight if Mark can assure me he'd already printed those before honoring me with them."

GRAHAM HAD JUST DROPPED his jacket onto the back of a chair when I entered the incident room. The tables, as much as I could discern on slowly passing them, did not hold the travel brochures. Of course, even if Margo had found Mark immediately on leaving my room, he would have had to re-bag and reseal them before returning them. And he had missed his chance for a while, for Graham—shirtsleeves rolled up and coffee mug within easy reach—showed all the signs of a long afternoon at work. But, ever optimistic, I glanced at the tabletop. No brochures.

"Oh. Hello, Taylor," Graham said, as I sat down.

I murmured my greeting, afraid my voice would break. Were all criminals this nervous? Graham didn't seem to notice my tenseness.

"A few lads from Bakewell are on their way over. They'll help with our investigations. Just pray we don't need to call in more officers from other divisions. Simcock really *will* explode then." He threw his pen at the computer monitor and sighed heavily. "God, it just keeps piling up, doesn't it, Taylor?"

"How to you mean, sir?"

For an answer, he tossed a plastic evidence bag at me. Mark's seal, I noticed, was not on it. Instead, it displayed the seal of a Scientific Officer, which, technically, was the proper procedure. Ordinarily Mark—as a sergeant—wouldn't have tagged anything from a crime scene, but we were stretched a bit thin, and Mark had been pulled in to work on the scene in Joel's house until reinforcements arrived. That's when he had spotted the brochures. And tagged them. And borrowed them. Lucky for Mark all around.

"Airline tickets?" I said, instantly regretting the obvious statement. Graham nodded, calling my attention to the date and names on the tickets. Again I echoed the evident. "Joel Martin Twiss. And..." I turned the packet over so I could view the other ticket, "Hannah Marie Leftridge. Hannah!"

"Do anything for you, Taylor?"

"Besides fill my head with the sound of wedding bells, you mean?"

"Most people would've raised a suspicious eyebrow and conjured images of a fortnight's illicit rendezvous."

I shoved aside my own vision of Mark and me. "Yes, sir, but there *are* the two wedding rings we found."

"Did Hannah Leftridge happen to drop the news to you when you questioned her—either before or after the fire?"

"No, sir. I didn't expect this, to be honest."

"I hope *she* expected it." He reached for his can of beer and took a long drink.

I must have blinked at the unexpected gesture, for Graham said, "I know it's early, Taylor, but perhaps you won't brand me a drunk when you learn I was nearly run off the road a bit ago." He smiled at my expression and said, "Up near Piebald Tor. I was rounding a tricky bend, when a car appeared in front of mine, forcing me to the left. Nearly slid off the road. Damned idiot never stopped. Took me a good quarter of an hour to dig myself out. Oughta be a law," he said, smiling.

I felt far from smiling. "You sure you're all right, sir? Shouldn't you see Dr. Rice? Whiplash isn't funny. You might've strained your muscles?"

"I'm fine, Taylor. I was more concerned with my car, but that's all right. Minor scrape to the left rear wing where it scraped against the stone wall. Thank God the wall ended where it did, or I would've been smashed against it."

"This other car, sir...did you see what it was, who was driving? Can he be had up for reckless driving?"

"It was a dark green four-door saloon car, Taylor, and there are hundreds of them about. And though I hate to admit it and end up sounding like a probationer, it all happened too quickly for me to see the driver, though I had the impression—don't ask me why—it was a man. Not that it matters, for I'm still in one piece. So no need for a police line-up or house-to-house search. And don't look at me like that, Taylor. I know you and Margo. And as to the reckless driving charge—that's a no-go. I don't think he was driving particularly reckless. It's hard going up there, roads not particularly cleared. No, Taylor, it's more a question of a skidding car than a negligent driver."

"Still—" I began, but Graham cut me off with a frown. "I know alcohol's a weak crutch, Taylor, and strictly speaking I shouldn't, for I'm on duty, but—"

I looked around the room. Margo was the only other person there, and I knew she wasn't going to say anything. "Simcock will never get wind of it, sir," I said, watching him crush the empty beer can. "At least you're ok. Your car can be taken in."

"Yes, but there's just something about the first dent." He sighed, and I knew he was thinking about the smooth body of his Insight, the red metal dented and scraped with grey limestone. "Well, if that's all the excitement I encounter on Bramwell roads…" He tossed the crumpled can into the waste bin. "This would never happen in Tahiti."

"Speaking of which…" Looking at the tickets again, I read aloud the couple's destination. "Athens. Expensive honeymoon."

"You would be so crass as to put a price tag on moonlight and romantic beach walks, Taylor?"

He sounded like Margo. He also seemed far away, as if he was walking those beaches in the moonlight. The window, or what lay beyond it, again claimed his attention. I knew he didn't see the snowy landscape or feel the cold seeping through the glass. He strolled some foreign shore, heard some distant drummer. I left him to his palm trees and calypso music, and went to talk to Hannah—but not before I investigated the site of Graham's accident.

DESPITE GRAHAM'S calm air, I wasn't too sure about his accident. We had stirred up things in the village—emotions, secrets, stories that villagers wanted to keep hidden. If Graham had dug too deeply to suit someone… Well, it wouldn't be the first time either of us had been the target of a vengeful or fear tactic.

Margo sat beside me, listening to my thoughts, returning her own answers. The drive up to Piebald Tor was uneventful, even if Margo did complain about the cold. I'd cranked up the car heater and windscreen demister to high, but it did little in the face of a car that had been sitting out in wintry temps for nearly 48 hours and a heated conversation between Margo and me. She kept leaning over the steering wheel to wipe the glass clear. "What makes you think find anything up here? Graham told you the other car skidded into him." She tapped on her passenger window. "I can believe it, Bren. What if we get stuck up here? We should've brought Mark."

"Mark? Why in God's name—"

"Bren, even you have to admit that there are times when muscle—in whatever form—comes in handy. And Mark's physique is pretty impressive."

"So we'll phone in for help if we get stranded. But no Mark." I stared ahead, my body leaning forward, my hands gripping the wheel as the tires fought the rutted snow. "Besides, I don't know what we're looking for."

"And you don't want to look like a berk in front of Mark. Or man," Margo added quickly. "So you honestly think Graham was the target of an upset villager? You sound like a movie scenario."

"I'd rather sound like that and be sure of Graham's safety than to sit in Bramwell, sipping hot tea, and wish tomorrow that Graham wasn't in hospital."

"Like I said, movie scenario."

We rode the rest of the way in silence, not because we had nothing to say, but because we were looking for the accident site.

Clumps of dried tufted hair-grass poked out of the snowy drifts, their white plumes an autumnal memory, for the biting wind had scattered the flower heads long ago. Bracken and helleborine, once colorful, nodded their drab brown stalks at us. Outcroppings of gray stone dotted the landscape where the wind had swept away snow. As the car approached a steep incline, Margo pounded on the windscreen, yelling, "This has got to be it! Look! The small bit of stone wall, the tight turn. Even the tire marks. Careful, Bren!"

I was about to reply when my car slid away from the turning road. Margo gripped her seatbelt, said something that sounded like "Our Father, who art in heaven," and breathed heavily as the car stopped inches from a millstone.

I switched off the car's motor, unbuckled my seatbelt, and grinned at Margo. "At least we're still on the road proper. Shouldn't have any problems getting back."

"Where's Nanook of the North when we need him?"

"Come on." I stepped outside and immediately pulled my cap over my ears. The wind whistled through a chink in the stone wall. Margo joined me, pointing to the millstone.

"Why anyone in his right mind would just fling that thing so close to the road…"

"I don't think it was flung, exactly."

"OK. Discarded. Derbyshire's famous décor. Who's at fault, the road makers or the mill workers?"

"I never was any good with chicken-or-the-egg things. Come on. The sooner we find something, the sooner we'll get back to that hot tea."

"What are we looking for? Would you give me a clue? As brilliant as I am, I work much better when I have a direction. There are hardly bound to be bloody handprints. Graham said no one was hurt."

I had been walking toward the confusion of tire tracks but stopped when Margo joined me. I shrugged, then pointed toward the grey stone wall. A smear of red paint stood out like blood on snow. "Something like that. I know this is probably hopeless, but I just can't shake the feeling that Graham was targeted."

"You mean someone followed him up here and lay in wait just to run him off the road? Seems risky, Bren. You couldn't be certain your car wouldn't end up in the ditch, too. Why not track him in the village, knock him on the head at night?"

"For one thing, that would be obvious. Up here, in these conditions, his crash could be classified an accident."

"Fine if the bloke lives through it all."

"I don't really think the driver stood much risk. Here, look at it." I pointed to the curved part of wall and then to the tire ruts. "Graham was on the inside of the turn, heading away from it. The road angles downhill, where Graham would be, and turning sharper than the other driver."

"And the other driver, even if he did skid more than he hoped, would have Graham's car to buffet his slide."

"So if his car was caught in a rut, he could blame the skid, which is perfectly legitimate."

"If it's so legitimate," Margo said, blowing on her gloved hands, "why are we out here looking for a hit-and-run? I know, I know. So you can sleep tonight."

"These are great impressions," I said, gazing at the car tracks. "Rather pristine."

"No one in his right mind would be coming up here. By the way, why *was* Graham up here?"

"Didn't say, but no doubt he was checking out something."

"No doubt. And *you,* I can tell by your thoughtful voice, want to follow the tracks of the Car in Question."

I smiled. "Well, since you suggest it…"

"*I* didn't suggest it. *You* were suggesting it."

"And you know when to accompany your smarter, if older, ranking officer. You know, Margo, this could be a big break for us."

"Yeah, if the big break's not a leg when we're getting out of here." She had turned back to the car when she grabbed my shoulder and pointed behind me. "Good idea, but too late, as they say."

A snowplow exhaling black exhaust against the white landscape was chugging up the road from the direction in which Graham's assailant had gone. I groaned and shut my eyes. "For once I wish the highways department wasn't so bloody efficient."

"Wishing will not make it so, Bren. Well, without our compass, as it were..."

"We must depend on our own observation skills."

"I wish we had the tire tracks to follow, instead. By the way, did Graham mention their cars hitting? If so, we could comb the countryside for a dark green saloon with red paint on the right front wing."

"He didn't say, but I looked at his Insight before we left—only the rear damage and no signs of green paint."

"So no impact with Car Number Two. Great. Should be easy to find this car. We've only got the entire kingdom to search."

We walked slowly, peering at the road and the wall. Snow dusted the top and face of the wall, icicles fringed the stone edges. I knew Margo was uncomfortable and probably inwardly cursing me, but she had turned on her professional police mode and worked silently. I was just about to admit it was a daft idea and to suggest we head back to the car, when Margo called to me from the far end of the bend. When I joined her, she pointed to a sheet of paper leaning against the wall. We looked at it for several moments before I said, "Damn. Wish we had an evidence bag."

"You could wait here while I drive back for one."

I caught the pronoun order and said it would probably be all right if we lifted it carefully. Grasping the page by my thumb and index fingernails, I gingerly pulled it from its snowy anchor.

"Page from a book," Margo said as I turned it over. "What would a book page be doing up here?"

"Litter, like everything else?"

"Could be. What a strange thing for litter, though. Usually it's beer cans and empty crisps packets. Why a page? That means deliberate destruction. I hate to see that. Books, I mean. They're so valuable."

"Guess it could be from just about anyone," I said, starting to scan the paper. "From just about any time, too."

"But it's not wet, Bren. I mean," Margo said, her voice coming faster, "if it had been out here a while, wouldn't it be wet or frozen or torn or something? Looks brand new."

I nodded, my brain taking in the printed page. "It's from David Willett's new book. See? It's the dedication page with his name on it."

"Still could've been out here a while."

"No. Not on sale yet. His coming-out book party is this weekend."

"So," said Margo, leaning against the wall as the snow plow approached us, "is *this* why Graham was forced off the road? Doesn't make sense. *Got* to be a coincidence, us finding this here."

"But no one has access to these books yet, Margo."

"Except the author, David Willett."

"And Magdalína Dent," I said slowly, recalling the scene in Pineapple Slice. "David was bringing over a carton of books for the book signing party."

"And, if you're going in that direction, Hannah Leftridge has *more* than a carton of books in her shop."

THIRTEEN

MARGO BEGGED TO BE dropped off at the incident room to powder her nose, but I suspected she wanted to warm up. Entrusting her the page, I asked that she not say anything to Graham yet and parked my car. Margo hugged the paper to her chest as she called out her thanks and disappeared inside the building.

The exterior of Hannah's bookshop held suggestions of what had overtaken it last night. Grey and brown scorch marks imprinted the walls, fanned out from the windows and side door where smoke had billowed. Outside the investigation barrier, stacks of books lay on wooden planks, thick scatter rugs and newspapers, chairs and tables—anything convenient to keep them from the snow and to make sorting easier. The books themselves seemed no worse for the adventure. I picked up one, opened it and sniffed the pages. A faint odor of smoke, but otherwise unscathed. Dropping it back on the pile, I nodded to Ward as he set an armload of books on a tread of a stepladder. He had shaved and washed his hair.

A movement on the far side of one of the tables drew my attention. It was the poodle I had rescued, and its lead was tied around a tree trunk. Going over to the dog, I said that it looked cold.

"It's got its jumper on," Ward said, motioning to the blue dog coat. "Probably warmer than I am."

"May be," I said, stooping down and petting the dog. He strained at the short lead, his tail wagging, and licked my outstretched fingers. "But he still looks cold. Why is he here? Your dad around somewhere?"

"Not that I know. Mum shoved Laramie at me, said the dog needed exercise, and went off. So I'm exercisin' the dog."

I watched the poodle jumping and lunging at the lead, yapping in his excitement or frustration. "This isn't what I'd call exercise, Ward. Walk around the village is more in order, I should think."

"Look," Ward said, waving a book at me. "I got this job, ok? Her Highness gives me an order. I can't do two things at once. So I'm creative and get 'em both done. Anyway, Laramie's all right. I'll take him home soon."

I patted the dog and stood up. "You could at least let him sit on a rug or something. Has he had something to eat?"

"More than I have. Just finished a dog biscuit before you got here. Now, you wanna call the RSPCA and haul me in, or am I free to get on with my work?"

"Of course you're free, Ward. I was just concerned for the dog."

"Yeah, well, don't waste your energy. He's better looked after than I am. Now, are ya just browsin' or do ya want somethin'?"

Hannah, he informed me as he bent over the pile, had gone to Buxton to see about the insurance and help in cleaning up the shop. Her return time was rather nebulous. Should he tell her I had dropped by?

"I rather think I'll catch her up, thanks. Perhaps at her home this evening."

"Your call," he said, straightening from his chore.

"You have a big job, I fear, if you have to sort out your inventory."

He shrugged, leaned against the ladder and pulled out a cigarette. The ladder swayed dangerously, threatening to discharge its precarious cargo. Ward paid no notice, concentrating instead on the police constables who stood just outside the shop doors. They looked as efficient as a 'No Entry' sign. And as bored as Ward did. After taking a drag on his cigarette, Ward said, "Got a lot of books out the night of the fire. People helped."

Like Graham, I thought, remembering his burns. "You didn't?"

"Not likely to, am I? Didn't know a thing about it. Not here."

"Out of town on business?" That provoked a laugh, so I asked, "On holiday?" Another laugh, though not as loud.

Ward said, "I'll save us both time, Sergeant. I rushed the calendar a bit. Had a dirty weekend. Was havin' it off with Paul. Paula Lindbergh," he added, as though I'd get the wrong idea. "That's what I call her—Paul."

"You spent *all* night with her?"

He smirked, shrugging as though that explained the situation. "You know how it is, Miss. You go to bed and next thing you know, it's mornin'."

"And you were at Paula's?"

"Not on your life. Still lives at home with her mum. Naugh. She came over to my place."

"Which is…"

"What am I—under suspicion of somethin'? Other than rapin' a minor? Which I didn't—and which she ain't. She's over the limit, so what we do is nobody's damned business but ours—got it?" He bit off his words, staring at me as though defying me to contradict him. I didn't answer, but waited for him to continue, which he did in a calmer, quieter voice. "Anyway, what can I say? We don't have witnesses, if that's what you want." He laughed, as though his statement provoked some kind of memory. "So that's why I didn't bloody well help at the shop last night. I was occupied elsewhere."

"Fortunately, people helped before the fire service arrived."

"You faultin' me for not leapin' out of bed and burnin' my hands like a lot of others did?"

"Not at all, Ward. I just applaud those who were able to help. Hannah obviously could have lost a lot more than those books." I gazed toward the heap of discarded books near the pavement.

"Hannah could've lost everythin'," he agreed, flicking ash onto a stack of books. "But, yeah, she was lucky. Most of it was confined to the back room. Buildin' seems safe enough."

"Nice that you weren't burnt out of a job."

"I can find another."

"So books—"

"They're not my life, let's say."

"You don't like books?"

"They're all right—some of them. But a lot of what gets printed…"

"Waste of money?"

"Who cares about that junk that's dished out?"

"Like what," I asked, picking up a book on birds.

"Like that," he said, tapping the book.

"You're not interested in birds, then?"

He drew another puff on his cigarette. "You got bleedin' birds around. Who needs to know what the hell kind they are? They're here. Your knowin' if they're a wren or buzzard don't make no difference to the bird. They'll get along without your peerin' at 'em."

"Some of us just think it's fun to see how many different varieties we can spot, that's all." I returned the book to the pile. "What *are* you interested in, then?"

"Book stuff or me?"

"Oh, you. If this isn't your end-all, be-all occupation—"

Ward relinquished his study of the constable to look at me. I wish he hadn't. He seemed simultaneously to disrobe and disarm me.

"Well, it ain't bein' no copper, nor no bird watcher. I got my mind on somethin' a bit more excitin' and lucrative. Racin'. Bike racin'. God, what a rush! *Vroom!*"

"You done anything? Have any experience?"

"Oh, I've been around the circuit a bit. Nothin' professional, you understand, but I've won a few. You oughta come up to my flat and see my trophies."

Only, the way he said it, made me think of etchings.

"That's why I'm here," he said, smiling. "Savin' up me lolly so I can turn pro. Big time, Miss. It brings in the birds, too. Not that kind," he said, tapping the bird book. "Somethin' about a man in a uniform…" He winked, then laughed.

"I wish you luck, Ward. Turning pro is hard work."

"Don't I know it. I had a bundle saved, only I had to pay off a bloke. So now it's back to square one, as they say."

"Bit of a knock, that."

"We've all gotta weather the rough times, Miss. And mine are about over. From then on, watch me—no responsibilities."

As if to remind him he still had one, the poodle barked. Ward mumbled something under his breath about always having to give up his own time to tend to others, and I went over to the dog. He was pawing at something half buried in the snow at the foot of the tree. I stooped down, patting the excited dog, and dug my gloved fingers into the cold whiteness.

"What's that damned dog done?" Ward asked, throwing an armload of books onto the tabletop.

"Just wants attention," I said, blocking Ward's view with my back. I lifted the object, flicking off the snow, and carefully pocketed the item. Standing up, I said, "Same as anybody, Ward. We all need attention and love."

"Yeah, well, seems to me he gets too much of it. My parents are always fawnin' over that dog. I mean, look at that ridiculous coat it's wearin'. Dogs have fur. That keeps 'em warm. Ya don't see foxes and such bothered by the winter, and they sure as hell aren't all coated up."

I let his comment pass, knowing a discussion was useless.

I had just turned to leave when I saw a pile of Christmas books on a table. Passing over the ones on home decorating and holiday cooking, I picked up the book that had originally intrigued me. St. Nicholas through the ages. The saint had changed costume with each century's demands of society, certainly. But what intrigued me was his story. I re-read it several times, my mind developing the implications of what lay before me in black and white. Excited, I gave Ward the money and turned toward the incident room when Scott's "Oh, Officer!" halted my steps.

He stopped his patrol car opposite Ward's temporary display, and I walked over to the driver's side of the car to greet him.

"Recover the goods yet?" I asked as Scott lowered the window. His white shirt nearly glowed in the sunlight.

"God, Bren, it's only been one day. Give me a chance. I'm not a 'tec."

I leaned against the car and smiled. Though the same age as Graham, Scott had no desire to rise much further in rank. He liked the variety of work that a response driver dealt with. It fueled him, he said. Each day different, directly connecting him to people. That, plus his sense of responsibility to make a better world, got him out of bed. As I said—his inner monitor of Duty without conceit. "So you're whiling away the day at Bramwell on the off chance you'll spot the perpetrator in the pub, then. Or is it the beer and prawns that call?"

He ignored my attempt at humor. "If I were a probationer, I'd have my eyes on your friend, there."

"Who?" I looked behind me, expecting to see Margo or Mark.

"Your book seller friend. Ward Hale."

I leaned forward slightly, peering around the car's windscreen. Ward had been watching our conversation, for when I stared at him he bent over a stack of books and pretended to straighten them. "You're joking."

"Not right now."

"*Ward?* What's he ever done—other than ride around on a noisy bike?"

"Granted, it's not in the category to get me a handshake from the Divisional Commander—"

"I'm glad of that! I like the lad."

"—But he's had his moments in the spotlight. Drunk and disorderly, petty theft, fights—"

"PC Coral, you shock me!" I laughed at Scott's scowl, then said, "So Ward's a bit of a tearaway. He's no worse than many who have finally grown into responsible adults."

"Time will tell, Brenna. I can only go from experience and our short but stormy acquaintance." He exhaled loudly and looked at me. His green eyes were the color of shamrocks. "That's not to preclude his mates, you know."

"I know he runs around with one or two others—"

"One, in particular. But go on."

"But do you think they're into car thefts? I can't imagine Ward doing the smash and grab bit. He'll not get started with that, Scott. He knows how many beans make five."

"Glad to hear he knows his arithmetic," Scott said, deliberately misunderstanding me. "But he's young. He may learn. Especially if he keeps hanging about with his guide-and-mentor."

"You can't be serious, Scott."

"Guide-and-mentor's been convicted for selling illegal drugs, for a start. What's the problem that you can't connect the two offenses, Brenna. Theft followed by moving stolen property—"

"—In order to have a few quid to purchase more drugs, yes. I know where you're leading me. But from theft of articles to selling drugs—Scott, do you actually believe Ward—"

"You lead a sheltered life, Brenna. You should get out more. There's a great film showing at The Apollo, in fact. If you've nothing on—"

"You're married, Scott."

"I was *going* to suggest," he said rather emphatically, frowning, "that you take a deep breath, turn 21st century, and invite a male friend out."

"Thanks, but the pickings at the moment—"

"Why not him?"

"If you're trying to hook me up with Ward—"

"Not the bloody hell likely to, am I? No. I mean *him*."

I turned and sucked in my stomach as Graham's car narrowly missed me. I could just discern Graham's apologetic smile and mouthed 'Sorry' before he sped by. "Not the safest place," I said, trying to regain my grace.

Scott laughed, put the car into gear, and said, "You referring to traffic or to dating your boss? Never mind. No need to answer. I can guess. Well, duty calls. Can I drop you?"

"I've *been* dropped, thanks very much. Many times. Good luck with your search. And remember, it's section three of the Act."

"Three *point six*," he corrected as the car glided into traffic.

FOURTEEN

MARGO COLLIDED WITH me as I opened the incident room door. I apologized and told her breathlessly that she was just the person I needed to see.

"No offense, Bren," she said, "but I'd like to hear that from a male lip."

"Anyone in particular?" I watched Mark Salt stand up and stretch.

Margo followed my gaze and patted my arm. "No, thanks, Bren. I know he's every girl's wish, but I leave him to you. I've got my sights on someone else."

I shook off Margo's hand. "I wish to God, Margo, you'd stop referring to Mark like that. And that you'd stop trying to make us a pair."

Shrugging, she said, "All right. So you're holding out for a higher rank. So what's all the excitement? You lose some weight?"

"Very funny. Take a look at this." I dug into my pocket, my gloved hand clumsily withdrawing the object the dog had found.

As I held it out for Margo's inspection, she said, "What is it?"

"Hopefully, a clue."

"Where'd you find it? Why didn't you bag it? If Graham?"

"I found it in the snow at the base of a tree. And I didn't bag it because I was afraid a dog would scratch it and that a nosey parker would dig it up and get rid of it if I left it there. And Graham, if we're lucky, won't hear of these irregularities if you help me."

She angled her head slightly to look at the cross. It was a

piece of jewelry—gold with silver filigree running down the cross's middle, rather like a strip of lace on a sleeve—about an inch long. The loop at the piece's top gaped open. As though it had been caught on something or pulled off. "Shouldn't you give this to a Scientific Officer to bag? What about photographs? And prints?"

"You seen this before?" I said, ignoring her, watching her face for recognition. When she shook her head, I asked, "OK, maybe not this particular article, but something that it might go with."

"Little early for Easter."

"There are other times than at Easter that people wear crosses."

"So, who's been to mass, then?"

"God, Margo, are you being intentionally obtuse? I'm not in the mood for games."

"Graham have you over the coals last night?"

"I'm trying to ascertain if this is a clue either to the murder or the bookshop fire, and you—"

"All right, all right. I just think it's a funny bit of jewelry for anyone to have, that's all, gold and silver. Where'd you find it again?"

I told her, then asked who she thought might have something like this.

"Well, I suppose we could ransack Joel Twiss' wardrobe since we don't know his taste in jewelry. At least we'd be warmer there than at that daft wall. I'll never warm up." She rubbed her arms. "Okay, okay, it was just a joke. Lacking that, I'd say our friendly vicar's wife or David Willett. Because," she added quickly as I opened my mouth to question her choices, "I don't believe it's Trueman's—this looks decidedly feminine—but Eden might logically have something like that. And David's St. Nick apparel might be minus a bit of decoration."

I pocketed the cross and grabbed her arm. "Let's find out."

DAVID WILLETT WAS shoveling his driveway when we drove up to his house. His friendly greeting changed to puzzlement as he watched Margo get out of the car. He knocked the snow off his cap, replaced it on his head, and asked us what we wanted. Margo stood slightly behind me, watching David's face as I showed him the jewelry. I could hear her softly clearing her throat, ready to throw in her own questions. When David denied owning any cross, Margo said, "Have you ever owned such an item?"

David shook his head, his eyes fixed on the item. "You've got the wrong person. This looks rather like a bit of woman's jewelry. I don't cross dress. Why you asking me? Did somebody tell you something?"

"What would someone tell us?" I asked. David pressed his lips together, standing mute. Turning to Margo, I said, "Mr. Willett evidently hasn't been frequenting the local gossip spots. You recall what we heard, Constable Lynch?"

"If," David said, pulling his shovel next to him, "you're referring to anything you overheard in the tearoom, you would be better off to pay it no mind."

"Why is that?"

"Do I have to spell it out? I should've thought it obvious."

"Nothing wrong with restating the obvious," I said. "Puts us all on the same page."

The reference to a book passed unnoticed. He either knew nothing about his destroyed book or had rehearsed his reactions well. David exhaled loudly. "As much as I like Magdalína, her place is a watering hole where old biddies and loose tongues congregate to inflate themselves at the expense of others."

"It didn't impress me that way when I was there. What about you, Constable?"

"I thought it a warm, cozy spot to have tea," Margo said, smiling broadly. "Kind of restful."

"The only thing restful about the place," David said, "is

when it's closed for the day. Anyway, why are you giving so much weight to this cross, whosever it is? I already told you that it looks feminine."

"Could have been torn from your costume," I said, recalling the elaborate embroidery, sequins and faux-gems that littered the garment.

"Could've been lost any time," he countered. "By *anyone*. It's a piece of female jewelry, for God's sake! Why connect it with the fire, for that's what I suspect you're doing, since it was found outside Hannah's shop."

"Must have been lost very recently," I said, holding the cross by its edges in front of David. "It was very near the surface of the snow."

"So?" David laughed. "Could've been shoveled up. Kicked up by people walking by even."

"Near a tree trunk in the little pocket park?" Margo asked before turning to me. "Perhaps Mr. Willett knows more about the weekday use of the park than we give him credit, Sergeant Taylor."

"Which seems remarkable," I agreed, "for one who is normally in school at this time on Friday afternoons. Perhaps he gets his knowledge from those same gossip-mongers."

"Though why he should be interested in park population is beyond me. Do you think that he needed this information in order to devise the best time to torch the bookshop?"

David's face blanched and he raised a hand. "Now, wait a damned minute! You accusing me of arson, based on this—"

"We're not accusing you of anything, Mr. Willett," I said. "We merely want to know if this cross is yours, and if so when you lost it."

"I told you it's *not* mine." David's complexion had turned bright red and he gripped the handle of his shovel. "Of all the ludicrous ideas. Just because a cross was found near a tree near Hannah's shop, you try to fabricate its importance as a clue.

Anyone could've lost it, at any time. So lay off me or I'll sue you for false arrest."

"We're not arresting—"

"And if you persist in this accusation," David continued, "I'll ring up my solicitor. I'm a gentle man by nature, but even gentle men can be pushed to the limit. All this nonsense about depth of snow…"

"I've never known the natural world to lie," I said, my voice quiet in great contrast to David's anger. "Would you say, Constable, that it's possible to drop something on Wednesday, for example, have it snow six inches, and then find that object within an inch of the surface on Friday?"

"Mr. Willett was thinking the item was disturbed prior today and thereby rose close to the surface, where you found it." Margo picked up the cross and looked at it, as though searching for David's name. "Or perhaps a mole tunneled there and inadvertently pushed it up."

I shook my head slowly, as though I regretted breaking the bad news. "Fiction, I'm afraid. The surface of the snow was packed, flat and smooth."

"Perhaps Mr. Willett knows a science teacher at his school who can explain this freak of nature to us."

We paused, looking expectantly at David, who was swallowing slowly. "There is such a thing as wind," he said moments later. "The wind could have shifted the snow. It does that, you know. You have only to look at the windward versus the leeward side of buildings, trees, tombstones…"

"There is that," Margo said somewhat unhappily.

"Rather like shifting sand dunes in the desert." I agreed. "But Mr. Willett's forgetting that the snow—"

"—was packed, flat and smooth," broke in Margo. "Like the rest of the area."

"All right," broke in David, "I give you your damned smooth

snow. I suppose you won't be happy until you've got me to confess or to show you my St. Nicholas costume."

"Do you mind if we look through your wardrobe?"

"You think I'm that stupid to have an incriminating piece of clothing still hanging in my cupboard? You think I wouldn't have burnt it or buried it?"

"Rather awkward to explain next year why you have no costume. Besides, you may have sewn something else in place of the lost cross by now." I smiled, wondering if he'd take the life line.

"Assuming I realized I'd lost that bit," he said. When neither of us replied, David sighed. "Fine. Go ahead. Get your excitement. Use the kitchen door—it's open."

I glanced toward the side of the house. "The door next to that car? Is that yours?"

David eyed me as though admitting ownership would land him in handcuffs. "Yes. Why? Is it unlawful to park on one's driveway?"

"Just wondered if you had guests we might disturb."

"No guests, Miss. I'm a lonely bachelor. Now, if you don't mind…" He grabbed the shovel, turned his back to us, and dug into the snow.

"White," Margo said as we walked up to the car. "Even if Graham mistook navy for dark green, he wouldn't have misjudged David's car."

"Looks used enough," I said, peering into the interior and noticing the piles of school papers and text books, an old cardigan, a few empty bottles of mineral water and a half dozen audio cassettes. "I doubt if he could have ditched his car so quickly, bought a new one, and staged it to look like it's an old family member."

"I'll run a check on it, just the same. Ready to play hide and seek?"

We found no clothing that suggested it had ever sported a

cross. But we had seen David's car and could most likely eliminate that from our list. When we had returned to our car, I winked at Margo. "Good as Batman and Robin any day."

"I would've said Abbott and Costello, but that'll do."

EDEN DEMERE HADN'T the forethought or guile to deny ownership of the lost jewelry. In fact, she'd shown Margo and me the surviving earring, even returning with the matching necklace.

"Typical of my luck," she said as I slipped the pieces into an envelope she had provided. "One of the few times I wear the silly things and it lands me in the thick of it. I've never been a murder suspect, Miss, and I readily confess I don't much like it." She leaned back in the settee in her front room, her eyes avoiding mine, and pressed her lips together, forcing the blood from them.

The room was oddly contemporary in this elderly vicarage. Chrome-framed posters of art shows and pop concerts complimented the tubular steel and glass furniture. Bamboo window shades and a large, white sheepskin adorning the floor were nearly lost in the other neutral tones of the grass-mat walls and tan carpet. It was a personal room with personal pieces, establishing family history and familiarity in the upheaval of following the owners from parsonage to parsonage.

"I don't think I said anything about your being a suspect," I said, watching her as she clutched her fingers together. She was dressed in a long woolen skirt and Aran knit pullover that echoed the neutrality of the room. A spot of blue and orange— an enameled pendant of a kingfisher on a silver necklace— broke up the monotony. "I asked if you could identify the piece and if you could explain how it came to be near the tree."

"Same thing, isn't it? I mean, I say I was at such-and-such a place on the night in question, and you take it from there."

"And just where do you think we're 'taking it', as you put it?"

She shrugged, glanced at Margo, then at me, and said rather

slowly, as if the trial had already taken place, "Holloway. Or wherever you drop women these days."

"Rather drastic, isn't it, since we haven't even determined if this has any bearing on the case?"

"There are ways. I've heard stories." She sat up, her hands on the chair arms. "Not that I'm accusing either of you two…" She reddened, as though she had said too much. "I'm sorry. This was all uncalled for. I'm just nervous."

"Oh, yes?" Margo asked. "If you're innocent—"

"But innocent people are locked up every day," Eden said. "You have only to listen to the ten o'clock news. And those DNA tests that prove some poor sod's been jailed wrongly and given his freedom after two decades…" Her voice dropped as she stared out of the window. "But no, I didn't kill Joel. Or have anything to do with the shop fire. I'd cut off my arms if it would help Hannah. Only it wouldn't."

"I agree," I said. "The best way you can help Hannah is by helping us. And that includes anything, however slight or ridiculous it may seem to you."

"Such as this cross," Margo said. "How'd it go missing?"

Eden sighed, evidently resigned to relating the story, and turned to face us. "I put on the damned things to visit a parishioner who lives in the hotel. And before you ask, this was yesterday. Around tea time, near as I can remember. She likes me to come for tea. You know how it is—gives her something to do while we're talking, lets her play hostess so she can repay me for my time and courtesy. I keep telling her it's not necessary. God, I know what living on a restricted income is like! But she insists, so I go."

"Can't see the harm. You're giving her something to look forward to. Must be lonely living at the hotel."

"It's got to be, yes. So I go every month or two and don myself up with her gift. She gave them to me several Christmases ago and, well—" She grimaced and slowly fingered the large silver hoop earrings she wore. They reminded me of the wedding rings found among Joel's effects.

"—to keep peace in the parish and with her, you wear them," Margo said.

Eden nodded and gave me the name of the woman. "I appreciate her kindness and thought, but they're a bit too fancy for me."

"You say she resides at the hotel. You walk there? Is that why Sergeant Taylor found your earring in the park across the street?"

"Obvious I did, isn't it? But I haven't worn them since…" She seemed to examine the ceiling. "Well, last Harvest Home, I guess. That's when I last visited her." Her fingers traced the curve of her silver hoop. "This is so embarrassing."

"I have a painting I drag out whenever my uncle visits. He expects to see it, and I don't want to hurt his feelings by not displaying it." Margo's eyebrows lifted expectantly as she waited for Eden's smile.

I thought how considerate Margo and Eden were, thinking of others rather than distress them. My dad hadn't been like that. He had no qualms about dumping several of my heart-given gifts at the church jumble sale or in the back of the cupboard. I had learned slowly that hand-made was not considered a treasure. Better the gift be bought than be sentimental. "So you walked to the hotel," I said, urging the interview forward.

"Yes," Eden said. "Seemed silly to drive one block, even with this snow. I stopped in the park to watch the birds." She smiled at me, remembering our earlier conversation. "I seem to be always watching the birds, now that Joel's gone. They're the only thing I have left of him." Her hand toyed with the bird pendant. "That was on the way back from my visit. A treat I give myself after making duty calls." She blushed suddenly, deeply, feeling the damning admittance. She searched our eyes to see if we chided her or were the type of people who would repeat a confidence. She bent her head briefly, studying her hands.

"I always bought a book or ice cream," I said, suddenly feeling close to this free spirit who was chained to obligation.

Taking a deep breath, Eden looked at me. "We all have our crutches."

"Nothing illegal about books and birds."

"At least it's not booze or drugs. God, how glad I am that I never got hooked on any of that! Anyway, that's the dull truth of the matter, Sergeant. I can't produce a witness, but I've confessed that the earring's mine. What does that do for your case?" She paused, her head tilted slightly toward me, her hand a fist around the bird pendant.

"Thank you for your time, Mrs. deMere. And thank you for being so honest with us. You've been a great help."

"I can't see how," Eden said, rising and following us to the front door. "But you know more about these matters than I do."

"So," Margo said when we were on the main road. "I repeat Eden's sentiment. I can't see how, either. What did we learn?"

"Body language, as Graham would tell me, speaks volumes even when the mouth remains mute."

"Mute? But she told us—"

"Figuratively speaking, Margo. What did she do each time she talked about Joel Twiss?"

"Can't say as I noticed especially."

"Fingered that kingfisher charm. On her necklace," I added when Margo opened her mouth.

"You think Joel gave her that charm, then? What's that prove? You saying she murdered Joel? I thought we were focused on the lost earring."

"It tells us she still feels something for Joel—maybe not as a lover, but as a good friend."

"And?"

"And while she may not have intentionally killed him, she may have accidentally done so. After all, Margo, the church is her turf."

DINNER WITH GRAHAM was becoming a comfortable habit, but it hadn't the excitement or intimacy of a Greek island rendezvous. We sat in The Four Marys pub, feeling the change from the hotel atmosphere would be a nice break. I guess it was, but I couldn't concentrate on the surroundings. Mentally and emotionally I was still with David Willett and Hannah Leftridge. Canned music filtered down from some unseen CD. I glanced at the stage but it was dark. Evidently the singer appeared later. Or on weekends. My dad's voice suddenly burst into our conversation, asking me again if I was prepared to starve in attics just so I could twank on Saturday nights. It wasn't until a loaf of bread was delivered with our soup that I realized Graham was talking. He held up the knife, his right eyebrow cocked. "Behold the ghost of Christmas Past."

"Sir?" I hated to admit it, but he baffled me.

"Wake up, Taylor. Christmas. Advent. Bread charity at St. Nicholas church. Bread knife. Knife in deceased's back. Dead body. Or is all this association too difficult to string together?"

"No, sir," I said, my face heating up. "It's just that, when you said ghost of Christmas Past, I thought you were talking of Dickens for a moment."

"Christmas Past in the sense that the village's St. Nick festivity is past. That's all. Perhaps I was too obtuse. Sorry, Taylor. It's been a long day." He finished cutting the bread and threw the knife onto the table. It landed next to my hand. He apologized again.

"That's alright, sir," I said, moving my hand, my body suddenly shaking. I looked around the room, noting the profusion of Christmas lights and paper chains. A few modern paper Santa Clauses were taped to the windows, while a three foot tall plastic one sat on the bar, glowing red and white from the electric bulb within it. They hadn't been here yesterday. I nodded toward the monstrosity. "I prefer our medieval saint."

"Likewise."

I was about to say something more when Mark Salt seated himself at the bar. He looked sure of himself, freshly shaved, every hair in place. I thought I could smell his after-shave from where I sat. He lit a cigarette and looked around the room, nodded to several people, then saw me. Holding up his hand, he wriggled his fingers and shook his head. I mouthed 'Thanks,' hoping he knew what I meant. There was no mistaking his wink. Or his meaning. I heard his laugh as I quickly reached for my drink and knocked it onto the floor. The publican hurried over and mopped it up.

"Sorry, sir. I'm a bit edgy this evening."

"Long day for you?"

"Not more than most."

"Just upset about the fire, then?"

"That shop is her livelihood. How's she to survive without it?"

"I ask myself the same thing, Taylor. But remember the piece of advice you had during your schooling."

"Don't get emotionally attached with the people involved in your case."

"It's not just a statement fabricated because some Chief Constable had nothing to do one rainy afternoon. There's reason for it. Which you'll find out, to your detriment, if you allow your heart to rule and you end up emotionally broken, like some of the clods who walk about, robotic, dull-witted and insensitive to everything in life. Don't become a misanthrope, Taylor. You're too valuable an officer for me to lose."

"Yes, sir." I fought the warmth that started creeping into my cheeks. "It's just that—"

"She has insurance, so she can rebuild without undue problems. She may even have money tucked away in the bank, so she can live off that until her reopening. I know you're feeling the vulgarity of her loss, Taylor, but you can't save the world single-handedly."

Which was what Mark had said when I had saved the dog. I glanced toward the bar. Mark was smiling at me.

I cleared my throat, leaning toward Graham. "I didn't like it even as a kid."

"Pardon?"

"That red suit. Looks more a fabricated bit of costume than clothing someone would actually wear. It always scared me."

Graham nodded and buttered his bread.

Silence fell between us as we concentrated on our meals. The softness of a Roger Williams piano solo crescendoed into a Manchester Jazz rendition. And while I normally would have enjoyed it, I found it difficult to hear Graham. Pushing back his plate, he said, "That looks like an interesting book, Taylor. May I?" He reached across the table as I was picking it up. His hand closed on mine. I could feel the warmth of his flesh and quickly pulled my hand away. The book fell onto his plate. I apologized, picking it up. Graham handed me his serviette, and I wiped off the back cover before giving it to him.

Turning over the book, he said, "Doesn't seem the worse for its adventure. Yours?"

I nodded, saying I'd just bought it that afternoon.

"I used to love Christmas. I probably still do, if I discard my prejudice about certain people." He leafed through the book, pausing periodically to study portraits of the various St. Nicks.

"From my meager knowledge, he really was a saint, feeding the poor. Too bad we've commercialized the man."

"Too bad we've done many things," I said, fingering the edge of the tablecloth. Mark was still at the bar, but his back was toward me.

"For instance." Graham leaned back, all concentration on me, the book in his lap.

"This is hardly the place or time for my personal soap box, sir."

"It may not be, but I'm interested."

"Please, sir. I'd rather not."

"As you wish, Taylor." He resumed leafing through the book.

"I bought it on a hunch," I said suddenly. Graham looked up, his expression asking me to continue. "Yes, sir. Something in the book attracted my attention, got me wondering about our case."

Leaning forward, Graham said, "And what captured your fancy, Taylor?"

"The sack, sir."

"His gift sack? I don't see—"

"No, sir. Sorry. I should have said his helper's sack."

"His helper? I'm sorry Taylor, but you've lost me. Where—"

"Nicholas of Myra—our St. Nicholas. He has a helper in many versions of his history. A dark little man. A grim-faced monk. Germanic, Austrian, Dutch, Russian... He appears in many countries' lore." I waited until he had found the appropriate page and had skimmed the story before I continued. "Quite ugly, isn't he? Demonic, if that's not too strong. Well, he followed our good saint about with a sack in many of the legends. Stuffed bad children into it." I paused, letting Graham catch up with my reasoning.

"And our murderer, you're suggesting, was trying his damedest to stuff Joel into that sack?"

"We're looking for his brother, sir. Could his brother have

found him and done this as a subtle comment about their childhood?"

The noise of the pub faded as I imagined the murder scene, the gloomy church, the snowstorm, the meeting of killer and victim, the cheerful pile of gifts. My scene faded into a fantasy of the real St. Nicholas and his somber servant. The coarse clothes contrasting with the saint's glittering robe, the gloom of night as the wizened helper sneaked into sleeping homes to steal unruly children, the snowy journey through a desolate wood. I pulled a red carnation from the bunch on the table, twirling it in my fingers as I blinked back to the present. Graham was staring at the page.

"What a hell of an idea, Taylor! You've positively frightened me." There was no laughter in his voice or expression, and his green eyes stared at me. "We've a few people concerned with St. Nicholas in this village, brother angle or not, I agree," he said. "A good handful make their living from St. Nick, or are involved in a benevolent way through him, yes. And as such, must be intimately acquainted with him in his various forms." He slowly closed the book and handed it back to me. "What are you thinking, Taylor?"

"What I'm wondering, sir, is who put all this information to use?"

FIFTEEN

"ALRIGHT, THEN," Graham said, pouring himself a second cup of tea. "Let's take them one at a time. Reel them off again."

Manchester Jazz faded away in a soft chord of clarinet, trumpet, trombone and piano. I repeated the names, giving him time to jot them down. "David, Nelson, Owen, the vicar, Olive, Hannah and Bayley."

"Fine," Graham said, looking up. "First is David Willett."

"History teacher and local writer turned famous."

"*The Ancient Art of Derbyshire Customs,* if I remember correctly. His publishing party is tomorrow evening, with the entire village invited."

"I leafed through his book at the bookshop. St. Nicholas is included in it, as is the more familiar Father Christmas, who is a character in most mummers plays. There are themes on him, certainly—as there are with his wizened demonic helper—but it's always the same character, no matter his name or dress."

"And you think that is enough to put David on your list?"

"No, sir. But he *does* play St. Nick at the church festivity each year. He has a sack—"

"Has it gone missing? Is it the one pushed over Joel's head?"

I admitted that it wasn't the same sack, but that didn't preclude David using another sack for the deed. "He'd hardly want to give the game away using his satin, embroidered sack."

"*Would* sort of point right to him, I admit."

"*And* he has an authentic costume, sir. *Quite* authentic, to hear Hannah talk."

"Presumably taking a lot of research, then. Yes, David would learn something, but did he know of the—Germany, is it?—helper? What's its name, by the way? If we're going to delve into this thing, I hate to keep calling it The Germanic Helper. Seems rather impersonal if we're going to include him as part of the case."

"Take your pick," I said, holding up my notebook so Graham could see the half dozen names I'd scribbled down. "Various names, various countries of origin."

"Give me *one,*" he said, running his hand through his hair and looking like he'd spent an all-nighter. "Anything German, like Bruno?"

"Knecht Ruprecht, Belsnickel, Pelzebock, and Pelznickel are German." I paused, watching Graham's eyebrow raise in surprise. "Or there's the Austrian guise of Krampus and Klaubauf. Or the Czech version—Krampus. And there's Zwarte Piet in the Netherlands. Then, there are the female versions. You want to hear those?"

Graham shook his head, his eyes bulging slightly. "Spare me. Just give me a name, *one* name. So I'll know whom you're talking about. Whatever happened to your 'Bruno'? Too simple?"

"Since you've given me authority, I opt for Knecht Ruprecht."

"For heaven's sake, why? What about one of those shorter names. Wasn't there a Belspickle in there?"

"You're confusing the names, sir. You've concocted a new one out of Belsnickel and Pelznickel."

"God, we don't want another name! All right. Knecht Ruprecht it is. But I just might call him KP for short. Seems a fearsome mouthful, that. Knecht Ruprecht."

"Rather goes with his looks, I think. He first appeared in a German play in 1668. He dresses like a monk—dark, long coat of animal skins. He has a dirty floor-length beard and carries a switch."

"Presumably to keep the naughty kiddies in line. Where's the sack come in?"

"Black Peter has a sack," I said, reading my notes. When Graham questioned me, I said, "Zwarte Piet, from the Netherlands."

"Ole KP gets around, doesn't he? What's he do with the kids he snatches?"

"Black Peter takes them to Spain. I don't know about the others."

"Best not to ask, I suspect."

"I don't think a sack is particularly in or out of line with any of them. Some carry a sack or a basket in which to drop the offender. Others intimidate with switches or chains. They all seem demonic in their appearance—horns, long tongues, beards, dark cloaks…" I shuddered. "Why these two sides to the legend? Why have the good St. Nicholas and his evil helper?"

"Perhaps to heighten the goodness of St. Nick. Or just to dramatize that good and evil are everywhere, constantly present. You can contemplate the subject on your off hours, Taylor."

"Yes, sir. Next on our list is Nelson Parnell."

"Brother of Owen?"

"Owns a cattery in Chesterfield, but lives here in Bramwell."

"Nothing cute, I hope. I can't abide cute shop names."

"Supposed to be good memory-stickers. So you won't forget the shop. Anyway," I said, rushing on with police business as Graham snorted, "also a budding author delving into the same subject."

"So, if his research is at least equal to David's, Nelson would also know about the St. Nick/Father Christmas identity. But if he doesn't don the dress for the church festival…"

"Yes, sir. Would he know about Knecht Ruprecht? But we

can't assume he doesn't, just because David plays the saint. After all, Nelson's book research may be better than David's."

"I agree. We can't discount him, though we have no proof at the moment that he's knowledgeable. We'll put him near the bottom of our list. Next is Owen Parnell. Our tearoom baker? Really? What's he done that's stirred your ire?"

"Don't know if it's ire, Mr. Graham, but it's suspicion. While not role playing as David does, Owen is in this St. Nicholas festivity as much as anyone else in this village. He bakes the bread each year, and the murder weapon—"

"—is our handy bread knife." Graham picked up the knife and cut another slice of bread. "Sharp, common implement found in many homes. Easy to come by. Long blade practically assures you'd hit your target." He set down the knife, offering me the bread, but I declined. It seemed tainted with Joel's blood.

"He had access to the scene when he delivered the bread. No one would think anything unusual with him in the church."

"Let's tackle motive and opportunity later, TC. I'd like to concentrate on our list of players first."

"I grant you Owen as killer may seem like a long shot, but we can't just ignore him."

"Not until motive or opportunity do so. Okay. Owen stays on the list. He could learn as much about the saint and his sidekick as anyone. He's been included in this Sixth of December thing for a while, as you said."

"Bound to pick up fascinating titbits, if he's at all interested."

"The vicar, Trueman deMere," Graham read off, then gave me a strange smile. "Your sense of equality, without trembling at high office, family ties or money, does you proud, TC. I assume in this instance you are thumbing your nose at the family ties."

"You mean he's the brother—"

Graham pointed heavenward and I reddened, hating myself for missing the joke. "What prompts his name on your list?"

"Same reason as Owen, sir."

"Been doing the custom for years; knows all about the sainted Nick—and perhaps all that goes with him. Right." He scribbled something down on the list and I said, "Would he have learned about saints in school?"

"As a child, you mean?"

"No, sir," I said, feeling the heat return to my cheeks. "Seminary, or whatever the Anglican name is."

"Ahh. Would he have learned about Knecht Ruprecht and his lot in Elementary Saints for the Beginner, you mean? I should hope so, though KP may be the bit for extra credit. I don't know if he'd be included in the course proper."

"Too much of a fairy tale, then?"

Graham nodded, but said the vicar was a strong possibility and we should consider him a suspect. "After all, he's a man. And any man, even clergy, sins. No one's immune. There have been clergy—priests, bishops, ministers—who have yielded to the call of the flesh."

I assumed he meant illicit sex, but didn't ask. The subject seemed too personal in a public place. More so, I felt, since office whispers hinted at Graham's own implication with a woman. Changing the subject, I said, "Olive Lindbergh."

"She who found the body. Can't deprive her of instant fame. She may know as much about the odd couple as anyone."

"She, too, has played the same part—decorator extraordinaire—as long as anyone can remember."

"So she has soaked up as much of the legend as anyone. Fine. Hannah Leftridge, bookshop owner. Prime suspect, perhaps?"

As much as I hated to admit it, I had to. "The information is at her fingertips, not meaning to make a joke of it, sir. She could easily find the information in any of the books in her shop."

"So could anyone, simply by digging about on the Internet, say, or library, but yes, Hannah may be our killer."

"And last, but not least, Andrew Bayley. Owns Idyllic Outings tour company, out of Buxton."

"And as a tour guide, interested in local customs, he's a suspect?"

"Yes, sir. His knowledge is quite extensive." I told him of Bayley's expounding on the Dark Man. "And though the Dark Man and Knecht Ruprecht are not of the same custom, it shows Bayley's research ability. He could very well know of St. Nick and *his* dark man."

"Was Bayley in the village on Sixth of December?"

I nodded. "After a week in Matlock, he returned November thirtieth to observe Bramwell's St. Nicholas custom."

"Nearly a week, then, in which to note people's patterns, plan when and where to kill Joel Twiss..." Graham's finger stroked the knife handle. "Sounds a bit far-fetched, a stranger appearing in the village to kill someone, but we've experienced worse."

"He could be counting on just that bit of far-fetched scenario to exclude him from suspect. 'Who, me? Why should *I* kill Twiss? I'm a stranger here. Just come on business. I don't even know the man!' Yes, sir. We've heard it before."

"And since he's been here a week in advance of the murder, people would be used to seeing him poking about. Let's talk opportunity and motive, TC. Murder was committed Wednesday evening between four and six o'clock. While we don't yet know motive, Bayley has opportunity. The people decorating the church had gone home, Olive Lindbergh was in the rectory with the vicar."

"Leaving the church unoccupied yet accessible. Easy enough for Bayley and Joel to meet, and for Bayley to kill him."

"*And* it was dark. Even if the snowstorm hadn't contributed to the early darkness, it was still sunset by half past four."

"Bayley could have easily slipped out of the church without

anyone seeing him. Most people were holed up in their homes, huddled by their fires or over their tea tables."

"And even if they *did* see him," Graham said, still fascinated with the knife, "why should they think of murder? Hadn't he been in the village for a week without anything like this happening?" His fingers lingered on the flat of the knife blade. I wondered what he was thinking. Over a roar of laughter from the bar area, I said, "Owen had nearly the same opportunity when he delivered his bread. I know it was earlier, but he could've slipped in later. And though I don't know motive yet, I *can* see him killing in anger, if not in premeditation."

"Volatile emotions, has he?"

I recounted my interview with Owen the evening of the murder. "The man's angry. Though if it's about his brother's book, or his own work, or the bread baking—"

"—or a love affair, or his aging parents..." Graham picked up the knife. "Endless list, it seems to me. But I grant that he could strike. He could've had the bread knife with him when he met Joel."

"But why he should be angry at Joel about his brother's book—or why Nelson should be angry at Joel for the same reason—is beyond me. Joel wasn't involved with the book."

"Maybe we need to focus on a different motive for Nelson and Owen. Leave the book out of it. It could be purely personal. A simmering feud, perhaps, or something more recent."

"I wonder if Joel could be his phantom brother."

"Half, through their mum, since their last names are different? We'll have to get one of the lads to uncover that part of the play. Next?"

"Olive and the vicar," I said, ticking off the names I'd written down.

"They vouch for each other, swearing they were both in the vicarage at the same time."

"But how long would it take to thrust a knife into Joel and cover his head with a sack if he was waiting, say, to meet one of them? One minute?"

"Not very long. Either Olive or the vicar could have made the excuse of running into the church to retrieve something, and killed Joel."

"Some excuse so ordinary, so common that it wouldn't have aroused suspicion."

"And therefore wouldn't have stuck in the other's mind," Graham finished. "Opportunity is a bit shaky, but it's there. So what about motive?"

"There again, sir, we'll have to dig a bit deeper into village life. Nothing screams as obvious."

"Maybe Joel burnt the biscuits for David's publishing party," Graham said, his voice flat with fatigue.

"That would give David Willett the motive, but what about opportunity?"

"Was David at home Wednesday afternoon?"

"I'll get Margo to check on that. But again, it could be a completely different motive."

"So this is all a waste of time—is that what you're telling me?"

"No, sir. We've established a list of plausible suspects. But until we know a bit more about personalities and histories, motive is a bit difficult to establish, never mind that most everyone seems to have had opportunity."

"I agree, TC."

"Oh, and sir, I checked through B.T. on Sylvia's alibi of the London call. She made it and the phone was engaged for nearly an hour."

"So ends *that* bit of speculation." He stood up and walked around to my chair—something he rarely did—and draped my coat over his arm. We could've been on a date at a posh restaurant, leaving to have coffee at my place. His hand lingered on the chair back as he asked, "Shall we drop our speculations for the moment and turn in?"

"Certainly, sir." Mark, I was happy to note, had already left the pub. A young man several tables in front of us seemed to be mimicking Graham's movements, for he held his date's coat while she wriggled into it. She flipped her long hair over the coat collar, and I could smell her perfume. They left quickly, he picking up the long-stemmed rose lying on the table, she clutching her small beaded bag. I glanced at my own black, regulation police shoulder bag and nearly cried.

Why couldn't this be the date at the restaurant, with a string quartet playing near a fountain? Instead I had canned music with a neon ale sign. I picked up the carnation, determined to hold on to some shred of my dream. Graham's fingers brushed against my back as he pulled out the chair, but it was nothing personal. His face held the concentration of our conversation.

Outside, after the warmth of the crowded pub, the evening air felt as sharp as our murder weapon. We slowly walked to our hotel, talking of nothing in particular. Our shadows, black against the white snow, stretched and waned as we passed beneath the glare of street lamps. A patch of yellow lay upon the pavement where light spilled from the village hall. The murder team was still working. Beyond the hall the sky appeared blacker, a part of Nature, and I could see a hazy moon nestled among translucent clouds. I stopped in the darkness, gazing heavenward, and sighed.

"Tired? Or waxing poetic?" asked Graham, standing close beside me. I could feel his suede coat on my bare hand. Wanting no stimulus for my deepening affection, I shoved my hand into my pocket.

"It's a Highwayman's night."

"The poem by Noyes?"

"Yes, sir," I said, slightly embarrassed at baring my romantic side. Especially in the middle of a murder case. "The sky seems to call for some ode or song."

"A psalm in praise of nature's beauty?" he suggested. "Or an elegy to midnight's masked lads—Zorro, Scarlet Pimpernel and the like?"

"Nothing wrong with righting wrongs," I said, rather too quickly and too defensively.

"As long as it's done within the limits of the law. Or have I just drenched the flame?"

I muttered that it was hard enough to kindle the flame these days without it being deliberately drowned.

In reply, Graham gazed into the sky and murmured,

"Do not ask how lovers sing,
souls and hearts attuned as one
through the joy of kindred spirits
or passion white-hot, chilling as their touch,
murmuring promises, love, desires
sweeter than heaven's chorus.
Do not ask how lovers smile,
nestled in the dark of night;
lips that part in breathless bliss,
eyes that hold the shining face.
Do not ask how lovers die
betrayed by masks of constancy,
deceived by smiling words
nurtured in the trusting heart,
racked by pain black as her soul,
jeers echoed from Hades' depths."

Graham had kept his gaze skyward throughout the recital, as if afraid of seeing my expression. I, too, had been reluctant to look at him, feeling the emotions born of experience. But after several seconds of awkward silence, I said, "Where'd—who wrote that?"

"Uh, a minor poet."

"Romantic?"

"Shelley, Byron, Wordsworth and the like? Hardly in that league. Minor, as to be obscure. Amateur. You won't find it in any collection."

"But how'd you—" Of course. Graham's tightened lips and downcast eyes announced the poem's author. I gazed at the sky again. "Well, he's caught the moods of love. I wish I could thank him."

"He probably knows," Graham said, zipping up his jacket. "Poets, living or dead, seem to sense those things, I think."

"Perhaps he's looking down on us from the edge of the cloud."

"He doesn't look down on anyone."

I swallowed, unsure of what to say. "You spoke the poem so well. You must like the poet."

"Most of the time I do. Ordinarily I wouldn't recite that in public, but you looked as though you needed that highwayman to come riding, even if the poetry didn't end happily ever after."

"The highwayman didn't either."

We walked across the street, carefully navigating the snowy tire ruts. As we approached the hotel, I said, "You must have written that when you were in great pain."

"It's that obvious?"

"I don't mean to pry into your life, sir."

Ward Hale staggered out of the hotel, his arm around a woman's shoulders. He waved at me, winked, and as he passed, yelled, "Paul and me'll be snoggin' in another ten minutes, Sergeant. You want I should have witnesses?" His hand wandered to her chin, pushing her face toward his, and he kissed her hard. Moments later, looking up at me, he laughed and pursed his lips at me.

"What's that about?" Graham asked, watching the couple walk down the street.

"Ward Hale, sir. Out for a romp with his girlfriend."

"So I gather. Looks like he's robbing the cradle."

"She's eighteen, sir, though she doesn't look it."

"Glad to hear that. I'd hate to spoil his fun and haul him, though the lady looked willing."

Their laughter faded as they disappeared around the corner. Graham cleared his throat rather obviously before saying, "This may be a bad bit of timing, but there's nothing suggestive in my question. Are you particularly longing for your bed?"

Despite the inference, I said "no." Graham took my arm and guided me across the street to the cluster of trees and benches between the chemist's and the bookstore. He brushed off the wooden seat and waited for me to sit before joining me. "To answer you, Taylor, yes. I wrote that a few years ago, suffering great pain after a great love. It's hard to distinguish them at times." He leaned forward, his forearms resting on his knees, and stared into the evening. "Writing is the great catharsis, Taylor. Diaries, journals, poetry, stream of consciousness. My passion cried out to poetry, though I'm not good at it."

So I was 'Taylor' again. Gone was the relaxed Graham who called me 'TC.' I opened my mouth to protest his writing ability, but Graham rushed on.

"We were talking of motive earlier. The motive behind this metered rubbish was my fiancée. Rachel."

Office gossip had been right. Graham *had* loved and lost. I looked at him. Though veiled in evening's dimness, his profile seemed sharp. Perhaps my eye was filling in the nebulous spots, already knowing his face. But I could see the straightness of his nose, the firm jaw line and slightly curling hair at the nape of his neck. Why had they parted?

"Rachel, for all her beauty, is one of those demanding women. Sorry, Taylor. I'll rephrase that—demanding *people.*"

I mumbled that I understood, unconcerned with his word choice.

"I was supposed to be home every night, available for parties, dinner and theater, holidays whenever the mood struck her. Of course, I couldn't be. It's impossible with our jobs. You know that as well as I do. Yet Rachel…"

The image of an off-hours Graham decked out in evening clothes was as jarring as my image of him in ministerial garb. Especially Graham at parties, laughing, drinking, mingling socially. Not that he was a misanthrope. But he detests crowds and noise and duty functions. He was the quiet sort who liked walks through woods and evenings by the fireplace. I was glad of the darkness so that I could study him without being embarrassed. "Wanted a round-the-clock husband," I said, finishing his thought.

"I can't fault her for that. When you love someone…" He dropped his head, staring at his clenched fingers. "Twenty-four hours isn't enough to hold all your ardor, accomplish all the things you yearn to do together. She entered our engagement expecting our marriage would be like those of her friends. But she couldn't understand my career. To her, work was nine to five. A schedule you could plan around and keep to. There were others on the Force, she told me, so if something arose when I was finished for the day…"

How Rachel would have detested Scott, I thought. The man so devoted to helping people that he didn't know a day had a finish.

"So your fiancée called it off, then." I brushed the carnation against the palm of my hand.

"Hell of a row, unfortunately. Hell of a night, too. Bucketed-down rain with lightning. She threw the ring at me and pushed me outside. I still think she has my jacket—unless she burned it."

I could picture Rachel tugging the ring from her finger, flinging it and the hurtful words at Graham. She would have continued screaming as she pushed him toward the door, her eyes bright with anger. The door would slam as her final statement of bitterness, the retort smothered, perhaps, by a crack of thunder. Graham would have looked for the ring, water running into his eyes and down his neck, his shirt plastered to his back. Hunting in the dark, perhaps, on his hands and knees. He would have eventually found it among the dead leaves or wedged upright between terraced flagstones. He would have pocketed it, feeling anger and astonishment and guilt.

"Can't say I blame her, Taylor. It's a rough life for the spouse of any detective. Even if you do pull regular hours most of your career, the call outs at night can destroy your relationship."

"It would be difficult to lie in bed, fearing what may be happening. Call outs aren't usually helping an old-age pensioner across the street."

Graham stood up, the mood shaken off. "Not that you're old age, Taylor, but it's getting late. Why don't we help each other across the street?"

Outside the hotel door, Graham paused, glancing at his feet. "Don't know why I'm so maudlin tonight, Taylor. Sorry. I'll see you in the morning. Get some sleep."

As it happened, I was later getting to sleep than I wanted.

SIXTEEN

TWO NOTES HAD BEEN shoved beneath my door when I got to my room. One was from Margo, saying she had returned the brochures with no one being the wiser they had gone missing. I silently blessed St. Nicholas, patron saint of spinsters, and tossed the note into the waste bin.

The second note was from Mark, telling me he had made reservations for dinner in Chesterfield tomorrow evening. I wadded the paper into a tight ball and slammed it into the bin, promising myself I would make my feelings known to Mark in the morning.

I tried to sleep, but a parade of book pages, crosses and faceless photos kept waking me. Finally, around midnight, I gave it up, dressed and walked to the incident room. Perhaps an hour at the computer would put me to sleep.

PC Byrd waved to me as I sat down at a computer, rather startled to see me at this hour, but asking if I wanted coffee. Telling him I was trying to put myself to sleep, I turned on the computer monitor and searched vehicle registrations for owners of dark green saloon cars. Half an hour later, I wasn't so much surprised at the great number of car owners as I was with how quickly the data swam before my eyes.

Needing to stretch my muscles and mind, I grabbed my jacket, told Byrd I was going to have a quick walk, and headed outside. Except for a rectangle of light spilling from the village hall windows and the meager line of street lamps marking the roads, the village sat in blackness. I looked up the street. Buildings so easily identifiable in daylight now huddled together into a dark, shapeless mass. The faint specks of light over doors or in windows did nothing to establish individuality, rather only bringing the starry heaven down to earth. As I was about to head in the direction of the Four Marys, I noticed someone slinking away from the corner of the hall. I yelled, but the figure only melted into the darkness. While I wondered whether I should advise Byrd or follow the suspect alone, the person crossed the street, careful to avoid the patch of light from the street lamp. He ran between the hotel and post office, hugging the obscurity of the walls. In his haste, he knocked over a flowerpot.

I ran toward the sound, certain he had no legitimate business at the incident room, wondering what he had been after, following the crunch of his feet on the snow or bare pavement. I paused momentarily before I slipped around the corner of the hotel, catching my breath and listening for his, hoping I wasn't about to be greeted with gunfire. Not a sound or movement came from the hotel yard, not a light guided me to his hiding place. I eased into the yard, my heart pounding, my mouth dry.

In the tangle of parked cars, rubbish bins and storage sheds I lost him. The intense dark seemed anchored to the courtyard, engulfing cars and me and everything else. I turned around slowly, eyeing doors and windows, considering where he might have escaped. Of course, he could have gone a dozen places, from doubling back to the incident room or to his own place. Was he even now peering at me from behind a door or cowering in back of a parked car? Even lurking in the shadows, waiting for me to walk by. Comforting thought. I decided to give up the hunt when I heard a dog whining.

Normally I wouldn't have paid it much heed. Dogs bark and whine quite frequently at night. But the pitch reminded me of

Colin's poodle, and I was curious enough to wonder what a dog was doing out at 12:30 on the village main road.

I found Laramie—for it was Colin's dog—tied to the news-stand outside Magdalína's shop. The poodle was cold and shaking, and jumped excitedly when I knelt to pet him. Ward, if he was up to his exercising mode again, was nowhere in sight. And Magdalína's shop looked closed for the night. So why was the dog out here and who had brought him? That was the last thing I remember before waking inside the fire-engulfed shop.

THE FIRST THING I NOTICED was the thick haze and heat. And that I could barely breathe without retching. I sat up slowly, trying to understand where I was, why the right side of my head hurt like hell when I touched it, and why the shop was on fire. A blast of smoke rolled over me, and I slumped down as quickly as I had sat up, coughing and holding my throat, groping for air along the floor. Loosening the zipper of my jacket, I looked behind me. A sheet of flame licked at the far wall, and a trail of crimson flared in a confusion of burning circles on the wooden floor. The noise barreled toward me from the wall. I pushed away from the corner where I had been dumped, shoved aside the tangle of chairs piled alongside me, and crawled on my belly to the front door.

The knob, though hot, turned and I tumbled outside almost into the arms of Mark.

Mark paused only long enough to give me a startled look and an expletive before he pulled me to my feet and half carried me to the pavement. He spat on one of his fingers, dabbed at my hair, and told me to stay put. It was an unnecessary order, for I was coughing too violently to move. Leaning against a tree, I watched the chaos before me.

A flood of faces, scarlet under the fire's flush, yelling in con-fusion and fright, crowded around the shop. Men ran and pushed and jostled, throwing questions into the air, acting without thought. As the mass shifted, I finally discerned Graham restraining Magdalína as she tried to enter the building. She beat at his hands, crying hysterically and lunging toward the fire. Small wonder, as the shop—like Hannah's bookstore—was Magdalína's entire life. Flames roared into the blackness overhead, as though trying to lick the clouds. A gust of wind showered the crowd with embers, and I heard a tree bough snap as it succumbed to the flames. Feeling guilty I wasn't helping, I threaded my way through the crowd, determined to rescue what I could from the shop. Graham motioned to Mark, who was emptying his arms of menus and table cloths, and pushed Magdalína at him. Then, shouting for everyone to step back, Graham hurried over to me and grabbed my arm, pulling me from the front of the building. As we retreated several yards, the shop sign crashed to the ground, the paint blistering before the flames consumed it.

Other than Graham batting several live embers that had settled onto my jacket sleeve, the rest of that evening played out as usual at a fire. It was only the next morning, after the fire was extinguished and the building cool enough to explore, that we discovered it.

We had cautiously climbed the stairs to Magdalína's flat, stepping over burnt furnishings and easing past bits of fallen ceiling. The body lay on the bedroom floor, head toward the window, as though trying to escape. Though badly burned, it was the body of a man.

I stared at it, unable to move or speak, though I heard Graham's voice and felt his arm around my shoulder. Moments later, I roused myself, apologetic and white-faced as our paper work suits.

"Is anything the matter, TC.? Anything I can—"

"No, thank you, sir. I'm— It's just a shock."

"Your first?"

I nodded, afraid I was going to be sick.

"If you need it…" He handed me his handkerchief and left me there, running downstairs to answer Trueman deMere's yell. I followed slowly, joining them outside, glad to leave the odor of charred wood and the disfigured body.

"My, God!" the vicar said on viewing the shop exterior. "I saw it last night, of course, but hesitated to come, thinking I'd be in the way. I had no idea…" He moved down the pavement, staring at the shop's blackened wall.

Though the back rooms and kitchen had been severely damaged, the building still stood. Fire had gutted only the rear portion of the building, but heavy smoke and water damage rendered the entire flat uninhabitable. It stank of wet ashes. I wondered how Magdalína would fare until the shop was restored.

"Did you see or hear anything before the fire?" Graham asked.

"*Before?* Like what?"

"Oh, unusual aroma of oil or petrol, argument with Magdalína…"

I walked over to the two men, avoiding the pools of ice-fringed water that lay among the charred debris, and thought of the dog last night and of the earlier scene in the tearoom. While Sylvia's words had not exactly been aimed at Magdalína, they might have sparked some row. Maybe something had happened after I had left.

"Petrol?" Trueman's face paled. "Is that how—you're saying it's arson?"

"I'm not saying anything until we know something conclusive, sir. I'm just sorting through the events of the evening. It's always a help when someone has seen or heard something pertinent."

"Yes, yes, that's so. But no, can't help you, I'm afraid. I was in the church for an hour or so after tea, then at home the rest of the evening, though I did look out when I heard the commotion around quarter to one, as I said."

Graham turned toward the church, cattycorner from the teashop. He seemed to be judging Trueman's statement.

"I *did* hear a bike," Trueman said, drawing Graham's interest.

"Oh? What time was that?"

"Just before midnight, I think. Yes. I'd just heard it and then minutes later the clock downstairs in the rectory struck."

"But you didn't recognize the bike, whose it was…"

"I looked out only because it had been noisy for such a long time. At least it seemed a time—it always does when you've been disturbed, doesn't it?" He paused, as though collecting his thoughts, then hurried on as he discerned Graham's attention. "Sounded rather like Ward Hale's. His is rather distinctive, I think. I can usually pick it out. Different pitch to the motor. One gets attuned to sounds when one is surrounded by organ and bell music, you see. Anyway, I heard this motor coughing for half a minute or so before it took life and the driver gunned it for a rather fast departure. Which, I think, was rather foolish, considering the present condition of the roads."

"He didn't skid or spin out?" Graham said.

"No. Which was fortunate as he had a rider with him. I assume it was female, as it was a shorter, much thinner bulk. Hard to tell at night, you know."

Graham sympathized with the situation.

"If it *was* Ward Hale," Trueman continued, "then your pillion rider's most certainly Paula Lindbergh. They're thicker than blood at the moment. Which also surprises me."

"Why?"

"I thought Paula was smarter than to take up with Ward."

"He been in trouble with the law?" I asked. "You worried she'll get into trouble for something he did, or concerned about her good name?"

"She's eighteen," Trueman said, sighing as though she had

just turned two. "She's smart enough to understand the consequences of her actions. But Ward's gone through women like…"

There was a brief silence. I suggested, "…like a kid in a confectioner's shop?"

Trueman nodded, blushing slightly. "Normally I don't set any store in village gossip—it's the work of idle minds and tongues needing to stir up some excitement—but a young woman left us a year ago. Around this time, I think. She'd been Ward's steady girlfriend, if you want to call her that. She leaves, and six months later returns."

"Pregnant with his child," Graham said slowly, voicing the conjecture. "Has it somewhere else, drops it on mum's or an agency's doorstep, and returns when she's back to her normal size. Makes sense."

"And village gossip," I said, "whispered Ward was the father of this child?"

"More than whispered, Sergeant. I heard the natter myself, good and loud, when I wasn't supposed to be listening, I expect. In a queue at the green grocer's, at an adjoining table at the Four Marys…"

I could imagine only too well the situation. The scandal eagerly imparted to prove superiority, the gleaming eye, the furtive look. Though not a subject of gossip, I'd come as close to it as I ever want to be when I was a probationer. As the only woman in my police class, I had endured the jests and comments and suggestions with as much grace as I could. It was, I knew, partly to test the weakest link, and partly reaction to the first crumbling of the male dominion. I eventually passed the police course and this macho test, and saw the disintegration of the wagging tongues. Except for my nickname, which— like Graham's—had evolved into a mere diminutive. TC, short for 'The Cop,' emerged from Mark's branding on the first day of class, mocking my desire to be a detective.

"And this probable mother…" Graham was saying when I shook off the memory.

"Unless it has some bearing on your case, which I can't see it having, I won't divulge it. It's not that I don't want to help, but this woman hasn't taken up with Ward after her return, and I don't want to embarrass her further or remind her of her sin."

"It may be more bad judgment than sin," Graham said so quietly that I'm sure Trueman didn't hear him.

I asked, "Would you have any reason to believe Ward or Paula would torch either the bookstore or tearoom? Are they hooligans, or just noisy wallies?"

"If you had asked me a week ago, Sergeant, I would have said Ward was your wide boy, fortified with whiskey muscles and Paula's adoration. If not adoration, at least the self importance of having a lovely woman wanting him. That, plus his mates, who roar into town every so often. But nothing major's ever happened before. Nothing more than a refuse bin pushed over, or a fist fight in the pub. You know the thing. So, unless Ward's had words with Hannah and Magdalína, I wouldn't know why he'd wish them harm."

"Could it be some sort of initiation?" I asked. "Some club or gang he wants to join? Is he that type?"

Trueman gazed again at the blackened wall. "I can't say. Is it the type of thing they do?"

"Depends on the gang or club."

"I can't see it, no. Ward's a bit of a loner. Oh, he goes out with his mates, as I said. And sees a lot of Nelson Parnell— Owen's brother. They're quite chummy, despite Nelson being five years older than Ward. But he prefers being on his own or with Paula. He's really not such a bad lad when he's on his own. Even shows the occasional manners."

"I saw as much of his Jekyll and Hyde sides as I hope to see," I said, "yesterday at Hannah's and before that at Sylvia's."

"I think he's trying to find himself. A lot of people struggle with that."

"That's true," Graham said, "but they don't tear up the town and torch businesses."

"Perhaps not," Trueman said, "and an indifferent mother doesn't help the situation."

Graham caught my eye. I could see he wanted to bow an imaginary violin. I quickly said, "So, other than a noisy bike and two anonymous figures roaring away from the general vicinity of the tearoom, you can't tell us anything definite."

The vicar blinked at me.

Graham came to his rescue. "Do you know anyone else in the village who owns a bike?"

"I should think several other people do. They're not that uncommon. But as for names, I would also say Paula Lindbergh—I've seen her and Ward racing together. And possibly Owen Parnell. Other than that…"

"Right. Thank you."

Graham had turned back toward the shop when Trueman said, "Some of the young people staying at the youth hostel have bikes. Would you be interested in them?"

We would, I thought, *if anyone saw them with a flaming torch.*

Mark motioned me aside, and I quickly left Graham.

"I hear you've been losing sleep," Mark said, amusement gleaming in his eye.

"Over what?"

"A few insignificant brochures."

"Insignificant?" I practically screamed the word. Graham turned toward me, astonished and puzzled. I turned to Mark, my head and voice lower. "Those Greek travel brochures you honored me with? If they're the ones Margo saw at Joel's house, I'd hardly call them insignificant. More like vital."

"Don't know if they're vital until they fit into the case."

"God, Mark, you've lifted possible evidence from the victim's house! Don't you know what you're up against?"

"Nothing much. I printed them before you received them. Hargreaves photographed them, so your prints won't show up in his snaps. I broke my own seal on the evidence bag, then resealed it, so I didn't tamper with anything that can't be fixed. So what's the problem?"

"Your career means that little to you, then, that you'd risk getting caught?"

"No risk," Mark said, dusting his hands of the soot. "Not when I'm the officer in charge of the evidence. Besides, I slipped the bag back on Vic's desk when the old boy wasn't looking."

'Vic,' or 'The Vicar,' was a name many of the police personnel used for Graham. It had been a source of derision when first invented, and though many still used it as such, it had mellowed into more of a nickname. Though no one ever used it to Graham's face.

"Speaking of risk," Mark continued, "what were you doing inside the tearoom when I came up? Playing at Wonder Woman again? Burning buildings are dangerous places, Brenna."

"I noticed you dashed inside several times."

"But I didn't get all choked up about it." He eyed me, as though able to see what had happened. When I merely smiled, he said, "Anyway, Graham'll be the one who gets all the aggro if the Super catches that on his desk and not with the rest of the evidence. What's he looking for, anyway?"

"I couldn't say. I'm not privy to his thoughts at the moment."

"Probably just as well. Keeps your mind on me. Speaking of me—"

"—your favorite subject—"

"—I assume you got my note. That time all right with you for dinner tonight? 8:00?"

"Sorry, Mark. I'm busy. Another engagement."

Mark nodded toward Graham, his eyebrow cocked in speculation. I decided to take the offer and replied that Graham wanted me to interview someone who would be back this evening.

"Just be careful, darling," Mark said, patting me lightly on the back. "Engagements can tell you too much about a person."

He left me, whistling Mendelssohn's "Wedding March."

"Could a candle have started this?"

I turned toward Graham, glad to talk about the fire. "Sorry, sir?"

"The tearoom was profuse with candles, I understand," Graham said, squatting on the pavement and looking at the items that had been saved from the fire. Among the clutter were several votive candle jars, their glass designs now smudged with smoke. He pulled on a pair of latex gloves and grabbed one of the votive holders.

"Red candles for Christmas," he said, eyeing the candlewick just discernable in the confined, melted blob of wax. "Candles on every table, adding seasonal cheer. Only this one evening, one candle is left unattended, forgotten at closing time. What do you think, TC?"

SEVENTEEN

"ISN'T THAT WHAT the glass is for? To contain the flame and eliminate this kind of disaster?"

"Could one of the glass holders have been broken? A hole that allowed melting wax to seep onto a table cloth, for instance? Were any candles free standing, TC? By a cash register or in a window?"

"I know what you're alluding to, sir, but…" I stopped, the vision of David Willett at the cash register suddenly clear in my mind. Nodding, I said, "There was one, I remember. And there was a near accident with it when I was there. Could have begun that way, the fire. But if someone had knocked over that candle, wouldn't it have been noticed right away?"

"Not necessarily. What if the candle had burned to a stub, the flame hardly visible, hidden behind a stack of menus or vase of flowers? The wax could have flowed down the holder, onto papers or such…"

"Magdalína was kind of harried when I was there. Sylvia came in, giving her a rather hard time, then she went to the kitchen to talk to Owen, then presumably ran after David. But I can't see a candle doing all this. Has to have started another way."

"We have opportunity," Graham said, sounding like a text book. "We need the miscreant. You favor anyone?"

"Besides our biking duo? Can't see them going into a tearoom. Pub's more their speed."

"Could always have jimmied a door or broken a window to

get in after hours, started a fire. Nice accelerant, this," Graham said, fingering a singed piece of pine roping.

"The shop was fair drowning in the stuff. Windows, door, wreaths on the tables."

"Surprised she got away with it. Or doesn't the fire regulations cover religious decorations?"

"Maybe it's the type of thing they turn a blind eye to."

"That's churches, TC. Open flames on the altar. Don't ask about regulations and we won't ban it."

I didn't know if he was joking or not, but accepted his statement. He tossed the candle holder back with the mess and stood up. "Too bad this had to happen right now. The publishing party for David's book was scheduled for this evening, wasn't it? Wonder what they'll do about it. Yes, Lynch?"

Margo had waited patiently for Graham to finish. Stepping over to us, she gave me the look that implied she knew how I was feeling. And frankly, I would have been elated to be with Graham, but I was still queasy about the scene. I would've replied to Margo's insinuation, only Graham was here. Turning toward him, she said, "They're ready to move the body, sir."

"Thank you, Lynch." He left me with Margo, which was not one of his better judgments.

"I hope he didn't see that smirk," I said, trying to keep a low volume on my annoyance.

"Didn't say anything about it, if he did," Margo said, smiling.

"Is that all you've got time for? Haven't we enough to think about with two fires and a murder?"

"Don't get your knickers in a twist, Bren. You're just edgy today."

"'Course I am! We're up to our necks in it."

"Don't know if the two fires *are* a crime. Not until the Home Office forensic lab and Jens Nielsen and—"

"What the hell difference does that make? We've still got a

body at this scene. And if it's proved that the fire is arson, we've got another murder."

"I've been talking to Magdalína and Owen, among others, and they're come over all queer about this. Everyone has. Even Mark, though he keeps up his swaggering façade."

"I wouldn't have thought he'd be affected."

"Well, he *is*, Bren. He's human, like everyone else. Only the difference is that the villagers have to live with this. They're wondering whose place will be next."

"They think there's an arsonist on the loose?"

"To hear them talk, they do. And who can fault them? Two fires in two nights. Plus a murder." She rubbed her arms. "God! Are we ever going to sort through this mess?"

"Does tend to put a damper on the Christmas spirit."

"If only they could do their St. Nick bit. Or have the book party. Something that screams of normality. You heard anything from Graham on that?"

"Where they going to hold it if he does give the thumbs up?"

"Hmm. I see what you mean. We've kind of taken over the village hall. What about the youth hostel? It's big."

"It may be big," I said, in no mood to figure out the town's party problem, "but it's filled with beds and knapsacks and people."

"I don't suppose they could hold it across the street." We both looked at the small stand of trees and benches. Graham's poetry suddenly echoed in my head.

"Don't be daft," I said, growing impatient. "It's hardly adequate. They've got elderly folk as well as babies. Besides, it's cold and wet. What if it snows again?"

"If you're going to shoot down everything I suggest... Oops. Graham's signaling for you. Hold onto your stomach, Bren. You look a bit green."

If I had had time, I would have said something catchy, but I couldn't wait that long to think of it. I've got another life.

"YOU'RE THINKING WHAT I'm thinking, sir," I said a scant half hour later when Graham and I had returned to the incident room. We had shed our boots and crime suits, but I couldn't shed the crime scene image. When Graham had told me the body was Colin Hale I asked him to repeat it, hoping I had heard incorrectly. I hadn't. I grimaced and bent over as my stomach lurched.

"You ok?" he asked.

Standing up, I said, "Lovely."

"He was found in Magdalína's flat." Graham's look telegraphed his inference.

"Don't jump to conclusions, sir."

"Hard not to. Her digs. Midnight."

"They could've been having tea," I said, "or talking about the St. Nick thing, all nice and innocent, when the fire breaks out. He runs to her bedroom, hoping to get out of the window. Nothing illicit in that."

"Then why did Magdalína escape and Colin didn't?"

I stared at Graham, my mind a whirl of scenes and snatches of conversations. "He was so sweet, sir." The breath caught in my throat as his words came back to me. 'I haven't given anyone flowers in a long time.' I knew right then that I would leave flowers on his grave—from one citizen and animal lover to another. I imagined the flowers, ice-tinged and very red, nestled on a snowy grave. "This just doesn't smell right, sir. Why couldn't he have followed Magdalína downstairs? If they were together, why was Colin trapped up there while Magdalína came through it all nice and safe?"

"And if they weren't together," Graham said, "what was he doing in her flat at midnight?"

"And where was she?" *And who hated me so much to drag me inside?* I wanted to ask.

I poured out our tea and thought how much nicer it would

be to sit in the tearoom, but that was behind us. What did they say about life going on? Graham took a long sip, not seeming to notice the liquid's scalding temperature, and cupped his hands around the mug. Even though the sun had been up for several hours, it did nothing to warm the frigid landscape.

I glanced at Graham. He was stretching and stifling a yawn. It was already a long day for him, and I knew it would be many hours yet until he headed for bed. I said, "So we're agreed, then?"

"Yes," he said, meeting my gaze but showing no emotion. "All indications point to it. Arson and murder."

He had echoed the situation voiced by me, his suspicions screaming to be justified or shown to be false. So now we sat, considering facts and speculations, trying to build or tear down our infant case.

"Ward Hale," Graham said after another swallow of tea, "got back to his place early this morning. Testimony from two neighbors and Mark Salt."

"Mark!" I said, rather too loudly. "Sorry, sir. How did Mark—"

"Out jogging at five A.M. Didn't know he was so keen on exercise."

He would have to be, judging by his muscles. I said, "I guess that's taken as read, then. One iron-clad witness. What's Ward say about his late night?"

"After telling us to get knotted? Just that he was out with his mates, messing about as usual."

"Did anyone see Paula Lindbergh come dragging in about that time?"

"What a suspicious mind you have, TC."

"He's mad keen on her, sir. Of course I'm suspicious."

"Must be hereditary, then. I've got one of the constables questioning her."

"He's got opportunity. Lives alone. Has that bike so he can come and go whenever he pleases."

"If it proves to be arson," Graham said, thinking out loud, "what's the motive? Wonder if that fire was set with Ward's life blood."

"Sir?"

"Petrol, TC. The juice that bike lives on. Petrol's a lovely accelerant, too."

"Petrol's also common. Anyone could have doused the area with it. Doesn't have to be someone keen on bikes."

"Ward's a ladies' man."

I must have looked confused at the apparent switch in subject. "Sorry? I don't understand the connection—"

"Bear with me, TC. Whether he really is or isn't a ladies' man, Ward fancies himself one."

"Trueman said there was a rumor about his involvement with a girl, about her pregnancy."

"We can't regard that as fact. But we can ask if our ladies' man had another lady."

"Besides Paula?"

Graham nudged the handle of his mug so it slowly rotated full circle. "What if he was having an affair with Magdalína?"

"*Magdalína?* She's got to be fifteen years his senior. Anyway, what makes you ask that?"

"Just throwing out suppositions, TC. We've got to start somewhere. Anyway, age may have nothing to do with it. A love affair turned sour can spawn a great passion for revenge. And arson is a revenge."

I understood the connection and swallowed, not liking the image of Magdalína as a slag. Because that would lower her to Mark Salt's standard of quantity, not quality. It smelled of cheap hotels, lies and deception.

"Magdalína Dent," Graham was saying as I left her on the hotel steps, "is a beautiful lady."

The old emotions, envy and annoyance, rushed back. Envy because I coveted Magdalína's trim, dancer's body. Annoyance because I couldn't get serious about my diet. Which, Margo would no doubt remark if I ever confessed to her, would have revealed a lot about me to a psychiatrist. But I wasn't ready to unveil childhood's misery. I busied myself with looking up something in my notebook while promising myself I would unfailingly start dieting after New Year. "So what you're trying to say, sir, is that Ward, involved with Magdalína, got jealous over Colin, coaxed Magdalína out of her flat, trapped Colin inside, set the fire—"

"Could have done."

"That's the motive? Clearing the area of his rivals? Is this Ward's favorite method of dealing with them?"

"Trueman's not likely to tell us. He wouldn't even divulge the name of the pregnant girlfriend. I'll put Margo on that little chore."

"Uh, sir," I said slowly, knowing I had to tell him. He looked at me thoughtfully, probably stealing himself for anything from holiday leave request to my announcement of the murderer. "I know a good partner divulges everything, even when it may seem trivial…" He had raised an eyebrow, waiting. This wasn't going well. I took a deep breath and said, "Last night. Well, this morning, actually. Around twelve-thirty, if you want to be accurate."

"What is it, Taylor?"

I told him about the shadowy figure, the dog and finding myself inside the burning building. Graham looked at me, asked if I was all right, then asked if I had formed any opinion on the whole thing.

"I thought about it last night, of course. Probably why I couldn't sleep after we left Magdalína's. But it all seems so daft. I mean, skulking figures at midnight, dogs as bait—"

"The bleating of the lamb attracts the tiger, TC."

"Some tiger."

"Did you have the impression that whoever it was had been spying on you?"

"I can't say, sir. Of course, if he had been there any length of time, he would've seen me put on my coat and leave. So why did he hang around?"

"And if he was after PC Byrd, why knock you out? And why drag you into the shop?"

"I don't suppose it could all be a horrible coincidence—you know, one person who runs away from sheer fright after playing Peeping Tom at the incident room, and another person outside the tearoom who saw his opportunity and coshed me over the head…" I looked at him to see if he accepted the idea, but Graham was frowning.

"The whole thing smells of premeditated murder, TC. Not to give you another sleepless night—sorry. Who've you been talking to lately who might have it in for you?"

"Besides the whole village?" I told him about the lost earring and the few interviews Margo and I had had over that. "The jewelry is a non-starter, sir. Belongs to Eden deMere."

"You're ruling her out of the Dastardly Deed due to her husband's profession? How unsporting of you. Clergy have killed before, Taylor. *I've* even felt like it a few times. You look shocked."

"I'm glad nothing came of your emotion, sir."

"Perhaps it did, and I have the torso buried in the back garden. Is that why I don't have a dog? My God, Taylor, it's a *joke*. Don't ring up the station."

I smiled feebly and said that I'd keep Trueman on my long list but didn't think the earring meant anything special. Graham laughed and I went on to confess the trip up to Piebald Tor and the finding of the book page.

Graham nodded, his eyes half closed as though in deep

thought. "As you say, the whole village. And aside from seeing the dog with Ward, we have nothing else to go on. That's not conclusive, TC, though I know you'd like it to be. Could be Colin who tied it there. Or Sylvia."

"Or another dog-sitter. But why outside Magdalína's at half past twelve? Isn't that unusual?"

"I'd say so, but maybe it isn't for Colin or Sylvia or Ward. We don't exactly know their schedule. It's unfortunate we don't have anything to work on, like a piece of cloth clenched in your fist," he said, smiling. "And you saw or heard nothing to identify this person?"

"No shuffling gait or gigantic shoe prints, nor harmonica music—no."

"But isn't it safe to assume that whoever our killer is has some connection to the dog? As we said, it would indicate Ward, Sylvia or Colin?"

"I would assume that, yes, sir. But I suppose it could also be one of Ward's chums." Hesitating, I thought of Ward's guide-and-mentor that Scott had mentioned. It seemed too absurd, so I said, "Ward could be innocent."

"Merely having the dog out for its midnight stroll? Far-fetched, Taylor, but I suppose within the realm of probability. And you just happened upon it during your midnight stroll."

"Like I said, daft."

"Well, I'm extremely thankful you weren't hurt, other than the bump on your head. For God's sake, TC, be careful!"

I mumbled that I would be and, changing the subject to something less personal, brought him up to date on the scene between Ward and Sylvia. "His rooms don't cost all that much—I checked. And he's got enough from his wage to pay for that, plus have a nice chunk left over."

"You hinting that he's using the extra change for something? I thought he was saving for a pro bike or whatever, so he can thumb his nose at Hannah and turn to the racing game. A bike like he probably wants will take a bit of saving for."

"That's as may be, sir, but what I'm wondering is who paid for the girl's abortion? Or delivery, if she saw her pregnancy to full term. Even if money wasn't the issue there, could she have demanded money from Ward to keep quiet about the whole thing?"

"She left the village, TC, so I can't see her blackmailing him."

"That's what *Trueman* told us."

"You think he's lying?"

"Not lying. But maybe that's what he believes. Maybe that's the assumption he gathered, either from the circumstances at the time or from the girl herself. She could have told him a different story to save face."

"But all the time…" Graham wrapped his hands around the mug again, as though he needed something to hold. "Who's likely to know about this? Girl's name, if she was paid off for keeping her mouth shut…"

"Besides her father confessor, you mean? I'd say a girl-friend whom she confided in like a diary."

"Hard to find if we don't know her name."

"I'll start with Paula. They may have been friends."

"Good. By the way, TC," Graham said as I started to get up. "If you'd like, you can skip this P.M. I'd rather you break the news to Sylvia and get your notes in order. This is just the P.M. on Joel Twiss." He broke off, scrutinizing my face, then said, "I'm just off then, right? I'll be back as soon as I can." He left quickly, as though he didn't want me to feel obligated to go with him.

I HAD JUST FINISHED writing up my notes and talking to Sylvia when Graham returned. He dropped his jacket on an empty chair and handed me the P.M. report. "Makes fascinating reading, if you're so inclined."

"Would you mind giving me the gist, sir?" I said, eyeing the thick packet. I wasn't in the mood to wade through all the medical description.

Graham smiled and picked up the report. "In layman's terms, then, Joel Twiss was knifed in the back. The knife, as we know, has a nine inch long serrated blade of the type used to cut bread. The blade, being quite long, passed between the ribs, through the lung, and into the right auricle of the heart. Blood coagulated around the knife blade and handle, and seeped onto his chest, soaking his clothing. That's why we didn't see much blood. Face down like that, the blood collected beneath him."

I swallowed, unsure of my breakfast. After an initial surge, my stomach quieted. I said, "Any signs of tampering with the body after death?"

"Rigor was well established, as well as fixed lividity. All point to death where he was struck, Jens assures us."

"So whoever killed him…"

"Did it in the church, under the very noses of Trueman and Olive."

EIGHTEEN

NEEDING SOME FRESH AIR, I left the incident room to talk to Paula Lindbergh. The late morning sun shone with a vigor I was not feeling, but helped disperse the gloom of the recent tragedy. Lemony light bathed the slate roofs where the snow had melted or fallen off. The sky struggled to shake off the grey clouds, for bits of blue mottled somber canopy. From the willow, I heard a redwing singing, its song like a soprano round of bells, descending in scale only to start joyfully again. I watched, delighted to see a bit of color in the otherwise somber landscape.

Across the street, Magdalína was coming out of the Garlic Clove restaurant. Normally, I wouldn't have looked twice, but Mark was holding a large bouquet of flowers—red and white carnations, small white tea roses, white mums and sprigs of fern and baby's breath. It might have been an ordinary scene, but I was suspicious of Mark's motive. The bouquet would've cost more than Mark probably spent on a night out with his mates. Certainly more than his weekly groceries. What was he doing?

He bowed, handed Magdalína the bouquet, and said something that caused her to laugh. Let him try something with Magdalína—it'll only land him in deeper trouble than he's in already, I thought, watching Mark help her over an icy patch on the pavement. Sleeping with a witness in an investigation was one thing, but if she turned out to be the suspect… Mark's days would be numbered in the Force; that was certain. Well, I wasn't surprised. First he breaks the seal on his own evidence bag…

A shaft of sunlight caught Magdalína's hair as she left Mark
and walked to the hotel. It was a lovely titan shade, with walnut
and sepia tints. Her grey eyes were black pools beneath her long
lashes. From Mark's attention, I assumed he shared Graham's
opinion. After all, she had a good figure—'stacked,' is how
Margo had described her. I glanced at my thighs, then at Magdalína's. Dancer's legs. That's what hers looked like. Margo
also would have told me to get over my envy, or lose the fifteen
pounds I'm always talking about. I watched Magdalína walk
into the hotel, wondering if I could emulate her easy gait. Mark
did not follow, having disappeared into the post office next
door. He had waved to her, calling out something that had made
her laugh again and shake her head. Did most men covet beauty
and a drop-dead figure more than humor, disposition and intelligence? Those characteristics withstood the passage of time.

I quickly walked to the hotel, hoping I wouldn't meet Mark.
After that little Sir Walter Raleigh episode, I doubted I could
speak civilly to him. The lobby of the hotel was empty as I
entered. Somewhere—the dining room or kitchen—a radio
station was changed, the snatches of music jarring in the calm
morning atmosphere. Breakfast odors still clung to the air, reminding me of family holidays in little hotels. I sat in the front
lounge, letting Magdalína get settled in her room, reasoning
myself out of my ill humor.

Joel Twiss' photo stared at me from the local newspaper discarded on the coffee table. I picked up the tabloid and scanned
the article headed 'Case of Killed Copper.' It highlighted the
St. Nicholas festival and the disappointment of the children and
old-age pensioners. At least the reporter stopped short of
hinting it was the police who snatched the bread from their
hungry mouths. I stuffed the paper under a sofa cushion and
went upstairs.

I nearly collided with Francis Rice on the landing. He

seemed older than he had Wednesday evening. There were puffy circles beneath his eyes, which were dull and red-rimmed. He seemed to stoop some, as though tired or carrying the weight of the village's problems on his back. Eyeing his medical bag, I asked if something was wrong.

"Oh, you mean this?" He held out his bag, tapping the worn leather with his free hand. "I was just paying a call on Magdalína. She's understandably upset, so I wrote her a prescription for some sleeping pills—temázepam, if you're taking notes or are wary that I'm out to poison her. It's a common medicine for insomnia. But you'll check with your police surgeon, of course."

"Hannah Leftridge needs no sedative?" I asked as Francis sat on the loveseat.

"If she does, she didn't consult me. Which isn't surprising."

"She's not a patient of yours?"

"I don't know whose patient she is, Miss Taylor. I merely meant that I would be surprised if she was taking something. She's a very strong woman. Nursed her husband through cancer, watching him slowly die, buried him, then kept her sister sane when their parents and the sister's daughter died in Israel—the result of a suicide bomber."

"When was all this?" I asked, remembering not to open my heart too much.

"Oh, the husband died four years ago, I believe. Yes. The parents and her daughter died last year."

"Very hard time for them."

"I think so. And through all this Hannah Leftridge never darkened my consulting room door. But, as I say, she may have relied on drugs from someone else."

"So Magdalína is your current concern. What about Sylvia Hale? Having lost her husband—"

"Again, Miss Taylor, I reply as I did to your inquiry about

Hannah. If she needs something medical, she's not getting it from me."

Recalling Sylvia's cool, steely exterior, I asked, "Could she seem dispassionate because she and Colin were divorcing? Would she look at his death as a release?"

Francis got up, stuffing his bag beneath his left arm. "Preposterous! Sylvia Hale may appear indifferent, but she harbors a well of emotions. She doesn't make a public scene of her feelings, that's all. You can't judge another person's passions but what they show, Sergeant. Many grieve in private."

I agreed, thinking royalty was a prime example.

"She's always been a strong woman," Francis said. "Even after her mother died. Good night."

He clumped down the stairs, his hand gripping the banister as he leaned against it. I scribbled the name of Magdalína's medicine into my notebook and went to see if she was still awake.

"I'm afraid I didn't see or smell anything unusual last night," Magdalína said in response to my question. She looked relaxed in jeans and a sweatshirt, clothes she wouldn't be wearing now if she was working in her tearoom. "I—I wasn't in the back of the flat. That's where the fire started, isn't it?"

A vision of the tearoom flashed through my brain: the fiery wall toward the rear of the restaurant, the smoke-packed air, the flame searing the floor in a loop design that screamed of petrol trails. I breathed deeply and said, "We haven't a definite report yet, but yes, I believe so, since the building is damaged more extensively there than in the front."

"God, I wonder how long it will be before I can rebuild. I've an insurance agent coming to look at it. But in the meantime, before I'm running again..." She bit her lower lip, as though keeping herself from crying. "Perhaps I should've kept Sylvia's cake, but now I'm glad I didn't. A few extra pounds may not sound like much, but when you're forced out of business…" She searched my eyes. "And you don't know how it started?"

"That, too, has yet to be determined. Do you recall any candles left burning? Or something in the kitchen, perhaps, left on? It's so easy to do in the course of a work day, never mind the rush of preparing for the party."

Her fingers traced the edge of a flower petal. It was part of the bouquet I had seen Mark present to her minutes ago. The flowers sat in a large, white pitcher bearing an impression of a pineapple. From the tearoom, no doubt. "I can't think of anything, no. I always extinguish the candles. Always. I have a checklist by the back door, you see. I've made it a habit to go through both the tearoom and kitchen before leaving at the end of the day. I actually tick things off when I do them. I—I'm fearful of fire, Sergeant. So I guess I overdo it when I close up."

"I can't see how you can do overdo safety, Ms. Dent. It seems rather a good idea to me."

"As much as I fear a fire in the tearoom, I acquiesce to candles. Especially this time of year. Besides being a cheap decoration, they're part of the season, aren't they? And they do break the gloom of our dull wintry days."

Along the High Street the trees dripped large clumps of snow in a steady serenade of plops and thuds. The last shreds of sober clouds hugged the eastern horizon, a smudge of grey on a listless background. Early evenings, even without the drab weather, cried for some spot of cheer and light. Eyeing the cluster of votive candles burning on a tabletop, I said, "So, everything was as it should have been when you closed up, then?"

Magdalína nodded. "I can't think how it started. I really can't. And I don't see how—or why—someone could've started it. I was home. I—I would've heard." She grabbed a tissue and blew her nose.

"Have you had trouble with anyone—neighbor, relative,

customer? Anyone threaten you, however slightly, even if you assumed it was a jest?" Hannah and her irritated customer came to mind, and I wondered if Andrew Bayley had wanted to work a deal for his tour trade with Magdalína. But Magdalína emphatically repeated no one she knew would've set the fire. They would've heard him.

"Someone was with you that evening, then?" I wanted her to tell me about Colin, to explain away the image of harlot.

Magdalína blushed and clasped her hands in her lap. "I didn't mean—that is, what I meant to say—"

"What you're meaning to say," I said, watching her fidget with the hem of her sweatshirt, "is that someone was with you last evening. Someone whom you're embarrassed to name. Married, is he?"

Nodding, Magdalína began in a small voice. "We hadn't meant it to become an affair. But it just happened. Very gradually. He—he's unhappy at home. And no!" she said, her voice quickly strengthening, "it's not just a line. He's treated shamefully. Not one ounce of respect from his wife or child. Not one ounce of love. He's stuck it out with them for longer than I would've thought decent. The child's living away from home, and the wife is able to support herself. So it's not as though he's abandoning them in their hour of greatest need." She stopped suddenly, her breath broken by sobs of grief.

I let her cry. It seemed the best remedy for her broken heart. Perhaps if Graham had been here instead of me, he might have offered spiritual solace, but I didn't think so. There were instances in a police investigation when the minister was out of place, and Graham knew that. Numerous times he had sat placid and unreadable while witnesses cried. I would've accused him of a hard heart. But that was before I knew him better.

"I'm sorry. I wouldn't have gone off the deep end like that, only—" Magdalína smiled at me, wiping away a tear that dangled from her chin.

I assured her there was nothing to apologize for.

"It's just the shock, you know. And the loss of someone I loved. Not meaning to sound pious, but these are probably more tears than he'll get from—"

"Sylvia and Ward Hale?" I ventured.

Magdalína blinked widely, opened her mouth, then thought better of it. She looked, instead, at the flowers. "I shall have to send some to the funeral. It'll be alright to do that. After all, he was a friend to many in the village. There will be other flowers. Mine won't be particularly noticed. And even if they are..."

"It's still a neighborly thing to do."

"Sylvia will only be concerned about names, anyway. Did her women's club send something, did she get acknowledge-ment of her loss from the garden club... God, if Colin had only left her weeks ago, when he was talking about it. We could've..." She sighed deeply and sank back into the chair.

"What could you two have done?"

"Left here—this village. Or bought a house together. Oh, I don't know. Nothing. A million things. It doesn't make any dif-ference now, does it? He's dead. And the funny thing about all this is that he was the first man I ever loved, who I ever slept with. I told you it was hysterical, Sergeant. At my age—I go to bed with a man, give my heart, and look what happens."

After she had cried for a while, I asked, "Do you suspect anyone at all of starting this fire, Ms. Dent?"

Magdalína looked up at me, her eyes—red and swollen from crying—searching mine. "What do you want me to say? That I suspect Sylvia or Ward of setting the fire?"

"I'm not *wanting* you to say anything. I just wondered—"

"You just wondered if I would finger someone for you, make

your job easier. Well, I won't because I can't. And it's not out of love for Sylvia or her wretched son. It's because I'm a law-abiding citizen. However much I cry out for Colin and want to see his killer punished, I can't just fling a name at you. No matter how suspicious it looks."

"You're accusing me unjustly, Ms. Dent. I have no intention of charging the handiest person, guilty or not, with this crime. I just wanted to hear your thoughts. Do you know if Sylvia knew about your affair?"

"I'm not sure. I would've said emphatically no before last night, but now…" She stroked the flower petal again before saying, "Doesn't seem the sort of thing she'd do, set a fire. Cut Colin out of her will, fabricate lies about him and me—that sort of thing is more her speed. But physically destroy my property? No."

"Is it Ward's?"

"If it weren't for those cronies he hangs around with, I'd have said no. But if he was egged on he could have done."

"Why would his mates have wanted him to torch your shop?"

"Haven't a clue. But you read about that sort of thing. Bored and out for a bit of excitement."

Could Ward or his mates be my attacker? Could Sylvia? But to drag me into a shop required strength, and even though Sylvia worked out, was she capable? And, more importantly, why try to murder me? What had I heard from my attacker to warrant my death? I said, "I have the impression that Ward and Colin weren't very close."

She laughed. "Were Charles I and Cromwell?"

"And which was Colin?"

"The issue isn't two long gone English leaders, Sergeant. The issue is that Colin has been killed in a fire that damaged my business. You find out who did that instead of pursuing Cromwellian personalities. And now, I really have to get busy."

She stood up. "I have to rearrange things at the bank. I'm afraid the tearoom will be closed for quite a while."

I thanked her for her time and left wondering how Owen would survive between now and the shop's rebuilding.

OWEN PARNELL, motorcycle helmet in hand, was just leaving his house, the end residence of a row of houses, when I arrived. Stark and grey, the houses squatted near the curb, running the length of the road until they collided with The Pineapple Slice. They seemed impenetrable, sprouted from the grey pavement and sky, as though they had always been there. Individuality of dwelling came through door color, a hint of curtain at the windows, or front garden designs.

Though we stood on his doorstep, talking of the fire, his immediate concerns, and Colin's death, Owen was no more civil to me than he had been Wednesday night. He kept glancing at his watch and sighing, yet he answered my questions readily enough.

"No," he said, looking past me to his bike parked on the road, "I don't know a bleedin' thing about the fire. Wouldn't I have gone to you coppers before now if I did?"

"Is that where you're going now?" I asked, nodding toward his motorcycle. "Feel more comfortably talking to Chief Inspector Graham or Sergeant Salt?" Owen seemed the sort who would talk to males if he could. At least for something important. I wondered how he coped with a female boss. But Magdalína's realm was the tearoom proper. Owen was master in the kitchen.

"I don't feel more comfortable talkin' to one of your lot than to any other," he said. "And if you have to know, I'm just now off to Buxton. Got errands to do. All right?"

When I asked him the standard question, Owen said, "Not likely to see a thing, am I? The shop's down the road from my house. 'Sides, if it were around midnight, I was asleep. Bakers have to get up early in the mornin'——or don't you remember?"

"With the shop closed for a bit, how will you get on? Magdalína won't continue your wages, will she?"

"Without money comin' in, you expect her to pay me?"

"I wouldn't think so. That's why I was wondering."

"She offered to pay me a part of my wage, yes. A percentage until we're back in business. But I couldn't take it. She's goin' to need everythin' she's got to rebuild."

"I understood she was covered for fire."

"And she is. But she's needin' money to live on."

"So do you, Mr. Parnell."

"Yes. And thanks to me brother, Nelson, I've no fears about that. He'll help me out if and when I need it. For as long as I need it."

"You're fortunate. Not many people have so generous a relative."

"He's a well of lolly," Owen said, making a deliberate show of looking at his watch. "Gets a monthly bit 'sides what he makes at his business. Now, I've got to leg it, unless I'm about to get the chop for settin' the fire."

"Was the fire set?"

"How the hell should I know? I figured that was what you were getting' around to, comin' over here."

"We've no evidence as of yet that it was, no."

"Then if you've no objections…" He slammed the door to his house and walked to his bike. The sound of his motor followed me down the road.

A PERSISTENT "Hey! Miss Detective!" stopped me mid stride to my car. I turned around to find Scott Coral grinning at me as he rolled down his car window. Wandering up to him, I asked what he wanted.

"Oh, nothing much. Just want to give you a present."

I screwed up my mouth, knowing a joke was probably

coming. "Well, it's too early for Christmas and my birthday, so that leaves something like Old Maid's Day."

"Why are you always so suspicious of me, Bren? Here I'm about to offer you a gift, and you're already looking it in the mouth and counting its teeth."

"I like horses, Scott, but I can't keep one. And unless it's one of those miniature ponies and you've got him in the boot..." I glanced at the car, nervous that I had somehow divined the truth.

Scott shook his head, exhaling in exasperation. "No, but it is an animal, that I grant you. Have any allergies to dander?"

Before I could reply, Scott lifted a cardboard box from the seat and held it out the window. There were holes punched in the box, and when I accepted it, there was an uneven shifting of weight and a quiet cry. When I opened the lid, a kitten looked up at me and mewed. I immediately let the box drop and held the kitten close to my chest. "Where'd you get him?"

"Wandering around The Pineapple Slice. I asked Magdalína about him, but she doesn't claim him. Doesn't know who he belongs to, in fact."

I nodded and held the kitten at arm's length so I could get a good look at him. There were patches of singed fur that spoke of his close call with the tea shop fire. Snuggling him against my body again, I said, "You taking him to the vet? Those burns should be seen to. I think he's burnt his paw, too."

"He needs a good home, Bren. He'll get patched up, but he needs a home. I was thinking that you—" Scott cocked his head and gave me that lop-sided grin that always melted my heart.

"I don't know, Scott. I'm not home regular hours."

"Cat's the perfect pet, then! Just put out some dry food and some water, and he's happy sleeping in the sun until you return. What about it?"

He kept talking to the cat, cooing at it and saying Mummy Bren would fix him a bowl of fish heads as a treat. I picked up the box and put the cat back into it. Thrusting the box at Scott, I said, "I'll take the cat if *you* take him to the vet. Find out when I can pick him up."

"You're all heart, Bren. You won't regret it. He'll be good company on those lonely nights when Mark's stood you up."

I gritted my teeth and said something uncomplimentary about ungrateful cads. As Scott rolled up his window, I called out, "And don't make Calhoun car sick."

I'D GONE TO Paula's house, a cottage on the western edge of the village, parenthesized by dense woods. My previous dealings with Paula had been brief, belligerent discourses, with Paula's denials or curse words standing in for intellectual replies. Now I was there to see if she knew anything about the unidentified pregnant girl.

Paula lived with her mother, a mousy woman who looked as though anyone could bully her into anything. Even the tea she served was weak, colored water, and matched the drab home furnishings. She bore the markings of an abusive marriage, with not only a bully of a husband but also a daughter who was learning to yell for what she wanted. Mrs. Lindbergh had lingered in the background during the questioning, constantly clearing her throat or clenching her fingers. *My interview could have been better,* I thought as I drove to a neighboring village beyond Piebald Tor. But at least I was treated to a civil tongue and reasonable answers—due to her mother's presence.

The roads had been cleared into Netherthorpe, but my little Expression had no trouble with the snow-packed lanes in the village proper. It was hardly worth the trip, for I stood outside the home, conducting the interview on the front steps. But as short as it was, the meeting was surprisingly helpful, and I thought Graham would be pleased with my progress. But a flash of reddish-brown in the woods halted my walk to my car. Standing statue-still, afraid to close my notebook or even breathe, I noticed a weasel emerging from a hollow log. I quietly walked over to a tree, partially hiding behind it as the weasel ambled away from me. It was searching for voles and mice among the snowy leaf litter of the forest floor. I remained frozen in place for minutes, watching it pawing and turning over rotten logs. When it had lunched, it moved on. Patches of snow had melted to reveal the carpet of spent leaves, acorns and dead flower stalks, the residue of a glorious summer. Overhead, the trees stretched charcoal-hued boughs toward the gloomy sky. I followed slowly, for the copse was thick with under-growth that impeded easy progress. I laid my notebook on a tree stump, needing both my hands to hold the dried stalks and tree branches so they would not rustle as I passed. A mistle thrush's song was the only sound invading the quiet.

The weasel moved on, leading me through the woods until I lost him in a pile of fallen tree trunks. What must have been forty-five minutes later, I was driving back to Bramwell.

NINETEEN

"WHAT DID YOU FIND OUT about the identity of the pregnant girl?" Graham asked as I took off my jacket. "I'm anxious to get this piece wrapped up so I can tell Simcock what progress we're making on the case. He's getting rather vocal about seeing results. Taylor?"

I hesitated, one arm still in my jacket, as he asked his simple question. Sliding off the garment, I mumbled something and sat down.

"Pardon? You have your notebook?"

I felt like a school child caught without her homework. But there was no dog to lay the blame on. My breath stuck in my throat; my cheeks flushed—a crimson flood that implied a problem.

He asked if there was. When I didn't reply, he leaned back in his chair, his arms folded, and eyed me as though he was waiting for his teenager to explain the wrecked car. When I fumbled for words, Graham said, "I take it you don't have the information."

"No, sir."

"What was so important that prevented it?"

"Actually, I have the information, sir, but just not with me at the moment."

"Why don't you have it? Where is it?"

"Well, sir, I can explain…"

"I wish you would, Taylor. I'm waiting." His eyes were darkening and his jaw line hardened, the muscle twitching as he prepared for the worst.

"Well, sir…"

"You said that. Tell me something I haven't heard, although I can probably guess what you're going to say."

"Yes, sir," I said, then grimaced. "You see, sir, when I interviewed Paula Lindbergh—"

"Sergeant Taylor's trying to say, sir," Margo said, quickly walking up to us. She eyed me, as though willing me to keep quiet, then addressed Graham. "Paula was rather rude. And after telling Sergeant Taylor where several of us personally could go—"

Graham raised an eyebrow. "I won't ask for particulars, but why this verbal abuse prevented Taylor from having the information with her is not clear." He looked at me, his lips pressed together.

"You see, sir," Margo continued, "when Sergeant Taylor asked Paula—"

"No!" I yelled so forcefully that Margo literally stepped backwards.

Graham, shifting his gaze from Margo to me, asked in a soft voice edged with impatience, "What's going on, Taylor? You two remind me of a very poor imitation of Laurel and Hardy—without the humor. The truth, Taylor."

I gulped, then rushed on. "I appreciate it, Margo, but I'm the one who screwed up. You needn't get involved." Graham was not smiling. He was massaging his temples, as though he knew what was coming. I said, more slowly, so he could understand everything, "I lost my notebook. I know it's inexcusable, but I laid it down somewhere and forgot it."

"I found it," Margo said. "It was—"

"How long was it out of your sight," Graham interrupted, then added, "I suppose that doesn't matter. Could anyone have found it?"

I shook my head. "I don't think so."

"Then how did Lynch find it if it's so well camouflaged?"

Margo said, "I saw Sergeant Taylor leave it. I was too far away to yell at her, so I just followed and picked it up. I was going to return it to her—"

"But I got to her first," Graham said. He exhaled deeply, then stood up. Glaring down at me, he looked even taller than his six foot-plus height. He didn't speak for several moments, as though considering what to say. I tried not to breathe, tried not to remind him I was there, wishing I could sink into the floor. I could hear the fax machine ringing while he considered my future. When he spoke, his voice was like ice. "I don't know which of you is the more accountable. Lynch, for lying to me, or Taylor, for losing part of your equipment, which could've proved quite damaging if someone had found it and read your notes. I understand, Lynch, you're Taylor's friend and thought you were aiding her, but lying to your senior officer…" He exhaled, slumping against the edge of the table, and ran his fingers through his hair.

I watched his face, the muscles of his neck and cheek tightening, the scar on his jaw more prominent as the skin drew taut, his eyes closing as if to focus on his inner voice. Several times his jaw moved—almost imperceptive—as though he was grinding his teeth. When he finally opened his eyes, he didn't look at Margo or me, but stared out of the window, seeking, perhaps, the answer somewhere beyond the walls of the incident room, or willing himself away from me. I wanted to hear his thoughts, not so I would know what punishment he was considering, but because his face was a battlefield of emotions.

"No one read her notes, sir," Margo said, breaking the strained silence. "I saw her leave it and I followed her, as I said, so no one—"

"That's not the point, Lynch." When Graham turned toward us again, his eyes were uncommonly dark, as though all his anger was drawn there so I could see it. His voice was sharp, and he clipped his words in his hurry. "What if you hadn't been there to see Taylor forget her book? What if someone else had found it?"

"But I *was* there, sir."

"Do you follow her around all the time, picking up after her?"

"No, sir."

"You were just lucky this time, then."

I said, "It's never happened before, sir. I swear it won't happen again."

"I should damned well hope not."

"Please, sir, don't admonish Margo. She's not to blame."

"I *know* who's to blame, Taylor," Graham said, standing up.

His voice seemed to build in intensity as he spoke through his anger. "This is something I'd expect a young probationer to have done. Not a sergeant. You know this is a highly emotional case of murder. We've also got arson and a manslaughter case to deal with. The issue is *not* whether you swear this won't happen again. The issue is that it *did* happen and that all our confidential information might have come into the wrong hands. I cannot believe your incompetence in this! Your carelessness might have jeopardized the entire case, at the very least, besides costing some officers their jobs." He paused, leaving me to conclude whose jobs would be on the line. "By rights, I should have you both up on discipline. You, Lynch, on prevarication and being an accessory to a discipline offence. And you, Taylor, for disobedience to orders, neglect of duty, and negligent use of official police equipment."

I swallowed, afraid he was about to follow through with his statement, afraid I was going to be sick. I stared at the floor, not trusting my emotions to look at either Graham or Margo.

"Have you any idea," he said, his voice low, more threatening in its slowness than the fury of his previous quick words, "—*any* inkling what disobedience to order or neglect of duty means?" He waited for my answer. I stammered something about 'compliance to orders' and 'absent without leave' and 'without good cause' before Graham interrupted. "Without good cause is the key word, Taylor. Do you consider bird watching a good cause while on duty?"

I barely took a breath, standing rigid before him, staring at his rigid jaw and constricted throat muscles.

"If you had been called to a traffic accident, that would signify good cause, Taylor. If you had assisted at a fire or witnessed a robbery, that would signify good cause. But abandoning your notebook to go on a nature hike—" He took a deep breath and turned toward Margo. "And you, Lynch. When a police officer knowingly makes any false or misleading statement, that is a prevarication. A lie, if you understand that word better. I want to make certain you understand me. Right?"

Margo nodded, her lips pressed together.

"It may seem trivial, Lynch, lying to help your mate, but if I can't trust your honesty in this, can I trust your honesty in something bigger? What happens if you're involved with a boyfriend or parent? Does honesty fly out the window? Do you have two standards for telling the truth?"

Margo's face flooded crimson and she lowered her head. Without waiting for her response, he turned back to me. "*You* tell *me,* Taylor, which one of you is the greater offender. And what you deserve. Is reduction in rank too lenient? Is a year of pay reduction too strong?"

I didn't know which was worse, but couldn't trust my voice to answer.

Evidently not expecting a response, he said, "But since it is a first time, and since Lynch was there…" He took a breath, as though struggling with his conscience and police procedure. "I'll let you—*and* you, Lynch—off with a reprimand this time. But if you ever do something like this again, Taylor, I'll have your guts for garters. Understand?" I barely had time to nod and whisper my thanks before he threw his pen at the table and strode from the room. Margo came over to me, her face white, and we watched Graham until he entered the hotel, his jacket draped over his shoulder.

"God, Bren," Margo said. "Jesus, I've *never* seen him like that. I didn't know what to say."

"I think you said enough," I said, taking a seat at the table. My hands shook as I tried to straighten my hair. "I'm sorry. That sounded mean. Thanks for trying to cover for me."

"Might've worked if we had been trying to explain to Mark."

"Even that wouldn't have worked with Mark, Margo. 'Paula was rather rude.' How'd you come up with that one?"

"All I could think of at the time. Here." She handed me my notebook and I jammed it hastily into my jacket pocket, not wanting to touch the object of my problem. Margo smiled weakly. "Sounds funny now, but when you're drowning…"

"Any port in a storm, I know."

"You think he's okay?"

"You want to ring up Karol to check his blood pressure?"

"She won't get here quickly enough. What a damned mess. I'm sorry, Bren, but I thought I was helping."

"It's *not* your fault, Margo. How many other friends would've risked their careers to help?" And, odd thing was, it could have been our careers. The punishments Graham hadn't mentioned were dismissal from the force or asking for your resignation. Scott, for all my joking about his knowledge of discipline regulations, would have been able to quote section Sixty of the Act. Not that it made any difference, but it illustrated his awareness of regulations—something that I was rather lax about.

"At least," Margo said, wiping her forehead, "it was Graham and not Simcock. We got off lenient. Reprimand."

I nodded, but wondered how my relationship with Graham would suffer. Of course he had every right to punish me, and I was afraid it still might come after he'd thought a bit about his sympathetic sentence. Would he assign me jobs of work any first-day constable could handle, testing me, watching me to see I was as good as my promise?

"Why'd he come down so hard on us?"

I probably stared at her as though she had asked the most stupid question in the world. "Pardon?"

"Graham. Why so angry?"

"What do you mean? I lost my notebook and you—"

"I *know* what we did, Bren. I mean, why'd he rabbit on and on about policy? Everyone in the Force knows he was up before the old Super and on discipline for one of his own cock-ups years ago. Doesn't he remember how it felt? Why come down so hard on us?"

I had forgotten, but Margo was right. It was one of the first things a new cop learned on arriving in B Division—after locating the food machines and break room, and which senior officer you did *not* want to be partnered with. Though Graham's offence wasn't known, the punishment was. He had suffered demotion. But he had struggled back up to chief inspector after five years. I chewed my lower lip, wondering what he had done to warrant this sentence.

"You hear me, Bren?" Margo's voice cut through my reverie.

"Yes."

"So, what do you think? About Graham, I mean."

"Maybe it's tough love."

"Doesn't want us to suffer like he did? I don't buy it."

I shrugged.

"Oh, Bren, what a mess. God…" The last word, whispered and sighed, said it all.

Picking up Graham's pen, I held it tightly, invoking every god and spirit and thing I held dear that Graham would not ask to have me reassigned. The room settled into the quiet that follows an emotional upheaval. Birds twittered at the window, the wall clock whirred in preparation for the hour strike, people resumed muffled conversations and managed half-hearted laughs. An electric kettle, perhaps flipped on during my conversation with Margo, now whistled enthusiastically. Grabbing my jacket, I checked the time.

"Where you off to, then? Chasing Graham?"

"After I have lunch. I won't be able to talk to him if he's still angry."

"God, Bren, you're either the bravest person I know or the dumbest."

"I'll tell you after I get back."

The wind felt good on my face after that fiery confrontation with Graham. I took deep breaths of the icy air, needing to clear my mind and emotions. Where should I go while Graham cooled down?

As if drawn by the memory of that quieter evening, I wandered to the pocket park opposite the hotel. The sun broke through a patch of clouds, the sunlight dazzling bright on the snow, and the world seemed a bit cheerier. Oblivious to my presence, two squirrels chased each other up and down an oak, their claws scratching along the bark.

I had not been there long when Graham walked up. He glanced at me, turned away, hesitated, then, as if struggling with his manners or conscience, came over, asking if he could join me. Murmuring he was always welcome, I sat up a bit straighter.

He did not mention the altercation, but leaned against the back of the bench, his face tilted toward the sun. We sat in silence for some minutes, Graham completely relaxed, I wondering what to do, wondering if I was about to join Margo as a constable. I had decided to ask if he'd like to have lunch when he asked me about my interview with Paula. I know my voice cracked, for I was still embarrassed about the episode. But as I spoke and saw Graham's attention, I warmed to the subject.

"Before I could even ask about the identity of the pregnant girl," I said, "Paula swore she had nothing to do with the fire."

"Why am I surprised?"

"And she didn't know who did, as she was home all night."

"Whose home?"

"Her mum's. And yes, she could have sneaked out without mummy ever knowing, but I don't think so. Paula looked genuinely scared."

"Might still look genuinely scared if Ward's prank got out of hand and they wind up being charged for Colin's death."

"I think," I said, clearing my throat, "she *did* stay home. There was something about her voice that made me believe she's telling the truth. Anyway, that can be decided later. But she did tell me the name of the girl who had left the village: Inez Mills. She came back in October after an eight month absence."

"Returned unencumbered, I take it?"

"Not pushing a pram, if that's what you mean, sir."

"Where'd she go?"

"Paula thought it was Liverpool, but couldn't swear to it. They're not the closest of chums."

"What does your womanly intuition say about that, TC?"

TWENTY

I THOUGHT GRAHAM would be happier without my intuition, so I continued. "I talked to Inez. She and her boyfriend live just north of here. And, miracle of miracles, Paula was right. Inez admitted to being in Liverpool and to being pregnant. *And* to Ward being the father. She also admitted she wasn't getting anything from Ward. She said she wanted nothing more to do with him, and even showed me her bankbook. No suspicious payments. Nothing screaming of a payoff. What's the matter?"

"A bankbook doesn't necessarily preclude handouts from Ward, or anybody else. You've heard of cash, I presume."

"So it proves nothing. At least we know Ward Hale is the father of her illegitimate child."

"Where is the baby?"

"Inez arranged for its adoption before giving birth. Afterwards, she didn't even look at it or want to know its gender."

"Sometimes I think that's best," Graham said. "Clean break, no haunting face in your nightmares."

A sadness—born of experience?—washed over his face. Bowing his head, he watched a sparrow hopping at our feet, searching the fallen pine needles for lunch. When Graham abandoned his bird watching, I said, "Well, that's as may be. But who paid for the delivery? If we've no bank record of Ward's benevolence—"

"Would take more cash than Ward's bound to get a hold of. What makes you think Inez or her boyfriend didn't foot the bill?"

"Her bankbook's rather pitiful, sir. And the dates go back before her delivery."

"How do you like Sylvia?"

I said that she was well off and would probably not miss the money if she did pay for the hospital stay.

"We'll have to check."

"*We?* Royal or plural?"

"Consider yourself queen for a day, TC. Or put Lynch on to it. She's getting rather chummy with the bank officials. She can write up that report in record time, with all the practice she's getting. Speaking of which, the report came in on the tearoom fire. Care to guess?"

"Arson."

"Two arsons in two days. I don't like it. What's happening here? Is someone angry?"

"But arson, if I remember my schooling correctly, is defined as a malicious, willful act. Even if we do find our arsonist, we need motive. And we have two different victims, sir. We would need a link between them."

"Besides our disgruntled tour operator, Andrew Bayley?"

"There's Nelson Parnell."

"Don't exclude *Owen* Parnell. His tongue's still sharp as a knife. What's fueling his anger?"

"First thing that comes to mind is defrauding the insurance companies, but our three suspects aren't involved in that."

"And we can eliminate business rivalry," Graham suggested. "Two different businesses."

"I don't suppose we have anything like intimidation."

Graham sighed, his breath sailing skyward in a huge, whitish puff. "I'd be more inclined to believe that, TC, if the businesses were the same. How about revenge or murder?"

"If you're hunting for that link, sir," I said, "I'd go with the revenge. Of the two fires, Colin's the only victim. I wonder if these were pranks that got out of hand."

"A bit of pyromania?"

I nodded, saying Ward seemed abnormally disturbed and might get a kick out of setting the fires.

"Sexually stimulated, you think?"

"Or hero status."

"Nearly the entire village would have to be classified there, TC. I couldn't list names of those who helped drag books from Hannah's bookstore. Or pulled chairs and menus from Magdalína's place."

He refrained from mentioning his own part in the rescue at Hannah's.

"And the liquid agent—petrol—is too common to give us much of a lead," he continued. "Doesn't take any brains to splash some on a pile of wood and toss on a lighted match."

"We needn't necessarily exclude Dr. Rice," I said, thinking of the village's most likely vote for Brains. "It's not the intelligence or lack of it that's concerning me, sir. It's the way the fires were set."

"The back of both stores, you mean?"

"Yes, sir. If the arsonist had wanted to really inflict damage, he'd have used more accelerant, or set the fires where they would have spread faster."

"Perhaps he set them at the back because they are out of public view. Less chance of being seen and caught."

"There is that," I said. "You don't suppose Colin was intentionally killed, do you? His son harbors some real anger toward him."

"That's supposing Ward knew Colin was having an affair with Magdalína. I wouldn't have thought Ward would be concerned enough to murder."

"Sylvia babies him. Although he seemed to resent it, he also seemed to put up with it."

"If you're getting into some Oedipus or psychoanalyst thing, TC—"

"No, sir. But if he dotes on his mum, and he knew Colin was having an affair or leaving Sylvia—"

Olive Lindbergh puffed up to us, her face as red as the beetroot in her string carrier bag. Glancing from me to Graham, she finally decided to vent at me, since I was the instigator of the original problem. Her forefinger jabbed at my chest with all the sharpness of her tongue. "What do you mean by scarin' my grandchild?" Her voice was as demanding as a defense lawyer's.

"When did I do that, Mrs. Lindbergh?"

"Just today. Few hours ago. When you was over to her home, askin' her your questions."

"I wasn't aware I'd frightened Paula, but if I did, I'll apologize."

"She's that close to cryin', her mum told me just now. Askin' all that about murders and fires and such. And her a slip of a girl who never done no one a harm in her whole life. It's disgraceful, I calls it. When law abidin' citizens can't walk the streets without bein' pestered—"

Graham cleared his throat and Olive stopped mid-sentence, startled. Standing up, Graham said softly, in great contrast to her umbrage, "I know Sergeant Taylor had no intention either of frightening or pestering your granddaughter, Mrs. Lindbergh. Perhaps Paula was overly sensitive to the Sergeant's questions, being such a delicate girl."

Olive's face softened and she shoved her free hand into her coat pocket. "You are a perceptive one, Mr. Graham," she said. "And you new to the village, too. But as I told Trueman just yesterday, time don't mean a thing to some folk. They walk around their whole lives without knowing what the church clock looks like. Anyway, you're right about my Paula. And I do accept your apology. I'll let her know that no harm was meant." She shifted the carrier bag to her other hand, eyeing me with more benevolence than she had, as though feeling sorry for my shortcoming. "Good day you both. And I hope you find your culprit." She waddled away, the bag banging against her substantial hips, her coat catching the tops of her boots.

I exhaled heavily. "Thank you, sir. I didn't think I was that heavy-handed with the girl."

"You weren't, most likely. But either Paula or her mother may want us to think so."

"Or Olive," I agreed. "Though why, I can't imagine. Is one of them hiding something?"

"A good question, TC. But until we get our crystal ball, I suggest we have lunch and then have a physical look at Colin's secrets."

SYLVIA HALE begrudgingly gave us access to her husband's desk. It was a large, mahogany model, with drawers consuming each side of the kneehole. DCs Byrd and Riley accompanied us, Graham thinking either we'd need more muscle to persuade Sylvia or extra hands to carry away evidence.

Margo was in the master bedroom, rooting among bureau drawers, when I walked in. She looked up and asked if I'd had a chance to talk to Graham after his explosion. I briefly related our conversation in the park. Margo sighed, as though my talk had also cleared her of complicity. "Lucky break for us both," she said, shutting a drawer.

I said, "Speaking of breaks...Hannah's had a tough one with this fire."

"What?"

"The publishing party," I said softly, imagining the cartons of David's books. "But they can hold it later. I know it won't have the same feel as if they had been able to have it this evening, but they aren't thinking of canceling David's party, surely."

"They'll have it. But Hannah has to reorder some of the books. A number were damaged."

"Seems like a lot of things have been damaged in fires. Maybe some flowers would help her."

"Can't hurt. Magdalína bought herself some this morning. What's wrong, Bren?"

I grimaced. "Flowers *this* morning?"

"Yeah. Why?"

"Carnations, roses—"

"Mums. Yeah. Why?"

"I thought Mark gave her those flowers."

"Mark? Why would *he* give *Magdalína* flowers? Oh," Margo said, the inference clear. "Say no more. The beautiful woman, the handsome detective…"

"The *berk* detective. But you don't know the half of it." I related the scene outside the restaurant. "But if he didn't give her that bouquet, why make the big presentation and pretend he did? What's he trying to prove?"

"Make you jealous, perhaps?"

"Jealous!" I said the word so loudly that I was afraid Graham would come racing in to see what had happened. Lowering my voice, I said, "Margo, you've had some amazing theories in your time, but this one is on the crackers list. You've gone round the twist if you believe that. Anyway, if they're Magdalína's flowers, how'd he get hold of them?"

"I'm not certain, but I think she left them at the florist's. At least, it makes sense. She reported her watch had gone missing this morning—a fancy, gold affair that her dad had given her. Engraved and handed down through the ancestors. She was looking for it, going into shops she'd been in Friday. Probably left the flowers there while she asked the clerk about the watch, had a bit of a look around. Mark, bless his little promotion-seeking heart, took the call and dashed out to have a look. I assume that's where he found the flowers and watch. A bit later, Magdalína phoned to say she had the watch, thanks so much for our help."

"So Mark probably had the watch wrapped around the flower stems, or hidden in the fern—some crafty means of keeping it from my view when he gave it and the flowers back to her. Probably why she laughed, too."

"He shines at the witty remark," Margo said. "I hope yours are equally brilliant."

I said my brain had been a bit sluggish lately, and walked into the front room. Byrd had just opened the lower left desk drawer and dropped a paper into a plastic evidence bag when he called to Graham. I came over, momentarily abandoning the stack of papers I was going to sort through.

"The recipe for Flying Saucers?" he said, taking the bag in his gloved hand.

"Wasn't that at Joel's?" I said, peering at the handwriting.

"Looks genuine," Graham said, angling it under the lamplight. "Not a photocopy." He handed it back to Constable Byrd. "After you've run them through the glue cabinet for fingerprints, have the handwriting compared to the recipe found at Joel's. That just might tell us something other than Colin Hale likes Flying Saucers."

"So, whose is the original?" I said.

"May be a bit hard to establish, Taylor. But we've worked minor miracles before."

I agreed and went back to rummaging in a metal file box. Graham looked up when I said, "Sir, I think this may be interesting."

Graham read the letter silently, then one paragraph aloud, as though the significance of the penned words would become clearer:

"You talk of letting the hurt heal, but you don't tell me how to do that. You talk of forgiving, of ignoring the past. But I'm not a Christian; I don't have your outlook, or your weakness, or your god. So you can save your breath. Normally, I'd tell you this to your lying face, but I'm afraid if I got that close to you, I'd obliterate it. What the hell—change your name, but that won't erase your presence on the family tree, much as I wish it could. Or does praying to your god grant this desire? If so, maybe Christians have something worth my converting for."

I looked at Graham as he handed me the letter. The room had grown quiet while he had read, and I was reluctant to break the silence, but I had to ask. "It's not signed, but do you think that letter's from Joel?"

"Our handwriting expert can tell us, Taylor, but offhand, I'd say yes."

"That part about obliterating Colin's face…goes with those scratched photos we found in Joel's home. And if they are brothers, which the family tree part hints at, what was the hurt that caused the separation?"

"Both brothers dead. Perhaps Sylvia would know."

"And why are they both still living in the same village?" I stared at the letter, wanting the handwriting to divulge the history of the quarrel. "If I felt that strongly about a relative, I'd move as far away as I could get. Doesn't make sense."

"Did Joel need to keep an eye on Colin?" Graham said slowly, shifting his gaze from the letter to my face.

"That would imply blackmail. What's he got to blackmail Colin about?"

"The fun's just begun, Taylor. While Margo's delving into that other little financial matter, get her to find out about Joel's and Colin's deposit accounts. That could tell us who—if anyone—

was tucking away a bit of change. And tell her to get Colin's safe deposit box opened. His birth certificate may be in it."

I walked into the bedroom and relayed Graham's requests. She gave me an idea of what I could tell Graham if I didn't value my job, and finished up in the bedroom before leaving the house.

We spent the next hour poking into Colin's life, examining correspondence, photo albums, engagement diary, company shares, bills, address file, business cards, desk blotter and the like. Sylvia came in with tea and biscuits, more out of curiosity or apprehension, I thought, than from hospitality. She watched Graham flip through the family bible, her lips compressed until they were white. Setting the tray down with such force that some tea splashed out of the teapot, she said, "If you want to read my diary or see my birthmark, let me know. Of course, we'll have to go somewhere private to view the latter."

I colored and watched Graham as he gracefully declined both offers. "I know this looks as though we're snooping, digging into things that are no concern of ours, but we're only doing our job, Mrs. Hale. We're trying to find irregularity or clues that suggests motive for arson and thus link it to your husband's death."

"If you're accusing me of arson—"

"I didn't say that, Mrs. Hale." Graham's voice had softened and he spoke more slowly, but there was no ridicule in his tone. Rather, it held sympathy and an understanding of the fright of a police investigation. Sylvia's eyes lost their defiance as he said, "I said 'motive.' There could be something in your husband's past that called for revenge. Or he may have been an innocent victim, caught in a crime to destroy the tearoom's company records. There are many motives for arson, Mrs. Hale, and we need to figure that out. And hopefully your husband's effects will help us."

When Graham had finished, Sylvia nodded, her eyes moist.

"I understand, of course. I'm sorry. It's his death, you see. It was so unexpected. What was he doing there?"

"Perhaps," Graham suggested rather thoughtfully, "he was discussing some business venture with Magdalína. Do you know if he was thinking of anything like that? I ask because we found the recipe for her famous biscuits among Colin's effects. Do you know why he would have her recipe?"

"I've no idea, Mr. Graham. In fact, this is the first I've heard of it. I always thought Owen had invented it."

"Maybe he did," I said, thinking through a scenario. "We don't know. Perhaps he gave it to your husband for safe keeping."

"Safes are for safe keeping," Sylvia said, as though the word sparked a memory. "If the recipe's that famous, why isn't it in a safe deposit box? Why would Colin have it?"

"Joel has it, too," Graham said. "Would you know why?"

She shook her head. "So it's spread around town. Who else has it? And if my husband created the recipe, why didn't he get recognition for it?"

"Good questions, Mrs. Hale. Perhaps we'll find out in time."

"If Colin developed that recipe," Sylvia said, her voice edged with roughness, "and I'd be surprised if he did, for he was never one to do much in the kitchen—but that doesn't preclude a deftness for baking, even though he didn't show it to me. But if Colin created those biscuits, why keep it a secret? And where's the profit from it?"

"Pardon?" Graham blinked quickly, looking like a startled fox.

"If his Flying Saucers are that famous and sell that well, where's his percentage of sales? Why were we living off my wealth?"

TWENTY-ONE

BEFORE I COULD close my mouth, Sylvia turned quickly and left the room. Graham nodded at me—a signal I was learning to interpret—and I slowly followed her. I found Sylvia in the kitchen, pouring herself a cup of tea. Flowers from well wishers sat on the counter tops and clustered near the back door. A stack of cards expressing sympathy spilled across the table, while a tower of cardboard boxes leaned haphazardly against a wall. 'Kitty's Corner,' I read, the black and white labels decorated with the silhouette of a sleek black cat. Mourning clothes, I thought. Tools to express grief. Receiving permission to talk to her, I sat at the mahogany table, shoved aside a heavy bakery box, accepted a cup of tea I didn't want, and asked about her last statement.

"Simple enough, Miss Taylor," she said, putting the lid on the sugar bowl. "We lived off my money."

"Was that usual?"

"For us or for others?"

Before I could answer, she said, "Of course for us. I'm feeling rather inhospitable, I'm afraid. Pay me no mind. We had started out as what I suppose a usual marriage dictates—with Colin bringing home his paycheck and investing it. But after a few years we could very nicely live off the interest of the account, so Colin decided to quit his job and devote himself to his hobbies and to me."

"And what job did he have that produced such luck?"

"He had an internet business selling pharmaceuticals. Got out before the big dot com crash a few years back."

My dad would have had something to say about new technology and fools rushing in where angels feared to start businesses. But he was a cloth-cap worker. He believed in the slow accumulation of pence to make rock-solid pounds, the type of money that came from reliable companies. Curling iron money, my mum called it, those old-fashioned, secure firms and commodities that would live as long as the Rock of Gibraltar. He had no computer in the house, no answer phone or mobile phone. Dependency on electricity, he loved to tell anyone, was dodgy—it failed; pen, paper and the Royal Mail didn't. I often wondered if he feared seeming foolish in front of us kids if he didn't manage to conquer these tools. He was tip-top with his hands, but gadgetry stumped him. Perhaps that's why my sister and brother occupied such a large piece of his heart—they had inherited the family gene of employing one's body for livelihood. I merely used intellect.

"Who knows?" Sylvia said. "If the boom had continued a bit longer we might have made enough to retire to southern France. Colin had always talked of retiring there. He loved the region. Had even studied French—"

Dad would never learn another language. As far as he was concerned, England had built an empire and had scattered her language to every civilized land on earth. And if they couldn't learn it to communicate with him…

Sylvia sniffed loudly, her bottom lip quivering as she broke off. She dabbed at her eyes with a facial tissue, giving herself time to steel her emotions.

"And his hobbies?"

She finished her tea, then said, "Writing music, for one. Paula Lindbergh, for another. Not that Colin had an affair with that tart—at least I don't think so. And a wife usually knows.

I say Paula Lindbergh was a hobby because Colin took his turn trying to reverse her journey toward self-destruction."

"You believe she was headed that way?"

Sylvia shrugged. "Seems a good start, from what I've seen. But I was not involved with that slut. Not personally, as Colin was. Only secondarily, through her ridiculous assaults on him. But she took enough of his time. Nearly every night. Right after tea until nine or ten o'clock. What he accomplished, I don't know. I just remember the tedium of waiting for them to finish so that we could have some time to ourselves."

"In what subjects did Paula get tutoring help?"

"Algebra, I think. Or it could have been elementary math. I can't recall. It was something like that. And English composition. Though why Colin was helping her with that, I can't imagine. He could barely apply pen to paper without asking me to check his spelling. Still, I suppose he was better help than none at all. And his punctuation was impeccable."

"Sounds rather idyllic—a willing teacher, free lessons. Why did Paula quit coming?"

"Some sort of row."

"What was it about?"

Sylvia yawned and flexed her shoulders. "They kept behind closed doors, so I don't know. But she has that type of personality, hasn't she? Unruly, wild, smart ass. And Colin never said. Just told me the day after that Paula wouldn't be coming for tutoring anymore. I must say, I was rather glad to hear it. She'd taken up hours of his time for months, and never said thanks, as far as I could hear. Talk about an ungrateful b—"

"This row—"

"Couldn't have been much or I would have heard them yelling."

"You were always home when Paula was over?"

"Besides not trusting her as far as I could throw her, you mean? I wasn't home every night, of course. I have my committee meetings to run, and I sometimes go out to dinner with a friend. But it was one of the nights I was here. I recall because I was waiting for Paula to leave so Colin and I could finalize our holiday to Jamaica. We needed to decide on dates in order to receive the hotel discount, you see. If it hadn't been for that, I wouldn't have remembered it. Besides, I'm usually in the back of the house, working on my needlework or scrapbooks or reading, and they were in the front lounge. Anyway, that was a year ago," she said, interlocking her fingers and stretching her arms above her head, "the next thing I heard was that our staunch vicar had taken her in hand. Though how his wife liked that, I can only guess. Nearly the same age, Eden and Paula. Eden must've been jealous. Shouldn't have thought that would have sat very well with the deMeres. Paula wasn't there that long, from what I hear. Perhaps another row. Whatever the cause, I can't see Eden depressed over Paula's leaving. That creature could upset anyone in a matter of minutes. And Eden isn't the person to withstand domestic upheaval, even if it *is* only jealousy."

I wondered if Eden had been resentful and if she had said something to Trueman. Was that the real reason behind handing Paula to Joel? "Do you or Ward walk your dog at night, say, around midnight?"

Sylvia stared at me as though I'd lost my mind. "Of course not. Especially in this weather. It's freezing. Why?"

As if I hadn't heard her, I said, "You mentioned assaults a minute ago, Mrs. Hale. What type of assaults? Was Paula physically as well as verbally abusive to Colin?"

Sylvia smiled and pushed up the right sleeve of her sweater, rotating her arm so I could see all sides of it. Four yellow bruises marred her otherwise unblemished flesh, remnants of what must have been deep, purple contusions. Holding out her arm to me, she waited while my hand hovered above the spots, mimicking the fingers that must have grabbed her there. My eyes met hers, and she shoved her sleeve down and folded her arms on her lap. "Like that, Sergeant Taylor?" she finally said after a moment of silence.

Nodding, I said, "Colin?"

"What good will it do now even if I say yes? He's dead. You can't prosecute the dead, no matter how abusive they were."

I mumbled my apologies.

"But Paula dished out a different type of abuse, physical as it was. She reveled in terror, in emotional control, I guess. Little, domestic pranks that made you more than nervous. Things like eggs thrown at our car and windows, objects taken from our garden, vulgarities spray painted on the garage doors. You know the type of thing."

"And all this started when Colin and Paula parted?"

Sylvia sighed. "Nearly right away, I believe."

"Why should Paula resort to this abuse, Mrs. Hale? Wasn't she the one who wanted to quit?"

"As I said, Sergeant, I really don't know. Colin would've been the one to ask…"

She left the implication unsaid, and I bid her good day, thinking that even if Paula had been the instigator in leaving Colin, there are some people who just can't stand being dropped. Would Paula have taken revenge on Colin through egged cars and graffiti?

I had just returned to the room where the team was working when Graham handed me the tea things, telling me to get them out of his way. I looked around the room, wanting a place to deposit them so I wouldn't have to see Sylvia again. The desk was handy and unencumbered, so, shoving aside Sylvia's copy of the St. Nicholas book, I deposited them there. It was then that I noticed her appointment diary open to next week's schedule. That and the next week were ruled through in red ink. The lines looked faintly like ledger lines, so, on a hunch, I opened the middle drawer and again took out Colin's current account book. Leafing through the book disclosed nothing. I pulled out books from previous years. In the one from nine years ago I discovered a large deposit. None of the years previous to that showed a similar amount. I showed it to Graham.

"Colin's percentage of sales?" he said, looking at me quizzically. "Or a one-time sale of the recipe?"

"Someone—Joel or Owen—liked it rather well, that's certain. We'll have to look at their statements for a similar withdrawal."

"There's nothing else, then? No," he said, giving the books a quick look as I said I hadn't seen anything else. "And nothing that looks like discrete monthly or yearly payments. I guess he *did* live off Sylvia's money." He handed the books back to me as I briefly related the Hales' financial situation. "Fifty seems a bit young to be retired, though it's not uncommon. Before you told me, Taylor, I would've bet he was an ordinary wage slave."

"During their ten years here, no one ever saw Colin ride off to punch a time clock. It was just assumed he had some support—an inheritance or something."

"He had support, all right," Graham said. He yawned and glanced at his watch. "I'm just about finished—physically, mentally and forensically. I'll be interviewing Nelson Parnell and Andrew Bayley. Get me on the mobile if anyone needs me. I'd like you all to stay until you've finished your respective jobs. Where you off to, Taylor?"

I stopped at the front door, pulling off my latex gloves. "Off to see some books."

"Fine. Just don't forget about Colin's P.M. procedure."

I nodded, and said I'd be there.

THE FRONT SECTION of Hannah's bookshop had been undamaged in the fire. The sign announcing shop hours was slightly smudged from smoke and weather, but still readable. I walked as close as I could to the door and peered at the sign. A large 'Closed' and accompanying Xs marked a fortnight's holiday beginning next week. I drove slowly to meet Graham at the post mortem, turning this information in my mind. The airline tickets found at Joel's corroborated my surmise—same dates. So who was jetting away with Joel?

WHEN I RETURNED TO the incident room after viewing the P.M., Scientific Officer Jerry Lawford was pouring himself a cup of coffee. As he reached for the sugar, I asked him about Joel's rings.

"The one fits his finger, and while that's not conclusive—he could be best man and have the same ring size as the groom—"

"It's suggestive," I finished. "Especially with his name on the airline tickets and hotel reservations. And the other?"

"It fits several dozen women in town, so that's no help."

"What about Hannah Leftridge and Sylvia Hale?"

"Short of an order to force them to try it on…" He shrugged, his blue eyes mirroring his predicament.

"Being uncooperative like that only adds to our suspicions. But maybe we can find out another way. Do you trust me with it?"

"I'm responsible for it, Brenna. You know that. Why you'd even think of asking—"

"I *know* it's yours," I said somewhat irritably. "If I swear on a stack of bibles or leave you my paycheck as insurance, will that do it?"

"If your paycheck was the size of Simcock's, perhaps I'd do it."

"Come on, Jerry. Will you or won't you?"

He eyed me as if he was calculating the risk and its consequences against my hard-earned pounds. Grimacing, he said, "I don't know. It's highly irregular. I could be shot for doing this."

I thought it was a pity Mark didn't have jurisdiction over the rings. He would've jammed it on my finger and dragged me off to a vicar. "I'll answer to Graham if anything happens to it—which it won't. Please, Jerry."

He made me swear I'd stand him a dinner at Buxton's best restaurant if I had trouble over the rings. I agreed, and threw in a promise of half my paycheck. Jerry went over to the evidence box and brought it back. He held the plastic bag in front of me, making me take an oath before relinquishing them.

"What was that about?" Margo came up to me as Jerry, muttering, walked back to the coffeepot.

"The man has developed no trust in police officers," I said. "You find out everything Graham needed?"

She handed me two bank statements: Joel's and Owen's. I glanced at them, and noticed one rather large deposit for each account a few days apart.

Margo said, "If I see another £, or grey business suit, or ledger line—"

"Graham will be thrilled you're developing your skills. He's still out, so you've got time for a cuppa."

"So what was Jens' verdict at the P.M.? I hope we don't have another knifing." She grimaced.

"Colin died of smoke inhalation," I said, handing her the report. "The body is not suggestive of murder. There are no marks on it from ropes or a blow to the head."

"We pretty much knew he was at Magdalína's of his own will."

"But we didn't know if he was knocked unconscious first, then the fire set so he'd die in an 'accident.' So the absence of rope marks, for instance—"

"Just a tragic accident. Well, I'm sorry. Murder's bad enough, but something that could have been avoided…"

"I still don't understand why he died and Magdalína escaped."

"Calls for another round of questions, I'd say."

TWENTY-TWO

"I'D GONE DOWN to the tearoom's kitchen," Magdalína said when I questioned her. "Sounds silly, I know, me having a kitchen in my flat above the shop. But I was out of lemons. Colin likes—" Her voice faltered, then resumed more determined as she corrected her mistake. "He liked lemon in his tea. I put the kettle on the boil, then went downstairs to find a lemon. I sliced it, put it on a dish, then thought about getting a few flowers from the tables. It took me another few minutes to collect those and stick them in a larger vase. By that time I smelled smoke. When I opened the back door, the flames rushed into the kitchen. I—" She bowed her head, as though in prayer. She very well could have been, for the room was quiet as a church. When she continued, I noticed that she had been crying. "I'm not proud of what I did. I ran to the front of the shop, screaming, bumping into tables in my fright. All I could think was to get out, to call up to Colin once I was outside, get him to the window at the front. There was no fire there. It was all in the back at that time. I don't know how long I stood there, screaming and crying. I don't know when people arrived, or who put in the call about the fire. I just remember the flames and the heat and the roar. I never saw him again," she said so quietly that it might have been a confession.

Had I heard Magdalína's scream when she had passed me in the front room of her shop? Is that what had roused me, stuffed behind the barricade of chairs, and saved my life? I looked at her as one does with a hero.

"I should've tried to reach him," she continued, "but the fire had cut off the back steps, the way I'd come down to the kitchen."

"And there's no other route—"

"Except for the outside stairs."

"The ones on the opposite side?"

She nodded, twisting her fingers together. "But they're in the back. And the fire—"

I remembered that living wall of flame, said that I understood, and that no one was holding her responsible for the fire or for Colin's death. Perhaps with the opening of the kitchen door the fire had spread faster, but I wasn't going to tell Magdalína that. She was suffering enough. I left, at least understanding why we hadn't discovered her alongside Colin's body.

"DON'T SEE STARS like this in Buxton." Margo paused in our walk around the village to look at the evening sky.

The night was inky black, with a handful of stars scattered over us. To the southeast, the moon hid behind a smear of clouds so low on the horizon that the bare branches of a clump of elm seemed to hold them aloft. Beyond the lifeless church, the woods hovered like something primeval, dark and mysterious and whispering of nightmares. From the direction of the youth hostel came the scent of a wood fire. I breathed deeply, thinking of other fires I had sat around, wishing I were enjoying one now.

"If it weren't so damned cold," Margo continued, flexing her gloved fingers, "it would be beautiful."

"It's still beautiful. You just need to wrap up more."

"I just need someone to keep me warm. Which reminds me." She grabbed my arm, turning me from my contemplation of the silhouetted church tower to face her. "Are you going with Mark?"

"I'm afraid to ask," I said, studying her eyes. "Going where?"

"You know. Greece. Spain. Wherever those travel brochures were for. He had a hotel selected, didn't he?"

"Double occupancy. Don't remind me."

"You know, Bren, you're not giving Mark a chance. He's probably very insecure around women."

"He give you this script?"

"He's probably all wind and water. If you took some time, you'd probably discover he's a pretty decent chap."

I was about to make another snide retort, but suddenly remembered the original incident with Colin's dog. Mark hadn't ridiculed me then, which he would have done back in our school days. I glanced at the hotel bench, as though experiencing his concern. Had I been too harsh with him? What had he actually done to deserve my distrust? I must have taken too long to reply, for Margo said, "Give him a chance. If not Greece, at least have dinner with him. Or *him*. And I don't mean work-related. Oh, and I've the results from the dark-green car search. I'll tell you later. Night." She smiled, gave me a wink, bid Graham good evening, and walked back to the hotel.

"Have I interrupted something?" Graham said.

I listened to Margo's footsteps fade while I tried to think through my new confusion. Graham and Mark were both handsome, I thought, glancing at Graham, but I did value humor and intelligence above good looks. And that's where Graham excelled. Or did he, I wondered, Margo's voice coming back to me. Mark might have these qualities; trouble was I always brushed him away. I really didn't know him.

"Good evening for a walk." Graham's voice sounded suddenly in my ear.

I stammered that it was, and looked at the sky. The moon had emerged, its silver light gilding the adjacent clouds and masking the stars.

"I'm sorry about earlier today," Graham said suddenly. I

looked at him. His eyes were steady and examined mine, as though reading my reaction.

"That's all right, sir," I mumbled, not knowing what else to say. "It was inexcusable, my losing the notebook like that. You were right—if anyone had found it—"

"It was inexcusable to lose your book, yes, but it was *also* inexcusable for me to handle my anger like that. I apologize, TC. I know you're a competent sergeant, and this was one of those rare occurrences when you cocked up. I had a bloody nerve to come down on you like that. It won't happen again."

I wished he would stop. I wished he had never apologized. He was embarrassed by the incident today, and I was embarrassed now that he had reminded us of it. I repeated my understanding and said I forgave his outburst. Quietness settled over us. I wondered how often he apologized to subordinates. Perhaps more often than I thought. Did his ministerial bent have anything to do with it? Forgive us our trespasses. I abandoned my speculation to stare at the moon.

"I used to star gaze a lot when I was younger," Graham said finally, dropping the painful subject and looking heavenward.

"I know what you mean, sir. I had a telescope as a kid. Don't know what became of it."

"I meant three, five years ago."

"Oh." I smiled as he grinned at me.

"It seemed a natural extension of moonlit rambles with Rachel."

"Oh," I said again, less enthusiasm in my voice.

"Though getting her started was a bit like pushing a camel through the eye of a needle."

"Not the outdoor type, then?"

"We're not talking trekking or suiting up with mountaineering boots and snow gaiters. Just a walk in a meadow or down her road—as *we're* doing. A pleasurable pastime."

As much as I wanted to agree, I said, "My dad showed me a few constellations when I was around five. I still recall the thrill of picking out Cassiopeia for the first time by myself."

"You were obviously precocious. Rachel never got beyond the Great Bear."

Neither his voice nor face suggested he was joking, so I kept silent. The sounds of evening washed over us—a cat yowling, a snatch of a Beethoven recording, the bang of a dustbin lid. We walked partway down the road in silence while I thought about Rachel and what Graham had loved about her. I wondered if she was his opposite, small, dark-haired and vivacious. I wondered how they had met, if Graham had proposed during one of their starry walks. As we came to the corner, he said, "Church looks odd, dark like that."

It did. There should have been candles at the windows, throwing colors onto the snow. Glowing lanterns should have lined the path from the lych gate, etching cheer from the blackness. Most strange of all, I thought, was the silence. The doors should have been open, with "O Come, O Come Emmanuel" or some other advent carol floating into the evening. Instead, the somber bulk of the building sat as still as death on the hill.

We had always begun our neighborhood caroling with that song, and progressed more or less in seasonal order to end with "We Three Kings." As a child I had loved being included in an adult activity, the magic of the clear starry night, the tea and gingerbread afterwards in a warm home. How different St. Nicholas' was from the candlelit church of my childhood. I said as much to Graham.

"There's no reason B Division can't have a caroling group," he said, studying my face to see if I was serious. "If you're keen on it, organize one."

"And give the prisoners a concert? They'd probably have us up before the Chief Constable for cruel and unusual punishment."

"Not if you recruit your members well. Salt's got a good baritone. So has DC Fordyce. You've no reason to count yourself out, either. You said you sang in *Yeomen of the Guard*."

Ignoring Graham's counsel of Mark, I said, "Hard to find rehearsal time. We don't exactly work normal hours."

"Of course, if you're going to knock it down before you've even tried…"

"I suppose we *could* try…" I glanced at him. He was still serious. I said, "I can just imagine our performance. I'm about to hit high C when my pager beeps."

Graham laughed as though he could hear it. Or as though he had suffered an identical embarrassment.

"At least," I said, "the villagers haven't any similar problems."

"With any luck, they should be able to resume everything tomorrow. Including choir practice. I feel bad about tying up their activities."

"Which reminds me, sir. About the P.M. report on Colin… since he died of smoke inhalation, I assume you are not suggesting suspicious circumstances are tied to his death."

"Either it's true, or the murder was thought out very well."

"You're not thinking Magdalína planned the fire and Colin's death," I said, rather too sharply. Murder by stabbing, as in Joel's case, was one thing, but to die in a fire…I shuddered.

"Not really, Taylor. What was her motive in killing Colin? She wasn't in financial trouble, as far as we know, so there wasn't a reason to torch the store."

I agreed and said that made about as much sense as Owen setting the blaze to force himself out of a job. We had just turned the corner at Owen's house and were walking north again when we saw a flash of red and yellow leap into the sky. I grabbed Graham's arm, afraid I was reliving the past two nights, and yelled, "My God! It's Joel's house!"

The house was the last dwelling on the square of a dozen

other homes. Flames, already shooting into the black sky, grabbed at the bare trees and crackled as they ate the edge of the roof. Smoke poured into the air and seeped along the ground. I started running, following Graham, who was several yards ahead of me. As we got midway, he stopped abruptly and pulled me next to him.

"No! It's not Joel's. It's David Willet's house!"

I opened my mouth, wanting to scream or yell or curse, but could find nothing to express my anger and shock. Graham pulled out his mobile phone, punched in a number, and gave the dispatcher the building's exact location and what he could see. Logging off, he told me, "Stay here. I'm going to see if he's in there."

"Sir!" I screamed, my heart pounding in my ears. "Don't! Wait till help arrives! You can't risk—"

"I can't risk waiting, Taylor! You can call for help in evacuating neighboring properties." He ran toward the back of the house, where the flames had not yet reached.

I watched, fearful he wouldn't make it inside, fearful he would. If I phoned for help from our lads, it would be nearly ten minutes before they arrived. Graham needed help now. Help that was nearby. As he started kicking in the rear window, I turned away and raced down the road toward Owen's house. As I approached the corner, I saw the second fire. It was just east of Owen's; his brother Nelson's.

Pounding on Owen's door, I prayed he was home. What seemed like hours later, Owen jerked open the door, swearing that he'd kill whoever had woken him. I pulled at his robe, and motioned down the road. His tirade stopped as I screamed, "Nelson's house is on fire! Call 999. And tell them we need help at David's." I was already across the road, running to Nelson's, when I heard Owen screaming after me.

TWENTY-THREE

THE FIRE WAS confined to Nelson's tool shed, which stood thirty feet behind his house and next to his garage. Flames were well established on the near wall but had not reached the roof when I arrived. A mound of cast-off branches, dry leaves and spent flowers had been dumped against the shed's wooden door, a large rag or similar cloth burning in the center of this debris. The air, already opaque with smoke, held an odor other than burning leaves. Nelson's car, I noticed with fright, was parked within yards of the shed. If the shed fell onto it...

I grabbed the rake leaning against the shed and struck at the burning mound, separating and dragging the fire onto the snow until it was spread out several yards in diameter. I threw snow onto it before running to Nelson's back door. He answered my banging with a bit more graciousness than Owen had, then stepped outside when he saw the shed.

"Shit! What the hell—"

I told him Owen was reporting the fire, and asked him if he had a garden hose somewhere. By now the flames were licking at the shed roof.

"In there," he yelled, pointing at the shed.

"Any blankets?"

I didn't have time to pamper his confusion. I yelled, "Sheets, blankets, towels. Soak them in the bath and get them out here. We can try beating out the flames. I'm afraid for your car."

Nelson just noticed the danger. He stepped outside, as

though making certain of the distance, then dashed into the house. Seconds later, he had the car keys.

"We need to extinguish it," I said, running after him. I ducked as a tree branch fell on top of the car's bonnet. Even from several yards away, I could feel the fire's heat.

Nelson shook off my hand and yanked open the car door.

"The hell I'm gonna let this car burn. I just bought it." He was in the car before I could respond.

The engine started with impatience born of fear. Tires squealed down the driveway, leaving me with the fire. I dashed into the house and gathered every towel I could find in the kitchen. The sink was full of unwashed dishes, so I wasted several minutes piling them onto the counter. From the window above the sink I could see the shingles of the shed burst into flame with a roar. A finger of fire leapt to the weather vane atop the roof. The house's back door banged open and Nelson joined me. He snatched the towels from the counter, and stuffed them into the sink as he turned on the taps.

"There are more in the bath," he said, pushing the towels beneath the water.

I ran into the bathroom, pulled the towels from the racks, and threw them into the bath. I opened the taps full force, wishing they had the intensity of Niagara. As the water roared onto them, I yanked open the cupboard doors. I grabbed the wicker linen bin, dumped the dirty clothes onto the floor, and ran over to the bath. The wet towels seemed to weigh a ton as I drew them from the water, but I dropped them—heedless of the dripping water—into the linen bin and plunged the towels from the cupboard into the water. I grabbed the bin, banging my shins against it as I ran through the house, water marking my trail over wool carpets and linoleum. When I got outside, Owen was there, now dressed and hooking up a neighbor's garden hose to the outside tap. Nelson was slapping a wet towel at the flames eating the garage. Neighbors from several houses were squirting water onto the fire, their garden hoses looking ludicrously small against the growing volume of flame.

I lost count of the trips I made into the kitchen to wet towels, and the number of towels neighbors supplied. I do remember the cold from my waterlogged shoes, gloves and slacks, and the rawness of my throat from breathing in smoke. I also remember the dry leaves on the oak flaring as they caught fire over our heads, sailing into the dark heavens as wisps of embers or swirling to earth as charred skeletons. A falling bough had grazed Nelson's arm, and he had burnt his hand beating out the embers that had landed on his shirtsleeve. When I thought I couldn't fling another wet towel, the fire service announced its arrival in a blare of siren and light. The fire died fifteen minutes later.

In the silent aftermath, when neighbors had drifted back to their homes and Owen sat on the back steps to get his breath, I looked at the destruction. The shed was minus its roof and one wall. Charred lumber sizzled and popped, releasing tiny streams of smoke. Where the walls had not been eaten by flame, the paint was cracked and blistered like a giant patch of injured skin. I pulled off a fragment of paint and crushed it between my fingers, letting the powdery residue fall onto the ashes at my feet. Puddles of water glistened under the glare of the fire engine's lights. I blew on my nearly-frozen hands, peeled myself away from Nelson's thanks, and walked back to David's house.

THE HOUSE, bathed in the lamps from two fire engines and the portable lighting units, was still burning, though it seemed to be under control. Two large trees near the house were ablaze, looking like strange torches set into the frozen ground. Murky smoke gushed into the dark sky, obliterating the moon. The stench of wet cinders sailed downwind and mixed with the fragrance of pine. I rubbed my nose.

Graham, I was thankful to see, was on the pavement in front, holding back a struggling David Willett. I ran up to them, surprised I had any reserve of energy. Graham didn't notice my arrival.

"For God's sake, let me go!" David yelled above the roar of the generators, trying to pry off Graham's grip. His eyes were reddened and moist from crying.

Graham turned the man toward him. His face was as hardened as I'd ever seen it—his usually bright, green eyes dark with anger, his jaw muscle strained. His hair was grey with ash. Shaking David, Graham snapped, "You want me to handcuff you to this fence?"

"I've got to get in there," David wailed, as though Graham's threat held no significance. "I've—you don't understand. The party. My *books!* All my copies are in there! God, they're all I have! Let me go, damn you!" He swung at Graham's jaw, his fist making contact for I saw Graham wince.

I stepped up to them, as though I could help where Graham, taller and stronger, couldn't. He saw me, shook his head, and slapped David's cheek.

David stammered something, his eyes round with surprise, then looked at Graham. His arms went limp and he bowed his head onto Graham's chest and sobbed.

I walked over to Margo, who was standing on the path by the front gate. Mark, several yards away, was setting up the barricade. Margo nodded toward Graham. "Got his arms full."

Not knowing if she meant it literally or not, I merely nodded.

We watched the fire for several moments before Margo said, "Tough. For David, I mean. His house, his books…"

"Where was David? Did Graham drag him out, or—"

"Drove up a minute or two before you got here. He saw what was happening and tried to get inside. Can't blame him. His books—"

"Nelson Parnell also suffered a fire at his place."

Margo looked at me in horror, as though wondering what would be next. "Is he—"

"Except for a burned hand, he's okay," I said. "But his tool shed's shot. Part of his garage. Car would've been, too, but we got to it quick enough."

"What's going on here, Bren?" Margo turned toward me, her back to the house. She became a black silhouette against a red and yellow background. I strained to see her darkened face, my eyes hurting from too much smoke and soot and bright light. Her voice dropped to a faintness I barely caught, and there was a hint of fear that belied her tough cop exterior. "Why all these fires, Bren? Why two tonight? Who's doing all this—and why?"

No answer presented itself; no flash of insight sparked the confusion in my mind. I shook my head, feeling the losses.

Mark joined us, brushing the ash from his jacket. "Just about finished, I'd say. Hell, what a mess!"

The firemen were beginning to disconnect their hoses from the hydrants. The ambulance attendants were packing up the resuscitator and the medical supplies. Ladders and generators were being put away. The crowd hovering on the scene's perimeter was breaking up.

"Much damage?" I finally asked in the silence, still looking at the house.

"Who knows? Looks like it, doesn't it?"

I nodded. The house seemed a shell, for I could see the beam from an electric torch moving somewhere behind the front walls. The roof was jagged from fire and axe holes. The shrubbery around the house's foundation was trampled flat or torn up. It looked like a movie set. And morning would reveal worse realities. I turned away.

"You all right?" Mark stepped over to me, his hand resting lightly on my shoulder.

"Just feeling light-headed."

Margo said, "I should think so, Bren. You know she was at the Parnell fire, Mark?"

"No," he said, "but I could've guessed it. And probably fought it single-handedly." He grabbed my hands, turning them so he could see the palms. He ran a fingertip over a burn and I grimaced. "Burned, too. Hell, Brenna, I told you about Wonder Woman. When are you gonna—"

"I couldn't stand and watch Nelson's house burn!" I yelled, pulling my hands away and shoving them into my slacks pockets.

"You could've phoned for help."

"There *was* help. Plenty of help."

"Only not fast enough."

"So I'm supposed to chat with Parnell about football, talk about his recent holiday, ask him about his plans for Christmas while we wait for the fire engines—"

"You're being purposely obtuse, Brenna. You know that's not what I meant."

"You said I should wait for help."

"You could've been injured—or killed, damn it! I only meant that you should—"

"I've got better things to do, Mark, than stand here and argue."

"Go on, then," he said, his voice hissing from anger and frustration. "Bury yourself in your job. Hide behind your badge and your damned duty. Throw away your friends' concern."

"When have you ever been concerned about me, except getting me to sleep with you?"

"You've a conveniently short memory when it suits you," he snorted, looking down at me. "You don't choose to remember the dog incident, I take it."

I opened my mouth to retort, then closed it. He *had* been concerned, I admitted to myself. He had been as angry then about me risking my life as he was now. Mistaking my silence for uncertainty or vanity, he said, "Just remember that if you go on like this, pushing us all away, you'll die a lonely, unloved old maid." He turned as if to leave, then suddenly added, "Pardon me. I'm wrong. Your funeral *will* be crowded, with dog owners and the Super."

Again I tried to speak, but he ignored me, rushing on. "And the only reason the Super will be there is because he'll want to see what an ass looks like so he won't hire another one!" He strode off, making an impolite gesture above his head, kicking snow into the street.

Margo laid her arms around my shoulders and hugged me. "Bren, don't pay him any mind. He's just letting off steam. Upset about the fire, I should think. But God, I've never seen him so mad."

I watched him until he turned the corner by Joel's house and disappeared into the night.

Margo said, "I wonder if he's going to get drunk or something."

"Wouldn't put it past him."

"You think he'll be ok?"

"He's a big boy, Margo. It's his choice how he handles his anger." I hesitated, suddenly reminded of Graham's apology. But I doubted if Mark would offer one. It wasn't his style.

"I know," Margo said, "but God, Bren, he was angry."

I started in the direction Mark had gone.

Margo said, "You going after him?"

"He's needs to cool down. He won't hear anything I have to say. Besides, I don't jump up at his whistle."

"Then where—"

Graham was guiding David to the passenger seat of his car, showing the concern I'd been accused of. Had I overdone it? I didn't think so. Graham took David's keys and slid into the driver's seat. As he drove off, Margo repeated her question.

"I don't know, Margo. Anywhere. Nowhere. To think about gain and loss and profit."

MARK WAS NOT in the hotel pub, nor in the Four Marys. I had just seated myself at a table in the Snowy Cygnet when Graham walked in, evidently looking for me. Finding me at a corner table, he nodded, quickly bought a beer, came over, and asked if he could join me.

I pushed the bowl of peanuts toward him as he took a seat.

"Is it only midnight?" he said, glancing at the clock above the bar.

"Time flies when you're having fun," I said, looking around the room. Tubular, chrome chairs and tables gave the ancient interior a contemporary look. Mutton dressed as lamb. Track lighting above the ebony fireplace highlighted drawings and photos of swans dotting the white-washed walls. Normally I would have commented on the photo of a lone, black swan, but I didn't feel like joking. I took a deep drink of beer, ignoring Graham.

As he maneuvered his chair to get comfortable, I said, "You don't have to sit with me." There was one other couple in the room, the rest of Bramwell's residents either too traumatized by the fires to come out or standing watch at their own houses. "There's no lack of seating. By the fireplace, for instance. Maybe we should be there. Dry your wet clothes, thaw out the ice in my veins."

"I've had enough of fires for one night, I think. You all right?" He angled his head, as an animal will do when listening intently, and searched my eyes.

I stared at the table, my fingers tracing the dimples in the beer mug. "Why shouldn't I be? I've a home, a job I pour myself into, a pen pal in America…what else could an old maid want?"

"Taylor?"

"Sorry, sir. I forgot the goldfish, Hercules. Mustn't forget Hercules. He's part of the family. He adores me. Well, maybe it's a she. You know anything about goldfish, sir? Probably *is* a she. That would explain the adoration. Nothing male would dare come near me."

"TC—"

I cut him off—afraid he was going to get personal. If he did, I knew I'd start crying. "Pen pal's a smashing thing to have, sir. Especially on long, winter evenings. You can re-read his letters, imagine how he looks, what you'd do if you meet." Graham leaned forward, his hand reaching for mine. I hurried on. "But you wanna know the best part of it, sir? I'll tell you. Best part of having a pen pal is that you can lie and not be afraid he'll read it in your face. Yes, sir," I said as Graham laid his hand on mine. I tried to withdraw it, but his fingers closed around mine with a quick intensity. Trying to ignore it, I said, "Smashing, great lies. How old you are, how smart you are, your education, your people, your dreams, your funeral plans—"

"Brenna—"

"How much you weigh."

He nestled my hand in both of his, squeezing it so I could feel his warmth invade my cold skin. I pulled my hands free and stood up, knocking my mug and splashing beer onto the table. "But don't forget to talk about intimate things. That's what really binds a friendship. Girl talk over tea. Shared jokes with the lads in the back room."

Graham stood up, his eyebrows lowered. As he took a step toward me, I said, "Lies about your sex life. Don't forget that. And if you don't have one, get the details from a girlfriend. He'll never know." I ran out of the pub, half hearing Graham calling my name.

TWENTY-FOUR

I HAD AVOIDED Graham at breakfast the next morning, not brave enough to withstand Twenty Questions, should he instigate it. Several of our team were picking at their food, appetites suffering from nerves or lack of sleep. Mark was not in the hotel dining room, so the day was beginning well. I choked down toast and hot tea before reporting to the incident room. Graham was downing a mug of coffee. I drew a deep breath, crossed my fingers, and walked up to him. He said nothing as I quietly sat opposite him. Shoving the thermos jug at me, he tactfully avoided asking if I was feeling better. But he did glance at me a bit more intensely and frequently than usual.

"So," he said, setting down his mug, "give me your views on Nelson's fire."

I stared at him, surprised he was starting with so inconsequential an event. Not prepared to talk about it, I mumbled that it was obviously set after David's fire because Nelson's had just started when I saw it.

"I agree," Graham said, "and I wonder if you might have thwarted a possible third fire last night."

"Sir?"

"Being so quick on the scene, TC, you might have scared off our arsonist. He might have been hiding there, afraid to try for another one."

"Hadn't thought of that, sir."

"Another thing about that fire. Have you thought why

Nelson's fire was not set at his house proper? The other three fires were at buildings that meant a lot to the people involved—Hannah's and Magdalína's businesses, David's house…why Nelson's shed? Why not his house?"

"Could he have something in his shed that the arsonist wanted to destroy?"

"Like Joel's burglary loot?"

I shook my head. "Can't see it, sir. Why not steal it and move it on? If you've got a load of church silver or tellies or such, why burn it? Why not take it yourself?"

"Could our arsonist have been afraid of discovery? He's surrounded by the watchful eyes of the neighbors. It's more risky to burgle a shed with God knows how many boxes of stuff than to run through a darkened store."

"So you think Nelson's part of a burglary ring and his partner is getting cold feet or revenge? You recalling Trueman's titbit about Joel nearly catching one criminal?"

"I'm just fantasizing, TC. I don't know anything. But I do agree we need to question Mr. Nelson Parnell. It'll be interesting to see what the Scientific Officers find among the ruins this morning."

"I hope David can retrieve some of his books. That's a doubly hard loss—your household possessions *and* your first-published book. Where was he last night—did he say?"

"You thinking he's our arsonist?"

"Could be. Could've set the fires, then arrived home when we were there. Establishes witnesses to his innocent return."

"You saw him last night, TC. You think he was faking his grief?"

I admitted he would be a very good actor to do that.

"And being at the scene has nothing to do with guilt or innocence. If you think that about David, you'll have to think that about Nelson and Hannah and Magdalína. All three were at their fires, too." He took a sip of coffee, letting the scenarios play in his mind. The room was quiet this morning, with most of the murder team interviewing people about the fires or just plain late due to last night. Graham tilted the chair back, his legs stretched out on a neighboring chair, and wrapped both hands around the mug.

"But why these fires, sir?"

"You mean, who's benefiting from them?"

I nodded, suddenly recalling that's what I had intended to mull over after Mark's verbal beating last night. Instead, I had made a fool of myself with Graham.

"Let's look at it, then." The chair thudded forward and he put down the mug. Grabbing for his pen and notebook, he asked for my ideas.

"Well, sir, if we eliminate Nelson, it seems to center around books."

"Go on."

I hesitated, hardly knowing where I was going with my theory. "David's about to grab the limelight with his new book. Hannah's bookshop stocks it. Magdalína was going to host the publishing party in her tearoom. David's house was nearly destroyed—perhaps to get rid of his copies of the book, but I believe it was more personal than that. It was an emotional statement from the arsonist, telling David what he thought of him."

"Makes perfect sense, TC. And who would do this?"

"Nelson Parnell."

Graham took a sip of coffee. In the quiet I could hear the bells from St. Nicholas' chiming. An ordinary Sunday sound, designed to call the villager to worship and set minds on heavenly things. There was nothing heavenly about arson. I waited for Graham's response, my heart racing.

"Because he, too, wrote a similar book?" Graham jotted something in his notebook.

"Yes, sir. I know it sounds rather far-fetched—"

"Not at all. Jealousy or revenge pushes people to act strongly sometimes. More so if you've lost a competition, which may be how Nelson viewed this book thing. So how do you explain his fire, then, if this centers around David's publication?"

"Red herring. That's why the fire was confined to his shed. He didn't want to damage his house. And a fire made him one of the group. He could whine that he was being persecuted, too. Throw us off guard so we'd focus on someone else as the perpetrator."

Graham looked at me and nodded. "I do believe you have the making of a detective, TC. 'Course, it's up to the Scientific Officers to find the evidence—"

"There was a rag in the middle of the leaf pile. And the distinct odor of petrol. I know that's not proof—"

"Gives them something to start with, at any rate."

"Seems odd that Nelson didn't smell or notice it. He was at home and came to the door readily enough."

"Maybe he was in the front room," Graham suggested.

"Maybe…but I *do* know he was at a car dealer in Chester-field Saturday. Traded in his dark green four-door for a new white job. In the excitement of battling his fire, he told me he just got the car."

"I hate to rely on coincidence again, but it does sound suggestive. Interesting, too. But other than asking him politely to pay for repair to my car, we can't prove he tried to eliminate me on Her Majesty's highway."

"No, but I thought it fascinating. And, I'd bet my bank balance that—"

"Speaking of which," Graham said, handing me a folded paper. "Cast your critical eyes on this."

"What is it?"

"Colin Hale's bank draft. Notice anything?"

It took me a minute to decipher the statement, but when I

did I looked at Graham. He was smiling at my expression. "Yes, sir. A large deposit nine years ago. But why? What's the significance? Owen invented the biscuits."

"Maybe this will help. Mark found it last evening behind Colin's desk."

He handed me a slip of paper sealed in a plastic evidence bag. I angled it under the light. It was a bill of sale for Flying Saucers, dated the day of Colin's large bank deposit. It was also signed over to Colin by Ellery Hale.

I grabbed the bank statements for Owen, Colin and Joel. The same amount of money snaked through each statement: first Ellery sells to Colin, then, years later, Colin sells to Owen. That was the last date of transaction for that amount of money. I seized the bill of sale again. Its date coincided with the sum Colin paid Ellery.

"*Ellery* Hale?" I said, confused at the apparent newcomer. "Who's he?"

In answer, Graham handed me a birth certificate. "Retrieved from Joel's safe deposit box."

"*Joel's?*" I said, reading 'Ellery Austin Hale.' "Is he—"

"Same person."

"What's he got to do with Owen's recipe?"

"Remember the family photo album, TC?"

"Yes, sir. The faces of a small boy were scratched out." Supposition, like a winter sunrise, was slow in coming. I said, "Oh. Joel creates the recipe, sells it to Colin, who lives off the profits quite nicely and dazzles Sylvia with his creative genius. Then, years later, Colin sells it to Owen, who in turn benefits from the recipe."

"Almost as good as passing oil property through the family ranks."

"I agree. The recipe seems to have been valuable, switching owners three times and spreading wealth to all. But why the name switch to 'Ellery'? Why the secrecy? Was he a half brother?"

"Colin and Sylvia moved to this village ten years ago. Joel—Ellery, if you want to call him that—arrived one year later, the date on the sales receipt. It seems to make sense if we consider Joel's personality—light hearted, jovial, as though he had no cares, I believe Eden or someone said."

"He would be, with all that money Colin paid him," I agreed.

"Colin's murder would make sense if *Colin* stole the recipe from Joel—the scratched-out faces would support that Colin died first. Joel would be mad enough to kill anyone who benefited from his famous recipe as much as The Pineapple Slice does."

"But why would *Colin* wait all these years to kill *Joel,* if it's for revenge?"

"Colin has an alibi for Joel's death," Graham reminded me. "And anyway, we just said that Joel *sold* Colin the recipe, so theft and revenge don't come into it." Graham tossed the receipt onto the table and muttered, "So who *does* come into it?"

I opened the photo album again, stared at the faces and tried to imagine the hatred behind the obliteration. If this was Joel's album, and his face was untouched—as evidenced by 'Me' written beneath each pristine shot—why were Colin's ruined? And why had *Joel* been murdered? "Do you think it's some other motive than the recipe?" I said.

"Like what?"

Graham had listened, eyes closed and statue-like, while I told him of the Hales' vandalism problem. Now that I had finished, he stared at the note pad on the table and sketched a caricature of Colin. As he drew the last line, he said, "Could Paula have scratched out Colin's faces in the photos?"

I nodded, scarcely able to voice my opinion now that the theory had been spoken. "I don't suppose 'Ellery' could be a son of Colin's or Joel's…"

"According to the birth certificate, date doesn't fit, TC. Has to be Joel. Why? You keen on illicit affairs?"

"Of course not. I wish the whole world were happily married." Then, thinking he might misunderstand my comment in light of my chatter last evening, I said, "But it might explain the obliterated faces of the photos."

"Bastard son discovers his true parentage, seeks revenge…" Graham smiled much as he always did when listening to my babble. "Sounds rather like a book."

I admitted it did, now that I had expressed my thoughts. "If Paula *did* disfigure Colin's photographs—and she seems to have that sort of personality—she'd have the opportunity while she was tutored at Joel's."

"While Joel was out of the room, yes…but I can't see her snooping about the place, hunting for something on which she could take out her anger at Colin."

"He might have had the album out one evening. It's very likely, sir. You don't put up all your personal possessions simply because someone's coming over."

"Sounds reasonable," Graham said, tapping the notebook with his pen. "I wish we had some of those Flying Saucers. I'd work better for a few with my coffee."

"Isn't it odd, sir, that Colin has the recipe? Why does he have it if *Owen* eventually bought it from Colin? And we know he did—the dates of sale and the bank accounts tell us that."

"Can't say, Taylor," Graham said, throwing the pen onto the tabletop. "Maybe he kept a copy of the recipe when he sold it to Owen, remind him of the good old days or to have something to brag about to Ward. But let's leave the biscuits and worry about who killed Joel."

"And the recipe has no bearing on the murder," I said, "or Joel—or Colin—would've been murdered years ago, when it was sold."

"So what's the motive for Joel's death?"

We sat for some time, reading over statements, exchanging

theories. We had dismissed Hannah's role as murderer, jealous over Joel's time with Paula, and I was about to get a cup of tea when I read the last part of one of Sylvia's earlier remarks. I re-read it, aloud this time, trying to make sense of it in light of our case. "Colin and I aren't exactly co-warming our marriage bed. He's in the process of moving out. Taking up residence in the hotel. That's the usual thing after the papers are served."

Graham looked up, surprised. I ignored him and scanned my notes before finding the next part I wanted. Again I read it aloud. "...I still abhor lies and deceit..." My hand lay over the words, as though they were Braille and I could feel their impact. When I finally looked at Graham I saw the darkness of his eyes, the firm line of his mouth. He pulled the notebook from beneath my hand and read it before saying, "I'd forgotten about the impending divorce. Hell. It was staring us in the face for days and I forgot." He tossed the notebook onto the table and said, "Perhaps it is motive, but we've still no proof. We need it neatly boxed and tied up in tinsel before we can present all this to Simcock."

"Boxed?" I swallowed, suddenly afraid of my suspicions. "There were boxes at Sylvia's. In the kitchen."

"I have boxes in my kitchen, Taylor. Frozen food, containers from deliveries. But that's not what you're referring to, I can tell. What kind?"

"I had assumed they were mourning clothes. She's that sort of person. Fashionable, does everything according to societal rules, proper. But there were too many boxes. Yes, sir," I said in answer to Graham's raised eyebrow. "For all her wealth, they're from a fashionable Buxton store, quite up-market. And no matter how much Sylvia follows fashion or propriety, she wouldn't spend the kind of money implied by the cost and quality of the box labels on throwaways."

"Sorry, TC. I don't quite follow this. What's the matter with buying one or two black dresses?"

"She wouldn't spend that kind of money on one or two black dresses because she wouldn't wear mourning clothes that extensively, sir. We're not living in Victorian England when they dressed for a year of mourning. There were other types of clothing in those boxes."

"So she had just bought some winter clothes. Can't take her into custody on suspicion for that."

"But coupled with other damning bits…" I sat back, my mind racing over the events of the past few days. "Sylvia had ordered a cake before Joel's death, but didn't need it now. As if her plans had abruptly changed. And this was *before* it was common knowledge that Joel was the body." Suddenly afraid of my own inference, I looked at him. He was frowning, as though he pictured the entire plot.

"And there are the flour sacks, sir."

"What about them?"

"They were behind the store, piled up for the dustbin collection. I saw them when I was looking for David Willett."

Graham picked up on the significance and shuffled through our case documents, found the photos of Joel's body, and gazed at the sack covering his head and shoulders. "A flour sack. We knew that Thursday, of course."

Again I sorted through the case papers and pulled the sought-after one from the stack. "Long blonde and reddish-brown hairs were found on the sack, if you remember, sir. Magdalína has the reddish-brown."

"So we'd expect to find hers on the sacks."

"Owen is bald."

"Which eliminates his contribution. And the blonde?"

"Sylvia Hale is the only long-haired blonde I know of who's connected with this case. And she has a copy of the St. Nicholas book, so she knows about St. Nick's helper."

"Assuming she read that chapter."

"Assuming. Yes, sir."

"And you're also assuming that's when her hair got on the flour sack. When she picked up the sack to stuff over Joel's head." He rubbed his chin as he thought. Slamming his hand down on the paper work, he said, "It makes sense. But we're back to motive again, Taylor. Why would she murder Joel Twiss?"

Trueman's words suddenly whispered in my brain, so loudly that I thought perhaps the man was standing behind me. I repeated them to Graham. "Trueman said Joel would've been a great actor. Is that how he kept Sylvia and Hannah from knowing about each other, stringing each woman along in regards to a supposed marriage?"

"You're thinking of the wedding rings. The one did fit Joel's finger, we knew that. But the woman's—"

"There's another reason to believe Sylvia killed Joel. She had reserved the next fortnight in her diary. I saw it on the desk yesterday. She mentioned she and Colin were about to divorce, yet she is about to leave on a two-week holiday. The diary suggests it; the buying spree for a new wardrobe suggests it." I paused, forcing a swallow. Scott Coral had discovered Sylvia's wedding dress, yet hadn't known the significance of it. I shook away the visions of the torn dress and said, "Her own words about hating lies and deceit suggest it. Even the cake suggests it. Plus, I'll give my monthly wage if that bakery box I saw in her kitchen yesterday didn't hold that cake. I shoved it aside. It was heavy."

"Damn it, Taylor, a woman can buy a cake without being guilty of murdering her husband. But I agree. In combination with everything else… What about her alibi? You confirmed her call with her London friend, didn't you? What's that do to your theory?"

"Only Colin and Francis have substantiated alibis, sir. They were at a dinner and seen by dozens of people. They stayed for the entire event, which broke up at nine-thirty. And though

Sylvia's call was logged with B.T., she could have left the phone off the hook, gone to the church to kill Joel—"

"Convenient she has a record of her call to establish her alibi, yes." He picked up the phone, punched in the number, and told the hapless person who answered to rush a DNA test on the blonde hair. Hanging up, he said, "We can at least check it out. Can you get a sample from her so we've got a comparison?"

"Short of stealing her dirty dishes, you mean?"

"She has to *give* it to you, Taylor. You know that. I don't want any slip-ups now that we're this close to an arrest. But Hannah Leftridge had those same weeks saved for her holiday, and you're not inferring anything from that."

"I think that's the pivotal point of the case, sir. Trueman, as I pointed out, said Joel was a great actor. Fine. What if he had changed his mind, for whatever reason, mid stream, and decided to dump Sylvia as prospective bride? What if he was really going to marry Hannah?"

"But Sylvia couldn't marry Joel. She's still wed to Colin, no matter if he was just moving out of their home."

He had crushed my theory—not from spite or ridicule, but through introducing logic. I tossed these suggestions over in my mind and took a long drink of tea. Graham continued his speculation.

"Maybe she and Joel had planned to wait out the divorce in Spain. We don't know their schedule. The wedding didn't have to take place the first day of their sojourn. They wouldn't be the first couple to room together without the benefit of clergy. They could've even planned to slide the rings on their fingers for appearance in the hotel. Then got married later, after their two-week honeymoon. We don't know when the wedding was planned, either."

I nodded, the scenario whirling in my head. It made sense. I had just assumed the wedding was happening right away, with the romantic bit at the end. But it could've been planned as Graham had said. Nothing barred a fortnight's romantic trip with the wedding after the divorce. "We're forgetting that Hannah Leftridge is a strong woman. Not muscular, but emotionally." I repeated Francis Rice's statement.

"So," Graham said, "if Hannah didn't go to our doctor for anything pharmaceutical to help her through her husband's, niece's and parents' deaths—"

"—and she needs something after learning Joel is the victim."

"—not a relative, just a small incident compared to her family tragedies—"

"Grief over the death of a fiancé?" I suggested.

"Bereavement over a future she can never have, too. Another blow that she might have trouble dealing with. After all, familial love is different from affianced love."

"And when Sylvia discovered Joel had changed his mind and was going to marry Hannah, she plotted her revenge. She was furious, if the torn dress means anything."

"Are you sure it's hers? Is it the same size?"

"I'll run a check on it through the dress shop. Surely they'll have a record of the purchase."

"That'd help immensely," Graham said. "A lot easier than getting every woman in Derbyshire to try the damned thing on. Half will be too busy and the other half will think the request suspicious."

"Somehow," I said slowly, thinking my way through Sylvia's action, "she got him to meet her in the church, and killed him."

"He would've gone," Graham said. "He had no reason to suspect murder."

I told him about Sylvia's bruises. "They couldn't be self inflicted, sir. I thought at first they might have been, to throw us off the scent, for whatever reason. She even hinted Colin had done it, but his personality doesn't suggest violence. I matched my right hand to the contusions—they're yellow, suggesting they're a few days old. The time frame fits in if she had a struggle with Joel Wednesday evening. It was a right hand that grabbed her right arm."

"Grabbed as he tried to defend himself. But wouldn't Joel— and I don't mean this in a sexist way, Taylor—but wouldn't Joel, as a man *or* as a former cop, be able to disarm Sylvia?"

"I thought about that too, sir," I said slowly, remembering a phrase of Sylvia's. "But she knows self-defense. Yes, sir. Took lessons. Wouldn't that be enough to overpower Joel—especially if he wasn't expecting an attack?"

"I would think it very likely, Taylor. Who are you phoning?"

As I punched in the phone number on the mobile, I said, "PC Scott Coral. I'd like to take a little trip with him. And afterwards, perhaps Sylvia and Hannah wouldn't mind dropping over."

TWENTY-FIVE

SCOTT DIDN'T SAY MUCH as we drove to the stone bridge. His eyes were serious and focused on the winding road; his hands gripped the steering wheel with unusual strength, his wedding ring tapping impatiently against the molded plastic. From his bloodless lips, I assumed he was silently chastising himself for not bagging the torn dress when he had first seen it. But how could he have known it might be a clue in a murder investigation? Now I just prayed it would still be there.

The weather, at least, was on our side, for sunlight flooded the moor, highlighting bits of dried grass and black stone fences that coursed the land like the dark bands surrounding each magpie's wing feather. The land rose and fell in dozens of earthly billows until the swells melted into the hills and gorges that comprise the Peak. Beneath the snow the terrain was dull and brown from winter's harshness, yet it would bloom into a spectrum of greens under spring sunlight and warm air. Kestrels, wheatears, and short-eared owls would flood the land with song, while harebell, heath and cotton-grass would splash the foliage with color. The change always amazed me.

I'd been watching a golden plover flying overhead, its white underparts nearly as indistinguishable as Scott's police vehicle had been against the snow, the golden flecking of the bird's head, throat and breast pronounced in the sun. It was a common sight on moorlands, but even so, I listened for its mournful whistle, as though seeking a companion in our commiseration.

"Now I know I was right about letting you have that cat," Scott said.

I must have looked bewildered, for he said, "Calhoun. Your asbestos kitten. You really are an animal lover, aren't you?"

I shifted my gaze from the bird to Scott. His eyes examined my face, reading me as expertly as if I were an opponent in a poker game. "Yes," I said, smiling, shy now that he was talking on a personal level. "How's Calhoun doing? I rang up the vet yesterday, but haven't had a chance today. Have you heard anything?"

"Star patient. Besides healing nicely, he's eating everything put before him. Won't be long until you've got someone sharing your bed."

I colored at this verbal blunder and looked out the window. The bird had disappeared. Silence hung between us like a thick blanket. Over the hum of tires on the road, Scott coughed and tried to ease the awkwardness by whistling.

"Just up this hill, now, if I remember right," he said moments later.

Wavy hair-grass and deer grass, massed in thick clumps, nearly obliterated the approach to the bridge, and I wondered how Scott could be so emphatic about the spot. Then, a standing stone—massive, two-man tall, bleached white by centuries of weather—jumped into view as we crested the hill. It held the skyline as well as my imagination, for it was the only erect stone in this Bronze Age stone circle. Its companions lay scattered in a rough circle where they had fallen. Moss had decorated the standing stone's northern side, but the remaining faces remained free. It was a better landmark than an easily-missed road sign.

Scott slowed the car to make the turn and nodded. "Right. This is it. Just the other side of this hump-back bridge. God, I hope it's still there."

I mumbled my agreement and grabbed onto the arm rest as Scott steered into the skid, braking the car a yard from the edge of the river. He probably experienced the same sensation snow-boarding, but I preferred a slower approach. I must have looked shaken, for he grinned, slapped my hand, and unbuckled his seat belt. "You should've been with me on the other side of Piebald Tor. Guaranteed to turn your curly locks white."

"I like them the way they are, thank you," I said, extricating myself from the belt.

"So do I, for that matter. Good color for a copper. You on for this, then?"

"As much as I would love to sit here and chat?"

"Right. Let's try not to let the side down."

He was out of the car before I could reply, eager and already concentrating with the same intensity he displayed for sports or his job. Stepping slowly and cautiously around the sodden bare earth, avoiding patches of ice, he searched for any bits that could be evidence. He was as cautious as a cat, as thorough and patient as any detective, careful not to leave footprints if he could avoid it, looking before he stepped. He might be a PC, but he had an instinct for this type of work.

I caught him up at the river and watched as he loosened his tie before stooping over the garment. The skirt of a cream-colored silk dress trailed down the gentle embankment, the hem submerged in the icy water. The upper half of the dress was, presumably, buried in the snow. A section of black tissue paper, sodden and leaching its dye into the snow, lay plastered to the iced mound, marking the bulk of the dress as clearly as an X on a pirate map.

"You bring an evidence bag?"

I must have interrupted some deep, self monologue, for his green eyes—usually so alive with his thoughts and emotions—stared blankly at me.

"Evidence bag," I repeated, nodding toward the dress. "I know you're the outdoors type, Scott, and can live on sea urchins and lichen while sleeping on a bed of thistles, but even you don't want that soggy mess in the boot of your car. You have a bag?"

"Oh, ye of little faith." He pulled one from his jacket pocket and cocked an eyebrow at me. "Besides, what would the Vic say when I bring it in covered with fish and chips grease?"

"After or before you start your new career?"

Scott laughed, but it was forced. Graham would indeed have Scott on discipline. And he wouldn't get off as easily as Margo and I had, with only a reprimand. I met Scott's gaze, which, though steady, seemed suddenly lifeless. 'Discreditable conduct,' perhaps, or 'neglect of duty.' The charge really didn't matter; punishment would vary according to the severity of the offense and would most likely be reduction in pay or rank, or an outright fine. I had seen punishments lead to further problems, such as drunkenness, which created another round of castigation. And Scott, for all his high ideals of duty and love of job, would feel betrayed. As though all his years of selfless giving hadn't meant a thing. And he would try to soften that betrayal in liquor.

But all this was a mind game, for Scott had the polythene bag, which he prepared now by writing in the required data. "You know," he said, pausing to look at me. "This dress isn't the only crazy thing attached to your case."

Ordinarily I would've made some snide comment such as "Oh, such as me?" but Scott looked so serious that I knew jokes weren't appropriate. I nudged him.

"The night of that last fire. The tea room. I know you weren't exactly looking for me, but I was there doing the proverbial street cop stuff of blocking the road, keeping at bay our curious citizenry."

"Don't belittle your help, Scott. It's as essential as the fire fighter's."

"Actually, I'm surprised I even came up with this," he said, snorting either in disbelief or in self-mockery, "but in all that confusion I recognized someone, and it took me a hell of a long time to figure out who he was and where I'd seen him before."

"You don't mean you know who killed—"

He smiled at my astonishment. "Nothing so dramatic. No. The simple act of seeing someone in a different setting from where you normally associate him. That's all I meant. That's why it took me so long to place him. David Willett. I saw him in the throng after it dispersed from helping at the shop."

"And why was he out of place? Where had you seen him before?"

"London. We were at the same club table playing poker. Didn't know he had influential connections. Or that kind of lolly."

"Didn't know you did, either," I said. I knew Scott played poker, but I didn't know he had so much money—or expertise in the game that he could wager in the four digits.

"Anyway, that's it, for what it's worth. One of the curiosities of the job. Probably would never have picked him out, except that I sat across from him for five or six hours. Funny running into him here."

"Don't know why we never expect to see people elsewhere. We're a very mobile society."

"But Bramwell is a small place."

He nodded, then returned to complete the bag information. As he was about to break into the snow to retrieve the dress, he winked at me. "Allow to dry naturally," he said, quoting the manual on preservation of evidence. "It'd take about a week, I'd say, for this lot. What do you think?"

"I think," I said, looking nervously over my shoulder toward the car, "a Scientific Officer should be doing this. Why didn't we pick up someone?"

"I repeat: Oh, ye of little faith. What's with you all of a sudden? You don't believe that part about the fish and chips—"

"Come off it, Scott. Of course I don't. I'm just—" I gestured toward the dress. "It's a bit overwhelming, that's all. A lot depends on this. If it *is* Sylvia Hale's, well…"

He stood up and came over to me, putting his arm around my shoulders and giving me a quick hug. "Sorry, Bren. Unprofessional, I know. The hug *and* the procedure. But Graham's not the stickler for strict conduct that Simcock is. Besides, we don't know if it does pertain to your case yet, do we? Could be a bit of litter that your conscientious street cop is now clearing away. Beautify Britain."

I nodded and smiled weakly. "We've paper back at the incident room," I said, remembering procedure dictated the natural drying of wet clothing on clean, paper-lined surfaces before packaging it in paper sacks for its transport to the lab.

"Right." Scott squeezed my arm.

"Call it residue from watching Scientific Officers work," I said, pulling a pair of latex gloves from my shoulder bag and handing them to him.

"Or imagining what Graham will say. Ta." He put them on and returned to the dress. It emerged slowly from its snowy mound—right shoulder and sleeve, back, left shoulder and sleeve—the icy surface cracking and splintering as it fell away from the garment. As the waistline came free, Scott stood up, pulling the dress up with him. He held it above the river, letting the excess water drain back into the stream. "Shouldn't think there's anything damning, such as blood," he said, noting my concern.

"Might be hair or body fluids."

"Didn't know this was a case of rape."

"Nor is it," I said, jamming my hands into my pockets and watching the drainage slow to drips. "But there could be—"

"Look. I grant you there *could* be all sorts of residue—hair, saliva, urine, grass, cosmetics. But I can't bag the whole bloody area nor screen the ruddy Derwent Reservoir or the North Sea. This damned frock's been out here at least four days that I know of. You don't think the river, wind and snow have washed away a good bit already? Anything on the skirt, like hair and grass, will have been swept off. The current's rough here, or can't you see that?" His voice had hardened, either at my stupidity or at the situation.

I blushed and avoided his eyes, glancing at the swift water that burst into white foam where it hit rocks in the sandy bed. The land sloped down from our right to a deep dale where the river churned over boulders that had fallen from the rocky cliffs lining the stream's path. It would be cool and shady in the summer, with willow and burdock and Queen Anne's lace, and lazy trout feeding in the quieter pools. To our left, the terrain coarsened as it claimed altitude. Vegetation grabbed the ground, and the wind whipped every living thing. Discarded millstones, hunting sheds, and ancient Roman encampments dotted the land, forsaken to the elements. Even graveyards, abandoned and forgotten, crumbled under Nature's persistence. Nice place for a sacrifice.

Scott's voice rose above the river's roar. "All I can do—all any good cop can do—is work with what I've got. I can't magically recall displaced materials, just as I can't wipe out crime single-handedly in Derbyshire. We work within the limits of the law and our means. And if it's not good enough, if we lose a piece of the puzzle occasionally, we don't let that stop us from future attempts. It's what keeps us going, this belief that we'll succeed, even if our hearts break right now."

He watched for my reaction, the dress held over the river,

the bird circling overhead behind him. Cream colored fabric. White for a first marriage, cream for a second. She was divorcing Colin...I left the speculation and returned to the work at hand, opened the polythene bag and held it while he carefully lowered the dress into it.

When it was sealed, he said, "Sorry. Didn't mean to give you my police philosophy in one short, loud burst."

"Don't be ashamed of your passion, Scott. It's what makes you a good cop."

"Speaking of passion," he said as he shook his head, "even if she didn't like the color or style, she could've returned it. Waste of money, that."

The garment was torn, as Scott had said, but the extent of the damage was even more than we had feared. A sleeve was ripped halfway from the armhole seam, the neckline was torn in several places, and the skirt hung onto the waistline merely through the seam at the back zipper. Even several of the pearl buttons were missing.

"Real, these," I said, pointing at the buttons.

"Like I said, waste of money. God, what a bloody waste. Who the hell would've done this? Good quality."

"Silk, too. A tad flimsy for winter wear, but evidently that's just my opinion."

"You don't think it's been here since summer, then?"

"Couldn't have been. The tissue would be reduced to pulp, or completely dissolved. As it is..."

He said something about recommending my promotion to Inspector when Graham had a free minute, then pulled out another bag. Winking, he scooped up the clumps of snow and ice that had fallen free of the dress and secured the bag. I thanked him.

We had a more difficult time procuring the tissue paper. Scott used tweezers to lift an edge while I maneuvered an unopened evidence bag beneath it. When we were finished, scraps of paper resembling a black jigsaw puzzle lay on the polythene surface. Scott was about to get up when I grabbed his arm and pointed to a black-edged card. It was partially immersed in snow and had lain beneath the tissue paper.

"What?" He bent forward, peering into the area we had cleared.

"Voilá! The plot thickens!" I took the tweezers from him and pulled the card from its snowy anchor. The shop's name was superfluous; the silhouette of a black cat would have been enough to tell me the dress had come from 'Kitty's Corner.' "Sylvia Hale just dropped a wad there. Do you think…"

"Don't have to," Scott said, grinning. He held out his hand, palm up, like a surgeon in an operating theater. I dropped the tweezers onto his open palm and watched as the fingers tightened around the tool. A minute later we were staring at a very damp sales receipt that held Sylvia's signature. "Do I hear the clank of darbies?"

TWENTY-SIX

HANNAH AND SYLVIA dubiously eyed each other and us as they sat at our table in the incident room. I had been nervous about taking the initiative in requesting their presence—after all, Graham was senior investigating officer. But he had no doubt overlooked the procedural irregularity in the pleasure of watching me learn.

The greetings over and tea poured out, I offered condolences again to the women on their losses. Both murmured their thanks. "I suppose you'll both be looking forward to a bit of a break from all this," I said, catching Graham's eye. "Getting away, even for a weekend, would be soul-saving, I'd think. Give you a breather from the tragedies. I noticed you, Hannah, have a fortnight's holiday coming up."

Hannah glanced at the wall clock, as though already feeling she had been here too long. "I—it's been planned for a month or so. I can't very well cancel or I'll lose my money. I suppose I should go, but with the store as it is…"

"Isn't there someone who could talk to the insurance agents?" Graham said, leaning back in his chair. He looked as though he was spending the evening in front of his telly. "Surely you've contacted them, done all the preliminary work by now. You can't leave it for a week or so until you return?"

"I suppose so. Though I'd feel funny about it."

"There's always Ward," Sylvia said. "He's a capable young man. And I'd say that even if I weren't his mother." She smiled easily, showing us a calm, relaxed face. I thought there were probably better people than Ward Hale to take charge of a store—like Attila the Hun—but refrained from offering my opinion. Sylvia said, "And you have a brother or someone who could step in, don't you? And the other clerk—I forget her name. Besides, how much business did you expect to do until the store is rebuilt?"

"I'm being overly concerned, I know. But with all of the merchandise scattered—"

"Lease a storage locker," Graham said. "You can store all your books in there and you won't have to worry about losing anything. Then you can go on holiday with an easy mind."

"I'll check into it, thanks." Hannah looked out the window, as though already seeing herself on holiday. Or at least away from us.

"And are you planning to get away?" Graham asked Sylvia, stretching out his long legs. "I should think that after all you've been through …"

"I may," she said, her voice lower, as though the subject was too hurtful to express. "I had planned a trip, too, but after what's happened, I don't know if it would look right."

Propriety again, I thought. Keep your place in village hierarchy. I followed Graham's lead. "I can't think anyone would blame you if you were to continue with your plans. Being away from the place of your husband's death doesn't mean you don't feel the loss, Mrs. Hale. You can grieve just as deeply in Portugal, for instance, as you can in Bramwell."

Sylvia blinked back a few tears and reached for her purse. I pushed a handkerchief into her hand. Dabbing at her eyes, she said, "God knows that's true. I haven't had a decent sleep since—well, sleeping alone after having someone beside you for thirty years of—"

"You've lost a great love."

The tears were real this time, free flowing as she no doubt thought of Joel. She used the handkerchief again, apologizing for her tears and blowing her nose.

"Please don't apologize," Graham said. "We're not heartless. Of course we feel your pain along with you."

"I think," I said, "that trip will do you a world of good, Mrs. Hale. You're probably about to have a nervous breakdown."

"Delayed shock, you mean?" Sylvia said. "Yes, I suppose so. I'd just like to bury myself in a warm climate, with no cares, no thoughts of what I have to do, or who needs me. A rest would do me good, I suppose." She looked at me, as though waiting for my approval.

"Well," I said, making sounds for the breakup of the meeting.

Graham stood up and held out his hand to Sylvia. She blinked, probably startled there had been no grilling, and handed me my handkerchief. It was wet. I laid it on the table, then stooped down. Standing up, I held up the wedding ring, giving them a chance to see it. "Just saw this. Is it either of yours?"

Barely looking at it, Hannah quickly shook her head, denying it was hers, though her right thumb stroked her left ring finger.

"If no one claims it," I said, "we would like to give it to someone. If it fits you and you'd like it after the proper waiting time…" I held out the ring. Although both women stared at it, neither reached for it. The silence became awkward. I murmured that it was a nice piece of jewelry and a shame someone had lost it. Still no takers. Graham said if it fit me and I wanted it, I could have it—better that than having it sit in the unclaimed property drawer. I thanked him and slid it on my finger as I held my hand in front of me. "Just about a perfect fit, though I'd probably change the diamond for a garnet or sapphire. Too flashy for my taste. Still, the band's nice."

Murmuring she'd like to try it, Hannah took it hesitantly and slipped it on her finger. It seemed a perfect fit. Yanking it off, she pushed it into my hand. "I don't really care for it. The stone's not to my liking, either. Thank you just the same."

Holding it out to Sylvia, I asked if she would like it if we couldn't find the owner.

Sylvia jammed the ring onto her finger, shoving it past the knuckle. It hung loosely, space between the band and her finger. When it was apparent it didn't fit, she pulled it off and gave it back to me, complaining the band was too thin. I slipped the ring into my slacks pocket and asked Graham if he needed anything else.

"I don't think so, Sergeant Taylor, thank you." He turned on the twin-deck tape recorder and waited several seconds before turning to Sylvia. "Sylvia Hale. I caution you," Graham said very slowly, so she would not misunderstand, "that anything you say may be used in evidence. Your failure to mention any fact later, relied upon at trial, may damage your defense. You are not obliged to remain here; but if you do, you may obtain free legal advice. Do you understand?"

"Why are you cautioning me? For what crime?"

"Involvement in the murder of Joel Twiss. You are not formally charged. You are merely cautioned about any forthcoming statements. Understand?"

Sylvia barely nodded, her face flushed. "Always so considerate, our police force." Sylvia stood up, took a step backward, and yelled, "Murder Joel? That's typical. Where's your evidence? When am I supposed to have done this? Why should I kill him? I lo—"

Graham explained our grounds for the accusation, then added, "The ring, as we just witnessed, does not fit your finger, but it does Hannah's."

"And this damns me?" Sylvia said, her eyes blazing.

"Not by itself. But it does show that you were not Joel's choice as a wife. He changed his mind, didn't he, asking

Hannah to marry him. When you learned of this, you were furious. To the extent of destroying your wedding dress." He nodded at me and I walked over to a table, picked up the bagged dress and sales receipt, and handed them to Graham. "This is familiar to you, I should think." He laid the exhibits on the table and talked while Sylvia turned a deathly white.

"Where'd—how—" She realized what she was about to say and suddenly shut up.

Graham continued. "It's your dress, Mrs. Hale. Your signature on the sales receipt, so you can't very well claim it was a gift."

Sylvia stared at the dress as though it had miraculously appeared.

"You wanted revenge," Graham was saying when she finally looked again at him. A slow nod confirmed Graham's scenario and she sat down. "You were so furious that you tried to rid yourself of every reminder of your failed wedding, including throwing this away in what you presumed to be an undetectable area."

"I should've burned it," she mumbled, wiping her wet cheeks with the back of her hand.

"Furious at Joel, you got him alone in the church on some pretext, and there you murdered him."

Sylvia's breath came quickly, as though she was fighting to stay calm. Color had flooded her face and the veins of her neck bulged as her jaw muscles tightened. After a moment, she said more calmly, "So I threw away a dress. I admit it. Does that link me to murder? My God, half the people in this country throw litter. You writing me a ticket for littering?"

"I'm taking you into custody for the murder of Joel Twiss. You have the right to remain silent. If you choose to give up this right, anything you say—" He didn't finish the statement.

"Have you any witness to this? Don't I have to be accused by a witness?"

"The witness," Graham said, "is our evidence. And the DNA sample you just gave us."

"What sample?" Her voice was wary, as though expecting a trick.

I held up the handkerchief. "Your tears and mucus. You handed this back to me very willingly. I have Hannah and DS Salt, here, as witnesses."

"So, what do my tears prove? Did you find them on Joel's body? Is that what you're trying to match?"

"We don't have tears, no. But we do have your hair on the sack that you jammed over his head. How do you explain your hair on that if you weren't at the crime scene?"

Sylvia opened her mouth, ready for a quick retort. When she could think of none, she closed it. Lowering her head, she admitted she had murdered Joel. "I had already planned to divorce Colin. That had nothing to do with my wanting to marry Joel."

"Then why—"

"It was all a lie," she said, raising her head. Her voice, too, rose in tone and speed as her hurt and anger spilled out. "My whole marriage to Colin was a lie. He told me he had created that damned biscuit. He told me we had nothing to worry about, that the money from Magdalína's sales would keep us comfortable for years. He lied. Joel had concocted them. If there's one thing I hate it's lies."

"And Joel's marriage to you?" I ventured, wondering what Sylvia had felt with this double punch.

"I'd bought my trousseau. Even the wedding cake. I was ready for our trip, for my new life. He laughed it off when he told me he had changed his mind. I was stunned at first, thought he was joking. Well, he would have done, that being his way. But he wasn't. He was dead serious. I couldn't stand that. Not after Colin's deceit. So I asked him to the church, told him I wanted to give him a wedding present. He came quickly enough, the pig. Asked me where his gift was the minute he walked in."

I shut my eyes. The scene with the knife flashing in the candlelight and the agony of it plunging into his back was all too real. I opened them quickly, however, on hearing a chair scrape across the floor and Hannah's voice.

"You bitch!" She leaned forward, her left palm on the table, her face distorted with anger and tears. She raised her right hand, but I caught it before she could strike Sylvia. Hannah tried to wrestle her wrist free, but I held it firmly. I could feel her pulse beating, the tightening of her muscles. Her words streamed in a dirge of sorrow and loss and passion. "You've always had to have everything, haven't you? Men, money, clothes, house."

Sylvia stared at her, her eyes large and astonished. She opened her mouth, but Hannah rushed on, her face reddening as she released her emotion. "So you killed Joel because he wanted me, because he showed some strength and resisted you. So you destroyed him and you've destroyed me—my happiness, my future. I hope they hang you. I hope you rot in hell!"

"You have no idea," Sylvia finally said when the room had quieted. Her voice was edged with a hardness I had never heard. "How could you? Little, bookish spinster. You've been a long time finding a man who could tolerate you. Oh, I've watched you, flirting with anyone you thought you had a chance at."

"How dare—"

"You thought you knew Joel. How could you, over cups of tea and a book? You've got to share life with a man before you really know him. Or share pillow talk. Oh, don't look so shocked. He wasn't as snow white as you tried to believe. He liked women. Just because he didn't share your bed doesn't mean he didn't share mine. And he would've kept on sharing it if you hadn't somehow lured him into marriage. What was it—half ownership in the store? Joel never could refuse money. Had to have been something like that."

"Obviously my money," Hannah said, "if it was that, was still more alluring than you."

"Believe it, if you want to, but—"

"That's enough," Graham cut in. He handed Sylvia over to Mark, who told her her rights again, then led her away.

Hannah lowered her head, covering her eyes with her hands, and wept. Now that she had voiced her anger, she seemed about to collapse. I handed her a facial tissue and shoved a cup of lukewarm tea toward her. Quarter of an hour later, we thanked her for coming, and apologized for the deceit. I asked if she was going to rebuild her store.

"After I get back," she said, walking with us toward the door. "But I'm going to take that holiday. I need to think through these past few days."

"A holiday does sound good," Graham said when Hannah had left. "But first we've got to make a call."

SNOW HAD STARTED FALLING as we walked to Nelson Parnell's. I drew the collar of my jacket close to my throat, not so much from cold as from apprehension and distaste. I was still reacting from Sylvia's confession to killing another human being; how could I concentrate on Nelson? But I had to. Not only was my safety, perhaps, on the line, but so was Graham's if Nelson became violent. Hadn't I sat through enough District Training School lectures about becoming cold and distant, and at times even cynical as we grew into the job? I glanced at Graham, at his tightening jaw muscles, and wondered if he had the same thoughts.

Dealing with Sylvia was one thing, but Nelson could be entirely different. If our suspicions were correct, he had taken a person's life, just as Sylvia had. Maybe not with forethought or malice, but the result of his crime was, none the less, a dead body. And that was what made me focus now on Nelson.

He was in his back garden, sifting through the debris of his tool shed when we walked up. Tools and broken window glass littered the area still damp from the fire. Two piles were being made, presumably the tools worth saving and those burnt beyond usefulness. He put down the nozzle of his garden hose—the hose itself burnt in the fire—and asked if we'd come to make out a report.

"Actually," Graham said, "we've come to take you into custody."

Nelson clutched the corner of the shed wall for support. He coughed violently, as though he had taken in a lungful of ashes. I meandered a bit behind and to the side of Nelson while Graham pounded the man on the back. Waving off Graham's effort, he stared and said, "Into custody for what? Joel's murder?"

"Not murder. For the unlawful killing and for arson. Though I suspect when you had planned the fires you hadn't planned on killing anyone." Graham stood there, his face placid, waiting for Nelson to speak.

"*Unlawful killing?* When? Who am I supposed to have killed? I don't own a gun."

"I didn't say a thing about a gun, Mr. Parnell, but since you ask about the victim, it's Colin Hale. He was at Magdalína's the night of her fire. Only you didn't know that."

Graham waited for Nelson to say something—denial, confession, questions. The man merely stood there, the snow settling on his head and shoulders. I watched the ash disappear as the snow coated the ground, concealing the dregs of the fire. It was a gentle snow, huge dry flakes that swirled to earth with the gracefulness of a ballerina. As Magdalína probably would dance, I thought, recalling her long dancer's legs... The snow fell faster, nearly obliterating the distant scenery. The driveway was a sheet of white, with sprigs of dry grass fringing its edges. I watched a squirrel dash to a tree, thinking him smart to seek refuge. The grey sky threatened more snow. Nelson seemed not to notice any of this. He looked at the driveway as though thinking about what to say, how to apologize to us and to those he had hurt. Graham murmured something about a court-appointed solicitor when Nelson coughed again, stooped down as he clutched his throat, and straightened up with a garden shovel in his hand.

Holding it above his head, Nelson said, "Keep back if you don't want to end up with a face looking like concrete. You, too," he said, turning his body toward me and shaking the shovel. *"Back!"*

Graham slowly held out his arm to me, coaxing me back as he said, "Mr. Parnell, threatening police officers will only add to your sentence. Why don't you put down the shovel and we'll talk—"

Nelson raised the shovel higher, as if he was ready to bring it down on Graham's head. "To add to my sentence you have to catch me first. And I don't think you will. *I've* got the advantage."

He glanced over his shoulder. His car was parked on the street in front of his house. He'd have to run for it, if that was what he was thinking.

"What's this going to get you?" I asked, as Graham almost imperceptibly touched the inside of his wrists together. I cleared my throat. "As Mr. Graham said, you're only causing more trouble for yourself."

"*I'll* decide that," Nelson said, staring at me and backing up slowly. "And as for you two, as much as I'd love to invite you in for tea…"

Nelson glanced toward his left. Graham had taken a step toward the tool shed and was turned toward the pile of serviceable tools. With a yell, Nelson brought the shovel down with an emphatic oath. Graham dodged, nearly losing his balance on the snow, and grabbed the branches of a nearby bush. Seeing that he had missed, Nelson brought the shovel over his head again, holding it as he would hold a long-handled axe, and was about to lower it onto Graham's head when I shouted.

As Nelson turned toward me, Graham reached for the shovel. Either feeling Graham's tug or sensing his movement, Nelson pulled the tool from Graham's grasp and brought it around toward Graham's back. The unwieldy angle caught Nelson off balance, for the shovel glanced off Graham's shoulders. I grabbed a small bag of potting soil and swung it at Nelson. He grabbed his midriff and groaned. That was when Graham threw him to the ground. I kicked the shovel away, handcuffed and helped pull Nelson to his feet.

He glared at us for several minutes, patches of snow plastered to the front of his jeans and jacket, his hair mussed. Graham again stated our allegation, but Nelson's only response was to ask if he could have a cigarette. "So you've nothing to say in response to this?" Graham asked, holding the lighter for Nelson.

"Nice weather we're having." He eyed Graham through the cigarette smoke, his lips drawn tight in a self-satisfying smirk.

"That is the extent of your statement?"

"Happy Christmas."

"Officer." Graham nodded toward PC Byrd, who came over, grabbed Nelson's hands and shoulder, and walked him over to his car.

When Byrd had driven away, Graham exhaled slowly. "He may speak to us later. But then again…" He stared at me, the tension of the past hours and the frustration of attaining no confession evident in his eyes.

We walked without speaking for a while before Graham said, "There's one comforting thing in this mess. At least when he dragged you into Magdalína's tearoom he put you near the front where you could get out."

"Some comfort." I smiled at Graham. "But yes, you could be working solo now if Nelson hadn't been so considerate." I glanced at the pavement and kicked a chunk of ice into the street. "We've both had brushes with danger."

"You talking about the car incident on Piebald Tor?"

"Poor Nelson. It takes real nerve to hang on to the car. There's a risk we will eventually see it or learn about it from a neighbor. And if he gets rid of it, there's a possibility we can trace the car sale."

"Too bad he couldn't get rid of Willett's books so easily."

"In spite of the arson and Owen's death and what he attempted to do to us, I feel sorry for Nelson, sir."

"You believe David Willett stole Nelson's work on customs and legends, then? So do I."

"Wonder if we'll ever learn the truth about Joel's alleged burglaries."

"Perhaps Nelson will eventually talk. Sometimes the right barrister can work wonders outside the courtroom." He laughed, probably at some private joke. "We may never know a lot of Nelson's story, of course. But don't let it keep you awake, TC."

He ran his hand along an iron railing. The snow fell in small clumps, marring the smooth, white surface dusting the pavement. I tilted my head back, sticking out my tongue to catch a snowflake. I pointed out a brambling, the bird's orange breast vivid against the snowy whiteness. I told Graham that it was a winter bird and, though common, was still exciting to see, and that its song was rarely heard.

"Pardon, sir?" Graham's words had cut into my narrative.

"I was just wondering who is the most hurt in this mess—Sylvia, Hannah, Magdalína or David. They've all suffered a loss."

"Hard to say, sir. For all of Sylvia's bitterness, she's an awfully strong woman. She says she hates being lied to, but she lied to us about Colin's finances—the pharmaceutical business. Probably thought it added another layer to her mystique, the aura of feminine wealth. I'd never have known from her demeanor."

"And yet even her iron façade cracked."

"I wouldn't have thought she'd be so affected."

"Cool exterior fooled me, too."

I agreed and followed him into the pub, where a warm fire was burning.